T0066790

Percival

Percival

The Mrodic Wars

Rajiv Chopra

PARTRIDGE

ISBN:	Softcover	978-1-4828-7357-3
	eBook	978-1-4828-7356-6

Print information available on the last page.

To order additional copies of this book, contact
Partridge India
000 800 10062 62
orders.india@partridgepublishing.com

www.partridgepublishing.com/india

Dedication

This book grew out of a blog that I was writing for my kids, Tanvi and Tuhin. It was a magical experience to write it, and to tell them the story as it unfolded. We experienced the magic together.

This book is, therefore, dedicated to them, and to the magic that parents and children share in the telling of tales.

Contents

Acknowledgements

This book would never have been possible without the support that I received from friends and family.

The first person I would like to thank, is my wife Simmi, who patiently let me share those moments with my kids when I would crawl into their beds, and relate the tale to them. She was, and is, my great strength and support in life.

This book would never have been possible, had it not been for my two children demanding further episodes every week, and for their urging me to rewrite the book.

My sisters, Neera and Preeti, for reading through the draft, and giving me encouragement and lots of support.

Finally, my age old friend, critic and partner in crime – Gita – who patiently edited the book for me, and who constantly urged me to keep writing. This rewriting would not have happened without her constant badgering and coaxing. That's what friends are for.

Chapter 1

The Beginning

Percival was a pig, and the proudest specimen of pig that could be found in all of Percival's Land, for that is where he lived. Percival's life was uniformly happy and followed a routine that was generally unvarying. His father had left him with enough money to keep him and the next two generations in comfort, and without the need for work. But work he did, for Percival loved money, and he loved to be important. Yet, he did not spend his days and nights slaving in the office. He worked at a comfortable pace, as and when he felt like. He had a sort of genius for making money, having managed to multiply his father's legacy to no considerable extent.

So yes, life was very comfortable indeed. Percival would wake up and lie in bed reveling in the smell of clean, fresh sheets. His butler, Mortimer, would bring in his tea, open the blinds and leave Percival to savour his morning cup whilst gazing out at his garden with its profusion of colourful flowers.

After breakfast -- and it was a leisurely breakfast -- Percival would sit out in the garden reading a book, and drinking coffee. At about 11 am he would be served coffee with a mid-morning snack. Then, if the mood took him, and only if the mood took him, he would stroll down to the office and work a bit. Lunch at noon, followed by a light afternoon nap, followed by tea and sandwiches. Then he would walk down to Bessie's house to pay court to her, returning for some wine and dinner with friends. Life was comfortable. Life was easy. Percival had nothing to complain about. The skies were blue, the clouds white; nothing obscured the scenery of his days.

Percival was a young pig, rather portly and with a full head of hair. His face was smooth, his nails well manicured. Soft hands extended to soft, plump arms. His clothes were beautifully tailored and freshly laundered. All in all, he was the picture of a well cultivated young gentleman pig ideally suited to a life of genteel indolence.

Bessie was the love of Percival's life. He spent much of his idle time dreaming of her -- her white skin, rosy lips, fine features and red hair. She was slim and lively. She came from distinguished stock and lived in a luxurious villa on the outskirts of town. Her home was not too far from Percival's own house on the hill. And it was his haunt in the evenings. It was Percival's desire to make Bessie his wife, and to see their children and grandchildren grow up in his house on the hill.

Yes, Percival's life was full of blue skies and white, billowy clouds, bright sunshine and colourful flowers. And Bessie.

Bessie was a romantic. She had been brought up on tales of chivalry, tales of knights and adventure, danger, smoke, dragons and wizards. While she let Percival pay court to her, something in her heart yearned for more than just another plump, rich gentleman pig who would be a loving husband to her, and who would look after her for the rest of her life. Life with Percival would be comfortable. But it would also be dull.

As with most clear days, there is always a dark cloud on the horizon. In Percival's case, it took the form of Basil and his infernal second-in-command, Thyme. Basil was big and burly, and quite the opposite of everything Percival stood for. He walked about with a swagger and a gleam in his eye. He was comfortably off though his riches could not compare with those of Percival. But he had something that Percival did not -- muscle, brawn, and the general air of an adventurer. Thyme was his helpmeet, his shadow. A fine-looking specimen, he followed his master everywhere, whispering things into his ear. Always scheming, always looking this way and that, shifty-eyed little Thyme always seemed to be able to control Basil's mind.

It appeared to Percival that Basil's main objective in life was to court Bessie, and he did this with his usual careless air. If there was a thorn in Percival's side, that thorn was Basil, and on nights that Percival could not sleep he would dream of Basil. Basil, a grinning devil, evil and mocking, daring Percival to beat him back.

On the fateful day that this saga begins, Percival awoke in the morning as he did every day, at the same time. As he sipped his morning tea, he gazed out of the window at the roses in his garden. But this time his eyes were fixed on the thorns. His mind was on Basil and Thyme.

"Bah!" he uttered, coming to a sudden decision. "This is indeed an intolerable situation. It cannot be allowed to continue. This nonsense must end, and it must end today.

I shall go to Bessie's home this evening and shall ask her to be my wife. She shall see the wisdom of agreeing to this. We shall be married in a quiet, dignified ceremony, and all will be well with the world."

He thought it over right through breakfast and over coffee. He did not go to the office that day, but after lunch went straight to the barber where he had a haircut, a manicure and a facial. He wore his best clothes and decided that a new top hat was in order. There was time, he mused, for one last stop at Corky's Top Hat Shop before he proceeded with quiet dignity to where Bessie lived.

The day was getting on. The late afternoon sun was giving way to the cooler rays of the evening. Percival entered Corky's Top Hat Shop. Corky was an old friend, and the owner of the shop. His was the most expensive top hat shop in town, and Percival was a valued patron and customer.

As Percival walked this way and that, trying on top hat after top hat, Corky's assistants scurried madly around him. The young pig preened in front of the mirror, looking at himself from various angles, poses and facial expressions. He was convinced he had to have it absolutely right when he proposed to Bessie later that evening. At last it was done. Percival chose a top hat... nay, The Top Hat... and perfected the courtly expression he wanted to have on his face during the romantic interlude that was playing on his mind.

Suddenly there was a loud crash and a bang, and the lights went out! Everywhere there were sounds of stands crashing, top hats being crushed, and squeals of anguish as customers were trampled underfoot. Corky roared with anger and surprise. He appeared frozen in shock and fear. Finally, his shouts dwindled to a gurgle, and then there was absolute silence. Percival stood rooted to the spot. He was petrified, though later he would claim he was merely waiting for the right moment to pounce on the perpetrators of this outrage.

There was no time for that, however. Percival felt a sack being thrown over his head... over his head and The Top Hat. This was intolerable! Absolutely intolerable! He stamped his foot in rage and frustration. He may as well have saved himself the trouble as he was trussed up like a little chicken and carried out of the shop. He felt the cool evening breeze rushing through the sack. He felt himself being carried to a nameless destination and his heart almost failed him. What was he to do? He tried to scream but a mere squeak emerged from his mouth. He held his breath; the odor from the sack was overpowering. As he was carried he felt the dignity of his position being sullied. His thoughts were everywhere... then suddenly he felt himself being flung into the air.

He landed with a thump. Now he squealed. He had never realized just how hard the ground was. Percival was convinced he had broken every bone in his body. As he moaned and wept about the sad state of his life, he did not notice that the bonds were being gently loosened. He lay there for what appeared to be a lifetime. Then, slowly, he moved his hands...

Chapter 2

A Wedding and a Honeymoon

Once he realized he could move his hands, it did not take long for Percival to free himself of his bonds. Looking down, he almost wept. For the first time in his life, he was grubby. Tears of mortification ran down his cheeks, and he could taste the dust on the tip of his tongue. He reached up with his hands to find that The Top Hat had been crushed. Crushed beyond recognition. The watch that hung ever so elegantly at his waistcoat was smashed.

Percival sat there in the dirt of the rubbish heap, his head drooping in despair. What was he to do? The more he thought about it the more he became convinced that this was the task of that horrid fellow, Basil. Then, a terrifying thought struck him. Was Basil, at this very moment, paying court to Bessie? This could not be, he reasoned, yet it was the only logical conclusion that could be drawn. Why else was he in a rubbish heap, stripped of the dignity he held so dear?

There was not a moment to lose. Percival got up, dusted himself off, and began hobbling quickly to Bessie's home. His knees hurt terribly, and there was a pain extending all the way from his bottom to the small of his back.

However, no bodily pain could compare to the pain that seared his soul. Hope and anguish spurred him on. He did not notice the astonished looks of passersby as he struggled to get to Bessie's house. Nor did he pay heed to their whispers and sniggers.

Entering Bessie's home, he was prepared for her sympathetic questions; indeed, he was prepared to lay his heart at her feet. What he was not prepared for was the sight of Basil sitting at Bessie's feet, her hands in his. His lips were touching Bessie's hands. His foul lips were touching Bessie's hands, and she appeared to be simpering. Percival was stunned. He stopped and rubbed his eyes. At that moment, he seemed transformed.

They say fear gives wings to our feet. Hope and despair certainly had the same effect on Percival, as he glared and snorted. Something dramatic had to be done. Without thinking, he darted up to the first floor landing, stood on the edge of the balcony and, with a roar, jumped. His intention was to swing by on the chandelier, catch hold of Bessie by the hand and sweep her away from Basil. His hand caught the chandelier and it fell along with Percival, gravity propelling both towards the ground with alarming acceleration. He came crashing down on Basil, the chandelier alongside him.

With a whimper and a moan, Basil went down. Percival kneeled on the body of his fallen foe, whispering sweet nothings into Bessie's ear. Romantic intentions mixed with incoherent ramblings of adventure, intrigue and danger. Before she could react -- she had been shocked into immobility -- Percival drew her to his breast and kissed her on the mouth. He had never ventured to be so bold, and the experience only served to inflame his heart. His hand gripped hers and he drew her to him.

"Quick! There is not a moment to be lost," he said. "Let us leave immediately."

"But where are we going?" Bessie asked in shock.

"To my home," replied Percival. "Quick, there is not a moment to be lost."

Percival drew Bessie towards him and ran into her back garden. He did not know where he was going, but he knew he had to move before Thyme came back from wherever Basil had sent him. Night was falling as they moved through the garden. Then, suddenly, they heard shouts and gunshots and Thyme's enraged voice. Fear now lent wings to Percival's feet and he practically flew over the back wall, Bessie close behind him.

In the days that followed, Percival did not venture out of his house. Bessie was given a separate room in which to sleep. Percival's sense of honour did not allow him to make her his wife until she had been properly married to him.

There was much to be done, and Percival's servants lost no time in planning a grand wedding. It had to be done quickly, before Basil recovered and disrupted the wedding. As he subsequently discovered, Basil had been seriously injured during the escapade. Percival's not inconsiderable bulk falling on top of him had caused a severe dislocation in his back, and he spent the days in bed, moaning and swearing revenge against Percival. By this time, the events of the evening had become common gossip, somehow serving to elevate Percival's stature in the town. Corky had managed to recover The Top Hat; it was put on display inside a case at a prominent place in the shop.

The day of the wedding drew close. Percival was found also making preparations for a journey. A journey by ship to The Exotic Island is what was needed. He had heard much about this place and had decided that it was to be the place for their honeymoon. He chartered two connecting cabins on the most expensive ship he could locate. One was redecorated into a living room, the other was to be their bedroom. If it was to be an adventure, by God the adventure would come with all the comforts that could be procured!

As the day of the wedding approached, a festive air began to seep into the town. The townspeople suspected that a marriage was due, and there were whispers around coffee shops and alleyways. While Percival had given strict orders for the time and the venue to be kept a secret, the townsfolk knew that he would have a wedding in the grandest possible style.

At last the wedding day dawned. Percival and Bessie made their way to the biggest church in town, the Church of The Holy Grail. People thronged for a sight of the happy couple; some tried taking pictures. Bessie had, by this time, fallen in love with Percival. She was convinced now that her future had to be with him.

The church was teeming with invited guests, with others trying to force their way in. Percival and Bessie walked down the aisle as the morning light filtered in through the stained glass windows. The atmosphere was solemn and dignified. Then, as the priest asked the obligatory question: "Does anyone here have any reasonable objection to the holy matrimony that is about to take place?", a darkness seemed to fall over the church, and a voice rang out:

"Yes, By God! I object! This here Percival is a usurper of my rights... I should be standing there, with that dame who is with him..."

"I am not a dame!" Bessie screamed angrily. "I am a lady!"

Turning to the priest, she said: "Father, please continue with the ceremony."

Then there was chaos as Basil began walking down the aisle with Thyme behind him. Once again, something snapped inside Percival. With a loud bellow, he charged down the aisle bearing down on unsuspecting Basil. The sight of Percival charging like a bull with inflamed nostrils gave Basil cause to pause. He froze. Too late, it seems, as Percival's great bulk came crashing into him a second time.

Basil fell back onto Thyme and the three of them went crashing and rolling out of the church. The impact of Percival's charge was so great that they rolled right down the church steps. Over and over they turned, finally ending up on the main road below. Percival was on top of Basil, who was on top of Thyme.

"Oooh!" gasped Basil, who felt as though all his ribs had cracked.

"Ooooh!" squeaked Thyme, who felt the double weight of Percival and Basil on top of him. Both Percival and Basil were big fellows, and the impact of both on his slim frame seemed to have knocked the very life out of him. "Oooh!" he squeaked again. "I am going to die..."

Percival crawled up and looked down with grim satisfaction at his two fallen foes who had to be carried away.

The ceremony was completed without further interruption. Percival and Bessie returned to the home on the hill as a married couple. Percival's happiness was complete.

The celebration continued well into the night. Well beyond the time that Percival eventually slipped into sleep. This is how it happened.

Percival had drunk a bit too much for him. After a few glasses of wine too many, he suddenly got up on the table and started singing a romantic ballad in honour of his new wife. The words of this famous ballad, alas, are lost in the sands of time, but the effect that it had on the listeners is something people talk about to this day. Our hero had the most awful, screeching singing voice that could be imagined. To say that his guests' hair stood on end would not be an exaggeration. For some, the pain ran through their bodies and there was no escape. Others dove for cover. Mercifully, as Percival stood on one leg waving the other about, he lost balance and toppled over. He disappeared from sight and was discovered only later thanks to the gentle snores that emerged from under one of the tables.

"Let him lie there. It is best," said Bessie with a thoughtful look. A shadow flitted across her face as she wondered whether her life was going to be subject to this unearthly screeching every so often. Ever the gracious lady, she turned to the group with a smile and said: "Let's continue with the revelry while my Lord Percival recovers from his!"

The next day, Bessie and Percival left for their honeymoon. Percival was carried on to the ship, to surface only after lunch. The Grand Mariner was the name of the ship -- the most luxurious of luxury liners that could be found.

The next few days were blissful and Percival was the happiest man on earth. He and Bessie were completely in love and spent their days looking into each other's eyes. The weather was perfect; the sunsets were as God intended them to be; the rising sun was God's way of saying 'Good Morning' in the kindest possible manner. The food, always important, left nothing to be desired. Percival was in clover indeed. What could be better than this?

After about two weeks, The Grand Mariner docked in at The Exotic Island. They had rooms booked at The Imperial Manor; now the happy couple could begin the second phase of their honeymoon.

The Exotic Island was indeed a unique place. Here, the weather was always perfect. It was a place full of lush green trees and dense vegetation. The trees were always full of flowers and laden with fruit. The roads were neat, clean and cobblestoned. The markets were dotted with charming shops, cafes and restaurants.

The male pigs of the island had blue hair; the female pigs pink hair. This was the only odd bit about the island, but, as they soon discovered, The Great Architect in the Sky had come up with infinite shades of blue and pink.

Bessie and Percival would wake up late. After a wonderful morning of lovemaking and breakfast in bed, they strolled around the town. After lunch, they retired to their rooms to emerge in the evening for a spot of drink and some dancing. Percival could not believe life could be so good. Back home, he had though his life was perfect; now he realized how mistaken he had been. He would look at Bessie like a lovelorn puppy, and she would indulgently stroke his face. Yet, somewhere deep down, Bessie missed the sense of true adventure. The thought would emerge from time to time and then would be gone like a puff of smoke. Nothing would be allowed to mar their wedded bliss.

One evening, the weather turned. The first time it had happened in living memory. After dinner, just as Percival and Bessie were planning which dance hall they should visit, the breeze took on a decidedly chilly air. Dark clouds started to form, and soon large drops of rain descended. This was something the citizens of the island were completely unused to as they began running this way and that.

Soon, the rain turned into a storm.

"Bessie, come quick... this way," screamed Percival. His teeth chattered in the cold. Night had descended suddenly, and the storm had blinded all his senses, leaving behind a blubbering mass.

"Hold my hand," he screamed again. "Let's get away from this horrible rain... I hate it, I hate it, and I hate it!"

"Come on Percy, pull yourself together," Bessie yelled back as she ran beside him wondering what had happened to his sense of adventure. Where indeed was the person who had landed on Basil's back with a thump, and had charged him during the wedding? For the first time, a fleeting sense of disappointment crossed her face.

They ran, not knowing where they were going until suddenly they found themselves in an unfamiliar part of town. The deserted roads had a foul air about them. Percival shivered. Suddenly, there in front of him was a handsome looking black door above which was inscribed, in gold, 'The Black Pub'.

"Come, Bessie love. Let's get a drink and then push back home after the storm has abated," Percival gasped.

Pushing the door open, they entered The Black Pub.

Chapter 3

The Black Pub

The Black Pub stood at the corner of Elm Street, in the northeastern section of The Exotic Island. Even now, many years after the incident, Percival has no recollection of how he and Bessie came to be in that part of the island that stormy night, or how The Black Pub suddenly appeared before them.

The Black Pub had a significant impact on Percival's life. Nay, that is not good enough. You may say that the events of the evening changed Percival's life forever.

Visitors to the island did not normally go to The Black Pub; it was certainly not your typical tourist hotspot. The northeastern section of The Exotic Island was the one section that was not kept clean as other parts of the island were. There was litter all over the place; buildings had broken windows and the streets were covered in filth.

Indeed, this part of the island was grey and dull. It was almost as though the rest of the island folk had forgotten the people living here. They were in a world of their own as they crept up and down the streets in torn, scraggly clothes. There was an overall sense of decay in these parts, with just a hint of menace.

Here, people feared for their lives. They would walk along the road watching out for the slightest possibility of being mugged, attacked from behind, kidnapped, or killed. Fear ruled the streets as soon as the sun's rays began to dip; the light was a dull grey by day.

Yet, if a lonely traveler were to walk along Elm Street and ask directions to The Black Pub, they would be answered with a gracious smile.

The owner of The Black Pub was one Dragor. No one had seen Dragor in years. They remembered him as a young lad, intelligent, smiling and good-looking. He was known for his politeness and humility, and was considered the catch of The Exotic Island. Then, one day, it seems, he went on a journey with a mysterious person with three eyes. When he came back, he had changed. He became muscular, grim and unsmiling, and went about with a (menacing?) fearful air. His body was covered in tattoos. His parents quickly disowned him, and then he disappeared. It was said he set up The Black Pub and ruled it with fear and, some said, magic of the blackest kind. Yes, the fear that Dragor's name invoked was enough to send even the bravest scoundrel into a white funk.

The door of The Black Pub was solid. The lantern above it cast a warm glow on its black wood and golden handle.

Inside, the traveler was greeted with music, slow and rhythmic. The drumbeat, interspersed with various melodies, was enough to put him in a nice, mellow mood.

The lighting in the bar was low, yet the light was warm. Red leather sofas lined the walls; above them hung several paintings, paintings that were at odds with the warmth of the pub. Several chairs and stools were placed around the pub in a whimsical manner. These too were covered in red and green leather. The wood was a uniform black across the pub. The bar, likewise, was made of black wood that had been polished to a shine. Alongside were comfortable stools, again covered in alternating red and green leather.

The one thing the lonely traveler would immediately notice on entering the pub was that the stools and chairs were all exceedingly comfortable. Having once sunk into the comfort of the cushions, the tired traveler would lie back with a sigh, without the slightest urge to leave until it was time for the pub to close.

The barman at The Black Pub was tall and stout, with a red cheerful face and a balding pate. He had been here many, many years yet no one had seen him age and no one had ever seen him with a full head of hair. His skin was firm and smooth, with not a wrinkle. When in the mood, he would regale the drinkers with tales of his travels across the world. He remembered the smallest details of places he had visited and people he had met. This was strange, especially if you consider the fact that he had been at the pub every day for more years than anyone cared to remember. How and when had he embarked on those travels?

These were questions that were pondered but never asked. There was something about the barman that was imperious and mysterious. Something about him did not invite questions into his life or his comings and goings. Mortimer was his name.

After a drink or two, the weary traveler would raise his eyes and look at the walls. His gaze would rest on the paintings that adorned them. He would come to realize that the paintings were in sequence, as though telling a story. A love story starting out innocent, in light, playful colours, gradually becoming darker as the story progressed through tragedy, farce and agony. The latter paintings were dramatic, the last one extremely strange. The canvas was painted black and had splashes of red on it. There seemed to be a question left hanging at the end of the story. A mystery yet to be explained.

At midnight, the lights dimmed and the warmth would ebb. A sense of menace crept through the pub. Dark shadows played on Mortimer and the others serving at the bar. Kreechurs, they were called. Their eyes gleamed red, their teeth shone white. At this point, if the weary traveler was still in the bar, he would feel a chill run down his spine and a sense of dread take over, as though doom were descending upon his short life.

Yes, it was in this place that Percival and Bessie found themselves. Close to midnight, it was, and the air in the bar was still warm. Shaking the water from their heads, they seated themselves. Percival ordered a drink for himself and one for Bessie.

"Barman, some warm toddy please," he called out in a cheerful but imperious voice. "And, here's something for your trouble, my good man." So saying, he dropped a few coins carelessly onto the table as a tip. He looked around the pub and exclaimed: "My, what frightful paintings... The painter must have been hard up indeed." He laughed loudly. "Another toddy, my good man!"

While Percival was oblivious to the slowly changing atmosphere in the pub, Bessie was keenly aware of it. She gazed at the paintings, walked around them, and finally stopped at the last one. She seemed fascinated and stood in front of it a long while. Then she walked to the centre of the pub and started a slow, sensuous dance in rhythm with the music. She seemed hypnotized. Percival sat there, gaping at her foolishly.

"Here now, Bessie," he said at last. "We'd better be getting back. It is late, and I don't think you should be dancing like this."

So saying, he got off his bar stool and started to walk towards her. It was at that moment that the lights went out, and there was a loud 'poof!'. The lights came back on, and Percival saw white smoke where Bessie had been. But of Bessie there was nothing to be seen...

"Here now, barman," Percival scowled. "This is not in good taste, my good man. What have you done with my wife? Come on now, or I shall have to call the police."

"The police?" asked Mortimer in a quiet voice. "They have not been here in years, have they now?" He looked around. Percival followed his gaze and seemed to notice the Kreechurs for the first time. They were a frightening lot, and they closed in on him. Their white teeth looked very sharp indeed!

"This is surely the end of me," thought Percival. He closed his eyes and appeared ready to faint.

Chapter 4

The Journey Continues

"Oooh!" groaned Thyme as he felt the bulk of Percival and Basil on top of him. He had never imagined anything or anyone could weigh so much, and was sure every bone in his body had been smashed.

Basil and Thyme were carried home and nursed back to health. As they recuperated, over the next week, Basil fretted and fumed. He could not believe that he had been bested twice by Percival. Twice! That too by a pig for whom he had no great respect. He plotted revenge. He sent his friends out for news of Percival's activities. Soon enough, he discovered that Percival and Bessie had left for their honeymoon to The Exotic Island. Without further delay, Basil decided he would set out to recapture the lady he felt was rightfully his.

Reservations were made for a cabin for Thyme and himself, and they were off. On arriving, they booked a room in a nondescript hotel so as not to attract attention to themselves. Then they began making discreet inquiries.

While Basil was off hunting for Bessie, Thyme found himself utterly enchanted by the island and the ladies on it. Ah, the shades of pink that he found in their hair! The perfume, the grace with which they walked... All of it made the most unforgettable impression on him.

One morning, as they sat down for breakfast at a charming little inn, Basil announced that he had spotted Bessie and that this was to be the evening they would recapture her and take her back home with them. As he waxed eloquent about his plans, he could not help notice that Thyme's attention was fixed on a young lady who had just walked in the door. Basil talked, and Thyme gaped. Not a word went into his ears. Finally, like a man transfixed, Thyme got up and walked up to the lady. He appeared to be in a trance. "Grnhgdnk," he muttered as he walked.

Sally, for that was her name, looked up at Thyme standing there fixed like a statue and said with a laugh: "Hello, my name is Sally."

"Hrnskendl," replied Thyme, stuttering like he was struggling to find the power of expression. Sally looked at him with amusement. There was something about him that was charming, innocent and irresistible. Love indeed seemed to bloom between the two, something that was quite out of the ordinary. Clearly, something had to be done.

Sally was a forthcoming young lady. Sporting hair a redder shade of pink, she was a good looking creature, and very strong. Her glance went past Thyme to Basil, who sat in his seat glowering like a young pig being forced to eat bacon, and she called out: "Why don't the three of us meet here for dinner tonight? 7:30?" With that she got up, planted a kiss on Thyme's cheek and waltzed out of the inn.

Later that evening, after Thyme had recovered some of his balance, and after Basil had been able to get him to focus on some of his plans for the evening, the two of them found themselves back at the inn for dinner with Sally. Sally and Thyme sat next to each other, and she slipped her hand into his. And so Thyme's heart was won, without him having to take the first step.

This was the evening the storm broke, and as they hurried along home Basil saw Percival and Bessie scampering for cover. He let out a yell and charged. Neither heard him through the sound of the storm. Yet Basil kept his eye on his prize and ran after them, with Sally and Thyme close on his heels.

Seeing them disappear into The Black Pub, Basil declared: "Let's stay here until the two of them leave the pub, and then we shall pounce." He rubbed his hands in glee. The prize was within his grasp. He was deaf to Sally's entreaties that this was not the place to be. She knew about The Black Pub and its reputation, and had no wish to stand there in the pouring rain waiting for two strange pigs to leave the pub. What was she to do?

Soon after midnight, when the chill was beginning to reach their bones, Basil heard what seemed to be a loud clap coming from inside the pub. It was like a gunshot, or a thunder clap, or a bomb, or all of them at once.

"Enough," he cried. "Let's enter and pounce."

With that, he charged into the pub to find Percival standing in the middle of it and next to him, a plume of white smoke. A group of Kreechurs surrounded Percival, their eyes menacing. Spittle dribbled down the corner of their mouths as they prepared to pounce on the helpless pig. Doom was at hand.

Basil gaped at the scene. Rescuing Percival was not part of his plans for the evening. He stood there stupefied, until Sally jabbed him hard in the ribs and said: "Do something, you fat pig!"

With that, she picked up a bottle and flung it hard. Her aim was perfect and her throw hard. The bottle landed on the nose of the Kreechur closest to Percival, and he went down with a yelp and a howl. Then there was pandemonium. No one had ever witnessed an attack on The Black Pub, and for a few crucial minutes no one knew how to react. Sally and Thyme threw bottles and glasses, and smashed lights. Basil took advantage of the confusion to dart into the crowd, take hold of a bewildered Percival by the scruff of his neck and pull him towards the door.

"Stop!" bellowed a voice, and Basil turned to see Mortimer towering behind the counter. He seemed to have grown and his shape was black and menacing. As Basil paused, a Kreechur dived to take hold of his ankle. Shivering with a new-found fear, Basil stomped down blindly. Luck was on his side; his foot came down heavily on the Kreechur's nose. The howl of pain distracted Mortimer for a moment, and this was all he needed to be able to dart out of The Black Pub dragging Percival with him. Sally and Thyme followed close behind, and fear gave them wings. They deposited Percival at his hotel and retired for the night.

The next morning found Percival still a blubbering mess, and the following days did nothing to alter his behaviour. Meanwhile, the trio made some inquiries and learnt that a ship had recently left the shores of The Exotic Island. A Red Ship, they were told. A blood-red ship with a white skull painted on its sails and hull. A ship of death, they were told, a ship of blood and gore...

"This must be the ship that has taken Dragor and Bessie," said Basil. "We must find it. But first we must rouse that blubbering idiot Percival from his stupor."

Percival was no better that evening, leaving Sally muttering between clenched teeth and wondering just what Bessie saw in him.

Later that evening, Percival sat down glumly to dinner. He downed a few bottles of wine and tottered off to his tub to have the last one in its warm comfort. The warmth and the wine had their desired effect on him. First he cried and wailed about the disaster that had been visited upon his head. Why were the heavens subjecting him, such a nice guy, to this form of treatment? Had he not paid his dues? Had he not contributed handsomely to all the churches and temples of worship?

After whining and moaning a bit, he roused himself with some fervor. If the heavens did not favour him, then, by Gum, he was going to take matters into his own hands. He stood up naked in the tub, on one foot, in what he thought was a heroic pose. Brandishing the now empty bottle of wine, he sang a song in pure doggerel. A few lines remained in his memory, and a few lines is all he sang before slipping and falling back into the water.

"The wife has been taken from me.
The life has been taken from me.

Shall I bear the cross?
Of course!
I shall sail the seas and ride the winds.
I shall light the fires of their sins.
They shall burn, they shall cry.
I shall hunt them till they..."

With that enchanting verse sung in his characteristic screech, Percival fell into the water and snored his way till morning.

When morning came, Basil and Thyme pulled him out of the tub with a roughness he felt he did not deserve. All traces of heroism had left him. What remained was a splitting pain in the head.

"Quick!" commanded Basil. "We have found a ship that will take us in search of Bessie. The captain, a most humble fellow, has agreed to take us on board."

"Yes," chimed in Thyme. "The captain is a meek fella. I wonder why he's named his ship The White Eagle."

There was no time to lose. Percival was bundled into his clothes while Sally cleared their hotel dues. The four were soon on board The White Eagle.

"We are coming for you, Dragor!" Percival said grimly. Somehow, he assumed that this had been his plan all along. And something of his cockiness in the tub began to return.

Chapter 5

On The White Eagle - 1

Indeed, the captain of The White Eagle seemed humble enough. Azazel was his name. He greeted them, hobbling along with a slight limp as he accompanied them on board. Azazel was tall, and it was obvious he had been powerful in his youth. His ragged clothes seemed to indicate that he had fallen on hard times.

"Poor fellow," thought Percival, as he walked up the plank. "Look at those rags." "Our tickets will probably buy him food for the rest of the year."

Meanwhile, Sally was a little concerned as they boarded the ship. She thought she detected the presence of a third eye on Azazel's face and, if memory served her well, Dragor was taken up by a similarly three-eyed gentleman called Threye. But there was no time to lose if they were to have any hope of catching up with Bessie. So she cast her misgivings aside and climbed on board. Modesty stopped her from sharing a cabin with Thyme, but she resolved to spend as much time as she could in his room.

The cabins were comfortable enough, though no way as luxurious as those on The Grand Mariner. Yet they were not about to grumble.

Soon enough, they cast off from port. The chase had begun!

Things were getting exciting and Percival soon recovered some of his sang-froid. It looked like they were the only passengers on board and were free to come and go as they pleased. Well, almost. There were some areas of the ship that seemed to be out of bounds, and this piqued the curiosity of the four young passengers. Yet, try as they might, they were always prevented from straying into those sections by the ever-so-polite shipmates.

.....

Days passed. Percival was seen drumming his fingers in boredom on the side of the ship.

"This is not so interesting," he said to Basil. "This ship needs some more entertainment.""

Yeah, that is so true, my friend," replied Basil. The two seemed to have grudgingly accepted each other, now that they were united in their common quest for Bessie. The arguments and fights could be resumed later. Now, they had to find Bessie and destroy that miserable oaf Dragor. Who indeed did he think he was, running off with Bessie! Percival grumbled to himself, as he imagined the retribution that would fall upon the miserable head of Dragor when they eventually caught up with him.

"Ahem," said a low voice next to them. "If it be entertainment ye folk are seeking, could we invite you to a small ball tomorrow night? It will be poor compared with those that ye grand folk are used to, but we would be honoured indeed if you would come. My wife and sister-in-law will join us if such honoured folk as yourselves would care to attend."

"Ah yes, Azazel, my good man," replied Percival with a slight supercilious nod of the head. "We shall certainly be there. Will there be food, wine, music and dance at your ball?"

"Yes, yes. It shall certainly be arranged. I shall take it as confirmed then," whispered Azazel, as he left them and shuffled off.

Basil stood there in deep thought. Had he detected a flash in Azazel's eyes? Did he see what seemed to be a third eye? Impossible, he thought, and dismissed the idea with a shake of his head.

The next day seemed to pass very slowly indeed. Finally it was time for the ball. Percival, Sally, Thyme and Basil dressed up in the finest clothes they had brought with them, and descended into the ballroom.

Their eyes opened wide as they entered. Nothing so far had prepared them for the magnificence that greeted their eyes. Azazel sat at one end, dressed in clothes of a splendid weave and cut. Next two him were two extremely beautiful young ladies; one with red hair, the other with light, silvery hair. Both were extremely fair to look at, with reddish-brown eyes. The red-haired one was called Jenna, her companion Trix. They were sisters, and Trix was Azazel's wife. All of them, the four travelers noted, had three eyes, eyes that could blaze like fire when needed.

Indeed, the middle eye had powers that were yet to be revealed to the travellers.

The ball began, and Trix traipsed up to Basil and asked him for a dance. Her walk was light, almost pixie-like, her laugh a silvery brook babbling its way to the river. Jenna, who was asking Percival for a dance, was more languid, almost fluid in her movements.

Basil and Percival glowed with pride. They puffed themselves up as they accompanied the two young ladies to dance. The music was slow and the girls' bodies swayed against theirs. The lights dimmed, and they pressed themselves up against the young gallants. In the distance, almost as though on another planet, Thyme and Sally were locked together in what was probably their marital dance. The ceiling changed to resemble an inky blue sky covered with shining, glittering stars. Basil and Percival felt as though they were the most romantic balladeers that had ever been born on their beloved planet. One forgot that he was married; the other forgot that he was dancing with a married lady.

They seemed to have entered a land beyond time, and they danced with a skill and abandon they did not know they possessed. Soon after midnight, the ladies pulled themselves away from their partners, whispering something into their ears. Basil and Percival smiled, and, holding the young ladies' hands, drew them up onto the ship's deck. They did not look back, or else they would have seen a gleam in Azazel's eyes and a slight smile play about his lips. It is almost as though he knew what was coming next. His still, hooded look held a portent of danger, malice and immeasurable cruelty.

The moon shone down on the water, casting an ethereal, silvery light. The air was cool, and it was as though they had stepped over into a land that was altogether magical. Basil and Percival pulled the young ladies close and brought their mouths down onto the red, waiting lips. Red lips that smiled; reddish eyes that gleamed. The ladies appeared as though they had been waiting for just that moment; as though their entire lives had been a precursor for the kiss that was to follow...

But it was not to be. Just as lips were about to meet, Percival and Basil found themselves being lifted off their feet and tossed into the shark-infested waters below. The last thing Basil heard just before he crashed into the water was Trix's silvery laugh and he cursed himself for being a fool.

Down, down went the young pigs, to be swallowed up by the dark swirling waters. Thrashing and flailing his arms in panic, Basil choked and got ready to die. Then, from somewhere, his sense of self-preservation asserted itself and he stopped thrashing about. As he started to rise, he felt something gripping his ankles, pulling him down again. He could just discern Percival clinging onto him for dear life. One hand was clamped around his ankle, the other swung wildly as did his legs. Basil's head broke water and he lifted his arms in despair, before the inevitable second descent.

Basil started to sink again; soon only his right hand was above water. A right hand that was gripped by another. Slowly, ever so slowly, he was pulled up and out of the water and into the berths at the bottom of the ship. He landed like an ungainly puddle on the floor of the ship, with Percival close behind him. Luckily for Basil, Percival did not land on top of him this time!

Gasping for breath, Basil managed to wheeze: "What the..? How the..? He gasped and spluttered as he looked up to find himself surrounded by a gang of what appeared to be men, with their feet turned inside out.

"Who are you?" he gasped. "How did you come to be here? Where are we?"

Percival, by this time, had managed to drag himself up. He looked down forlornly at his soggy clothes and began to wail.

"Oh, woe is me! Woe is me! This was my last set of suits, and it is ruined! What shall become of me? This is intolerable indeed... And, I stink!" He moaned, looking down at himself. Life was indeed miserable, he thought. What had he, a gentle pig, ever done to deserve this? When he had signed up for an adventure, he had obviously not read the fine print, he thought to himself. Adventures did not always come with fine bedclothes, dancing, food and the best comforts money and connections can buy. On the contrary, adventures stank! He was ready to go home and abandon Bessie to her fate.

"Ow!" He cried as Basil's hard foot landed squarely on his ample behind. "What was that for, you brutish lout?" he asked scowling.

"Worried about your blessed clothes are you?" snapped back Basil. "Look around, you fat fool!"

For the first time, Percival became aware of his surroundings. The room was gloomy, its occupants chained and bloody. Their emaciated bodies gleamed in the dim candlelight, casting strange shadows on the walls. The floor was covered in dried blood. Blood that had caked and congealed; blood that had soaked itself into the floors and had coloured it red.

"My name is Findar," said the man who had pulled Basil and Percival out of the water. "We are Lexters, and we come from The Land of Ice and Snow."

"Percival and Basil here," said Percival gruffly. "I must thank you, my good man, for pulling us out of the water. I must compensate you as soon as this ship gets us home."

"Home?" Findar laughed. "That is a joke. Do you know where you are?"

"Yes," replied Basil. "We are on The White Eagle and we were dancing with these two wenches, Jenna and Trix, before we found ourselves being cast into the water."

"Cast into the water? You are lucky," said another Lexter called Sindar. "I am the king's son," he continued. "We are indeed on The White Eagle. The captain is Azazel, who is the definition of pure evil, magic and malice. He is exceeded in his talent only by The Lord of the Mrodics, whom they call Threye. Trix is Azazel's wife, and Jenna is her sister. They are cruel, merciless creatures."

"You seemed bemused," said another Lexter called Brindar. "Have you never heard of The Mrodics, or Mrod?"

"Nay," replied Percival.

"Then," said Findar, "let us tell each other our stories."

Percival began his story, embellishing his own role with bits of heroism that he felt he did not possess at that moment. Meanwhile, Basil struggled to keep himself from rolling with mirth as Percival finished his story with a flourish.

Then the Lexters began their tale. They had, it seemed, set off on a sea-faring voyage one morning. They were not a sea-faring race, yet Sindar wanted to explore the great world beyond their own. They set sail on a bright, sunny summer morning. The journey went well, and they visited many, many lands. Life was good until, one day, the weather turned foul. It seemed as though the devil himself had whipped up the winds, winds that howled and screamed. The waves appeared possessed; the currents lent the ship a life of its own. It was tossed about like a tinderbox on the raging seas until it crashed onto a rocky island. This is where they stayed for the next few days, in weather that was alternately wet and scorching dry.

"It seemed as though someone was controlling the weather," mused Rollo, a big, fat Lexter. Basil looked at Rollo in wonder. He had never believed anyone could be bigger and fatter than Percival. But here was Rollo. Rollo who seemed to defy the deprivation the Lexters had suffered during the course of their adventures, and at the hands of the Mrodics.

"Yes," said Sindar. "One day, we saw The White Eagle sailing by. We jumped, yelled, shouted, banged tin kettles and prayed to be rescued. And indeed we thought we had been when the Mrodic ship pulled up alongside the island. We had heard of the Mrodics -- the cruellest race on the planet -- but there seemed to be no other way out. We boarded the ship.

Azazel was kind at first, tending to our needs and making sure we were well fed. Then, one night after a feast, we woke up to find ourselves in these dungeons. Since then, life has been a long series of torture and pain. Only Findar here has managed to get out from time to time to explore the ship."

"We must escape!" exclaimed Basil. "Our friends Sally and Thyme are on the ship as well, and will be in danger."

"Yes," squeaked Percival, quivering with fear. "But how?"

"Well," said Findar. "There is something we could try. The chances of escape are slim, but we could attempt it if you want."

There was silence as everyone looked at each other.

"Let's try it," said Percival finally, trying his best to sound brave. "What else can we do?"

Chapter 6

On The White Eagle - 2

There was silence. Everyone looked at each other. Finally, Basil said: "Well, let's go! What are we waiting for?"

Sindar looked around at the rest of the group, and said: "Let us indeed go. Findar, lead the way!"

Escape from the room seemed ridiculously easy; indeed many wondered why they had not attempted escape before. As they walked along the dark passageways of the ship, they were even inclined to laugh. Retaking the ship would be easy enough. A new courage took hold of them.

Had they assumed escape too easily?

The great ship appeared to sway as it rose and fell in synchronicity with the ocean waves. And the passages seemed to glow in the dark, widening and narrowing with every passing step.

"Quick!" gasped Brindar. "There is some fearful magic about this place." As they broke into a run, they heard footsteps behind them. They ran faster and faster. Faster and faster came the footsteps behind them; footsteps that knew the ship, footsteps that spoke of malice and evil intent. They turned a corner, and came to a flight of steps.

Up they ran. Brindar, Sindar and Basil led, with Percival and Rollo making up the rear. As the two larger men huffed and puffed their way up the stairs, the footsteps came closer. They turned to see a group of Mrodics behind them, their eyes gleaming evilly.

Percival paused, and the first Mrodic was almost upon him. At that moment his stomach turned with fear, emitting noxious fumes from his rear into the face of the advancing Mrodic. The Mrodic gasped and fell backwards onto the advancing group. This was the break they were looking for. With a quick look back at the gasping Mrodics our escapees ran on.

Suddenly Basil paused. A light shone under the door in the passageway. Putting his fingers to his lips, Basil signalled complete quiet.

Crawling closer to cracks in the door, Basil and Findar were able to just get a glimpse into The Candle Room. In the centre of the room was a huge oak table. On it a big, red candle burned steadily, casting shadows right across the room. The candle did not seem to diminish as it burned, although wax rolled steadily down it. The shadows in the room seemed to have a life of their own, as the flame danced this way and that. Sitting around the candle were Azazel, Jenna and Trix, swaying gently, their eyes closed, to strange rhythmic music. They appeared to be in deep, meditative thought. What were they contemplating? Neither Basil nor Findar had the power to look into their minds. All that could be seen from the shadows and lines on their faces was that evil was brewing. As Findar's eyes moved to Azazel, he sensed nothing but pure, implacable evil.

Suddenly, there was a massive pushing and shoving. Percival was making his way to the front of the group, his entire spirit guided by an insatiable curiosity. As he pushed his eyes into the crack, he exclaimed in a loud whisper: "Corky!" Basil's hand clamped down hard on his mouth. Yet, the whisper seemed to be enough. A small smile crossed Azazel's face, a smile that was transferred to Jenna and to Trix. They seemed aware that there was something out there. There was a slight shift in the way they swayed. The music changed ever so slightly; it became jagged and slightly harsh.

Suddenly, Rollo turned to find what appeared to be a huge shadow looking down at him. The shadow moved and covered the group crouching in the corridor. A darkness seemed to come over them. Everything went black.

When they awoke they were in a strange room. It was pitch black. The room did not appear to have any doors or windows. The walls and floors were cool, and felt metallic. There was total silence. As they crawled around bumping into each other, the prisoners spoke in whispers. Hope seemed to have drained out of their bodies, as they slumped to the ground.

A sob broke the silence; a sob that sounded like it belonged to Sally. "Sally?" croaked Percival. "Is that you? How did you get here?"

Someone cleared their throat. It was Thyme.

"After you and Basil left with the two women, Sally and I kept dancing. The music was romantic, and we seemed to get closer and closer to each other. It was beautiful. I suddenly felt as if I was with the woman of my dreams, and that whatever else happened, she was the one who would be with me. "Sally, will you marry me," I asked. As she said yes, I whooped with joy. Azazel looked across at me, and with a gentle look on his face asked me why I was so happy.

"When I told him the news, he stood up, clapped his hands, and called: 'A cake, a cake for the happy couple!' After a pause, he continued, 'I would have loved to marry the two of you, but I cannot. A cake will be my engagement gift to you.'

"The cake was brought, and as we cut and ate it everyone clapped and smiled and laughed with us. All seemed well with the world. Then, as we resumed our dance, the ceiling seemed to move around and around and the stars glowed with a fierce intensity. Round and round they went, until we began to feel dizzy. The floor whirled. Or was it us? The movement was hypnotic! Suddenly we sensed Jenna and Trix dancing with us, and the four of us sped around with a speed and rhythm that seemed perfectly unnaturally natural..." His voice trailed off into silence.

"What happened next," asked Findar quietly.

"Who are you," asked Sally with some trepidation in her voice. Findar quickly introduced himself and his fellow Lexters. Their story done, there was silence again.

"What happened next," repeated Findar.

Sally shivered. "A shadow seemed to fall on us, a dark shadow that blotted everything else out. There was no light, no sound, no thoughts. There was darkness, and when we woke up we found ourselves here."

"What's to be done now," Brindar asked. "Nothing," replied Findar. "We cannot escape from this room. I think we are headed for Mrod. We shall see what happens then."

The days passed. There was no way of knowing whether it was night or day. There was only darkness. Food -- good food -- appeared at regular intervals and was taken away. No one knew how this happened, and no one asked. They were all wrapped up in their own thoughts.

Death, the inevitable consequence of their adventures, seemed to be all that awaited them. They hoped that it would be swift, though this seemed unlikely.

Finally, something roused Percival. A bundle of confused thoughts erupted in him. Thoughts of rage, regret, self-pity and vengeance jostled for space in his mind and formed into something more solid. Like the strands of a rope. Somewhere deep in his mind was the realization that he had not conducted himself with the heroism that he would have liked to have associated with his own character.

"Woe is me!" he groaned. "Why did I have to leave my home and embark on an adventure? I could have had a short honeymoon on an idyllic beach somewhere and would have been back home right now sipping tea on my lawn with Mortimer bringing me freshly baked croissants..." His thoughts trailed away as his mind conjured up images of himself and Bessie happily sitting in their garden, the sun filtering gently through the trees. He thought of the flowerbeds with honeybees happily going about their daily chores.

He sighed and wondered again why god had forsaken him. What had he done to deserve this? Melancholic thoughts morphed into thoughts of anger, as he thought about Basil. Why did Basil always have to shove his stinking snout into affairs that were not his? Why had god not struck him down with a lightning bolt?

Was there indeed a God in heaven, wondered Percival. If there was a God, then this God was a selfish, ungrateful brute. How could he forget the offerings that Percival had made Does Sauron live? Does the Ring bind us yet? At his altar? How could he forget the donations he had made to the church, to help in its upkeep? What sort of selfishness was this? Had God become so greedy, so selfish, so mean that he had forgotten? Percival swore that after this horrid adventure he would not give God any more money. He shook his fist in the dark at the Invisible God of his thoughts. Then, realizing the futility of the situation, he wept. Tears gushed down his cheeks and he began to supplicate God. He promised more donations to the church, if only he could be freed that very instant. That, of course, was impossible.

And so Percival sank deep into himself, and his thoughts grew more and more morose. "We are going to be killed. Killed and eaten. My bacon will indeed be fried by this horrible fellow Azazel and his two wenches. There is no hope left..."

Thoughts were all he and his fellow travelers had. Tales ran dry after a few days, and a gloomy silence filled the room. There was no night and there was no day; darkness was their only companion.

One morning, they felt a thud as the ship ground to a halt. The door opened and light streamed in, light that had become so unfamiliar it was painful. The prisoners were rounded up and marched outside. Uncertain steps followed uncertain steps, as they walked along the planks leaving the ship. Their feet touched hard ground and they heard a voice say gently: "Welcome to Mrod."

Ahead of them they saw a creature with white skin and white eyes ringed with yellow. It had three eyes, like the rest of the Mrodics; eyes that appeared gentle yet hid a depth of evil. Evil he was and evil he had been for all of his thousand-odd-year life. They were face-to-face with none other than the infamous Threye.

Chapter 7

The Dungeon Of Thron

As the boat pulled up at the harbour of Mrod, the prisoners were herded, blinking in the sunlight, to the shore. They were standing on firm ground after what seemed like months.

"Welcome to Mrod, my friends," said a kindly voice. Looking up, they found themselves gazing into the eyes of Threye for the very first time. Threye was tall and slender, and his skin was white. Indeed it seemed to shimmer, as did his silver eyes. The expression on his face was warm and friendly, almost avuncular. Yet, the kindly tone in his voice was not fully reflected in his yellow-flecked eyes. Standing behind him was a beautiful Mrodic woman called Kale. She had black hair and black eyes; even her lips were painted black. She wore black clothes, her pale skin contrasting wildly with the black. There was an almost demonic aspect to her.

Next to Kale was a man named Esh. He was Jenna and Trix's father -- the Master Game Player in Mrod.

The three made up the welcome party, and as the prisoners were led to their quarters they could not help but think that this was a group born to welcome them to hell. As they shuffled along, Percival suddenly cried out: "Bessie!". Was he dreaming? Had he gone mad? He was convinced he had seen Bessie standing in the shadows of a tree. But it was a Bessie with tattoos on her arms, and studs in her nose. A Bessie very different from the sweet little thing he had known.

But then the apparition vanished, and Percival was left wondering if it had not just been a figment of his imagination.

As they walked, the prisoners couldn't help but appreciate the lush green landscape. Yet, green as it was it seemed as if the trees, flowers and fruits were all watching them through unseen eyes. The Lexters shivered in the sun, as a sense of eeriness crept into the marrow of their bones. Despite the bright strong sun there was a deathly chill in the air. Laughing and skipping with unseemly glee, Jenna and Trix led them to the prisons.

Azazel followed Threye and Esh into Threye's quarters and they were not to be seen for the rest of the day. Strains of music and weird chanting were heard coming from the quarters, and a thin white smoke seeped out from under the doors.

Back at the prisons, Jenna and Trix sat quietly watching the prisoners as they settled into their new quarters. They did not lack for physical comfort, but there was clearly no chance of escape. Jenna watched Percival closely, as though trying to analyse his soul. Trix's eyes flitted to Basil every now and then.

Time seemed to hang in the air for the prisoners as they waited for what would come next. There was an air of impending doom. Uncertainty seemed to pervade every cell of their being. They looked down at the ground, at their feet, up at the ceiling, at each other and then away. There was nothing they could do to escape their predicament. They cursed the day they had set off on their journey.

Towards evening, Trix suddenly stood up and tittered with glee. "You are all being given a rare honour. You will be asked to go through the Maze. If you succeed, you will have to play the Game of Heads against our team, led by my father Esh. It is rare indeed to be allowed to play this game against us. I doubt you will survive it. No one has." She looked around at all of them, and announced: "Well, my little friends, perhaps you should sleep now. I will come by in the morning to take you to the Maze." She walked off laughing, with Jenna by her side.

"What Maze?" asked Percival, the panic evident in his voice. "Does anyone know about this Maze?" He paced up and down the room, his face twitching nervously. It was apparent that he felt he had come all this way just to die in a Maze.

"Calm down," barked Sally. "No one knows what this Maze is. We will just have to wait and see, right?" She paused, her eyes showing anger, fatigue and irritation. "You are not the only one who is stuck in this bloody situation. Remember, we threw in our lot to try and help you find your Bessie, and all that you have done is to bitch and moan most of the time. Stop it, or I will kick you where it hurts the most!"

She glared, then burst out laughing when Percival quickly brought his legs together and covered his groin protectively with his hands. He looked comical and foolish, and the rest of the group burst out laughing. The laughter seemed to lift the atmosphere, and soon they were rolling around in hysterical mirth. So it was that when Jenna came in later she stood there mystified. "Mad! The thought of impending death had driven them all mad!" With a last look at Percival, she walked back to her own quarters for the night.

The prisoners were led away the next morning. "What a fine day to die," Basil whispered to Thyme who was walking next to him. "Let's see what the day unfolds," replied Thyme. Wondering at Thyme's unending supply of optimist thought, Basil shook his head and walked on.

They arrived at a shimmering wall and found themselves face to face with Esh. He was old, very old, almost as old as Threye. Yet he seemed young. Reddish hair flowed down to his slender shoulders, and his three eyes were flecked with red. His lips smiled a welcome, and his eyes smiled death. His canines were long, and seemed sharp.

Findar shivered and wondered if the teeth had been used to eat people like him. He looked deep into Esh's eyes. The two of them stared at each other until, shivering, Findar looked away.

"Welcome," said Esh. "You will now enter the Maze. Should you escape, you and some of the older prisoners here will join my team and me in the Game of Heads. The rules are simple enough. We start with the head of a previous prisoner. The objective is to be able to cast the head into a loop in your opposing team's side of the field. Along the way, members from each team will attempt to cut off the head of the person carrying the head, and to place it on the line at the end of the opposing team's side of the field. Quite an enjoyable little sport, I must say. We have played this game ten times in the last one hundred years. We have never lost a head, neither the game nor one of our own heads." Licking his lips, Esh turned and whispered something to the wall.

"I designed the Maze myself," he said as a door opened wide. "Enter my friends. You may exit from any door -- if you can..." Laughing with glee, he watched as the prisoners walked into the Maze. "Come my dears," he said to Jenna and Trix. "Let us join Azazel, Kale and Threye."

The prisoners walked along the smooth pathways of the Maze. They appeared relaxed; it seemed easy enough. They marked their path on the ground with little etchings.

Suddenly, the light dimmed and the walls seemed to acquire a life of their own. There was an anguished wail, and hands reached out to grab them. Faces with huge tormented eyes stared down from the walls. Thyme was drawn closer by what seemed to be an almost magnetic pull. As he approached a face, hands reached out and a mouth opened wide as though to engulf him. He inched closer and closer to the wall. His eyes had a glazed look and he moved slowly, very slowly.

The other prisoners stood and stared, transfixed and rooted to the florescent passageway, as Thyme prepared his face to be consumed by the gaping mouth. Just as he was about to kiss the face in the wall, something inside Sally snapped. She jumped at Thyme and pulled him away. The face screamed in anger; red, bulging eyes glared in frustration as Thyme fell away and onto Sally. They tumbled in an ungainly heap onto the floor, Thyme looking up at the ceiling blankly. Percival stepped up to him and slapped him hard across the face. Thyme emerged from his stupor.

"Quick! Hurry!" said Brindar. "Let's move on before we get stuck in this place forever."

They scrambled together and walked on. As they negotiated the turns, music suddenly started to play and they heard dogs barking behind them. They ran, and as they ran small blades seemed to emerge from the walls. Thin and evil, they tore at the pitiful clothing covering the prisoners and soon the floor was spotted with their blood.

"We cannot keep on like this," gasped Findar. "We need to find a way out." He paused. "Let the dogs come," he said. "We will fight them. If we keep running, we will cut ourselves and bleed to death. Let's walk slowly. We will find the light."

The Maze twisted this way and that, alternatively bright and dark, silent and noisy. Hope gave way to despair, and despair gave way to defeat as they slumped to the ground convinced that they had found their common grave.

Anger surged in Sindar's breast. "Damn that Esh," he thought. "If we ever get out of here I shall hunt him down in the Game of Heads and kill him. I will cut his head off, and shall watch as his life blood drains out of him. And I shall gloat over his dead body!"

He lay there for what seemed like forever, and as he lay with his face pressed to the ground, his eyes closed, he felt a cool breeze blowing about his cheeks. He smiled. The floor felt cool and nice, and his mind went back to his home and family. He thought of his wife, and how they had gamboled about during their honeymoon. He giggled with a bit of insanity, and dribble seeped out of his closed mouth. He was going to die, he thought, and never see his wife again. And then the anger was back. He opened his eyes and looked around.

Was that a door in front of him? Was there a chink of light under the door? Or had he finally gone insane? He crawled to his feet and slowly made his way to the door. Heart beating loudly, thoughts and hopes hammering at his brain, he crawled to the door and gently pushed it with his finger, hoping but not expecting it to open. But open it did; slowly, ever so slowly. Light streamed in. Blinking, almost blinded by the incoming light, Sindar realised he had found a way out of the Maze. Or, as he asked himself later, had the exit presented itself to him?

Whooping and screaming, he slapped himself and pulled his hair in a sort of wild delirium. "We're free! We're free! We're free!" he screamed and rushed madly about the same spot. He pulled Findar and Brindar to their feet. Percival looked up blearily, and then whooped for joy. They all ran around in circles, dancing and exulting with the joy of seeing the blue sky and feeling the breeze on their cheeks. They had given up hope, and yet life itself had presented itself back to them.

"Welcome back," said a voice. They wheeled around to find themselves face-to-face with Esh again. Esh spoke directly to Sindar: "So, you would like to face me in the Game of Heads?" he asked. There was a hint of malice, of expectant pleasure in his voice. Clearly, he was going to enjoy hunting down his hapless prey. "You shall have your wish. Trix and Jenna shall take you back, attend to your wounds, and then you will sleep. Tomorrow, along with the other prisoners who will be part of your team, we shall meet again on the field." He paused, adding: "And then, we shall play. And we shall see who gloats then!"

He looked at Sindar with a mixture of arrogance, anger and evil. Then he walked away.

The next morning, before sunrise, the two sisters arrived to wake the prisoners and prepare them for battle. They were dressed in white. "White was chosen for you," said Jenna to Percival, "to contrast with the red blood that will pour out of your body when you die." There was no smile on her face as she patted his uniform into shape.

"You may need this," she said and handed him a small knife. "Keep it safe. You may need this in the end."

The prisoners were taken to the field. Arrayed on one side were the Mrodics, in tunics of red and gold. In the centre of the field, on a pole, was a head, brutally impaled. There were Mrodics all around the field, cheering and shouting. In a box sat Threye, surrounded by Azazel, Jenna and Trix. He had his eyes closed and seemed to be in deep meditation. The players on the field were still. They appeared to be waiting for a sign. As the crowd fell silent, the tension in the air was palpable. Everyone was waiting for Threye to make his move as they sat there in anticipation of blood and gore.

Suddenly Threye opened his eyes, and the crowd erupted. Esh jumped up, grabbed the head, and before anyone could react had lopped off the head of a hapless prisoner. Running swiftly across the field, his sword moving this way and that, he began to cut off heads at will. Five or six people died before there was even a reaction. Rollo saw a Mrodic charging at him, arms raised, sword held high. He blinked and charged at the Mrodic. Instinct propelled him forward and he moved with a speed never before seen in him. The oncoming Mrodic paused momentarily in surprise, not having expected a counter-attack. That was all that was needed. Before he knew what was happening, he was down with Rollo on top of him. He gasped as he felt Rollo's immense weight come crashing down on him, and he felt his sword being taken from his hand. The last thing he saw before his head was separated from his body was the look of madness in Rollo's eyes, mad with the lust of battle.

Things seemed to turn then as Percival and his team got into the fight. There was desperation and little skill in their fighting technique. The desire to live propelled them on, and the battle swung this way and that. The Head too was tossed this way and that as heads from both sides rolled on the ground and were kicked about as though they were bits of rubbish on the field.

The Mrodics had not expected any resistance. Anger muddled their brains as they ran amongst their opponents, slashing and cutting. They lost numbers heavily, and the battle seemed evenly poised. In the stands, Threye and Azazel bent forward, looking keenly on as the game unfolded.

The sun rose in the sky, and sweat ran down the faces of Percival's team. It blinded them, and fatigue made them weak. They would have given up had they not been impelled by their desire to live. Suddenly Esh saw Sindar in front of him. His eyes blazed as he walked resolutely towards him, his third eye flickering as little flames escaped from it. His entire aspect reflected anger, murderous anger. The contempt he had earlier professed had vanished, never to return. He was single-minded in his purpose -- to obliterate all memory of Sindar from this universe. He was blind to everything else.

This blindness was his folly and his undoing. He did not see Percival creep up behind him, and stab him in the small of his back with the knife Jenna had given him. The wound did not kill, but it distracted him. Wheeling around in rage, Esh saw Percival standing there frozen, his eyes full of panic. This was the opening Sindar needed. He leapt forward, sword held high. The sun reflected off the blade, and the sword came down in a blaze of light. As it finished its downward descent it took Esh's head with it. The head rolled to the ground and bounced around. There was a deathly silence as Brindar swooped in, picked up Esh's head and rushed off to the Mrodics' side of the field.

The crowd was deathly quiet. This had never been known to happen. In the main stand, Threye was on his feet in anger. Azazel, Jenna and Trix stood behind him, their bodies tense with shock and anger as they saw Esh's head being carried off. His lifeless body lay on the ground, looking shrunken and insignificant. Threye pursed his lips, and with a wave of his hand snarled: "To the Dungeons of Thron!" He paused, and whispered: "This will be the end of them."

The match over, the prisoners were rounded up again. There was to be no respite, no celebration, as they were taken back to their cell by Jenna and Trix. The walk back was a silent one, as the two sisters were stiff with anger and grief.

"You are going to be taken to the Dungeons of Thron," said Trix grimly. All traces of silvery, tinkling laughter were gone from her voice. She was so accustomed to dealing out pain and death that it had never crossed her mind that one day she would be at the receiving end. She was accustomed to death, other people's death. She was not accustomed to dealing with death at her own doorstep, and she was not sure how she should deal with it. Anger shook every atom of her being; every instinct in her wanted to lash out at Percival and Sindar and kill them on the spot. Yes, death is what she wished for them. She pictured herself standing over their fallen bodies, sword held high, as their life's blood flowed on the ground and seeped into the grass. Her mind was full of thoughts of blood and vengeance; only a fear of Threye prevented her from attacking them that very instant. Oh what she would have given to defy Threye! She also knew that this was something she just could not do.

Jenna walked alongside Trix, deep in thought. Grief engulfed her, and she could not help but dwell on the fact that it was her knife that had caused her father to be fatally distracted. She wondered, with some trepidation, if Threye and Azazel would discover this. What then would be the consequences for her? Was it some strange attraction that she felt for Percival? If so, it was very odd indeed. Jenna had never been attracted to men before. Percival, whom she believed to be weak, was a strange choice indeed. Yet, what is it that rules the powers of attraction? What is it that moves our soul and our hearts? The rules, if indeed there were any, were arbitrary and unpredictable and there was never any accounting for the outcome. Odd though it was, Jenna felt a strange stirring when she looked at Percival. She remained pensive as she led them to the Dungeons of Thron.

They found themselves walking along a wooded path, with the sun filtering in through the trees. The breeze was cool; birds chirped among the branches. The atmosphere was peaceful. "Too peaceful," thought Percival to himself. "It's as though we are destined to see nature for the very last time. I wonder what horrors the dungeon shall bring. Fire, heat, pain, dragons, goblins, mischief..." He sighed and walked in silence, waiting, dreading what was to come.

Finally, they came to a hedge with a rusty old gate that swung open.

"We have arrived," said Trix grimly. "In you go, and may you all die painful deaths." She cast a venomous look at Sindar as he walked through the gate.

The prisoners entered, and the gates creaked shut behind them. They looked around and found that they were on the same path that had brought them here. What was so terrible about this place?

"Let's rest," said Sally. "We have had some really bad days. I think we need to lie in the shade of the tree and sleep."

"Yes," agreed Basil. "I have never felt so tense, so tired, so wrung out in my life. Let's sleep in peace for a while and then figure out our next move."

They trooped to a clutch of trees and lay down on the grass. The grass was soft, and the trees formed a cool green canopy over their heads. As they moved their buttocks on the soft grass, they squirmed with delight. Soft sighs emerged from them all, as they settled down to sleep.

Sleep came and had never seemed to blissful. Soon they were all in a deep slumber, the birdsong punctuated only by soft sighs and gentle snores. Sleep brings with it the power to heal and soothe the most weary and the innocent. Deep sleep comes to those who are clean in heart and conscience, and the group slept the sleep of the dead. Hours passed and the sun began to dip over the horizon. Its rays lit the clouds and painted them fiery shades of red, yellow and orange. The breeze turned cool, and Percival stirred. His eyes flickered open, his mouth opened in a huge yawn. He started to lift a hand to cover his mouth but found that he could not move. He was entwined in the roots of the tree! He was a prisoner!

Kicking and screaming, Percival thrashed about like a madman. Yet even as he writhed, the roots seemed to hold him tighter. He was in the grip of something evil, something malevolent; small spikes from the roots seemed to pierce his clothing and graze his skin.

His screams woke the others. All of them were in the same predicament, and as they thrashed about like wild creatures the trees gripped them tighter and tighter till it seemed they were all about to die. Finally, they ceased their struggles and fell back exhausted. Sleep now was impossible, and as they waited for night to fall they wondered what nightmares were in store for them. Yet night did not fall; the bright colours of the sky remained the same for hours. The red colours of the evening emitted warm uncomfortable rays. Sweat trickled down the prisoners' foreheads and into their nostrils, and hung on the tips of their noses.

"This is unbearable!" moaned Findar. "If this is indeed hell, we are here."

"What do we do?" screamed Sally in agony. "Damn these trees," roared Basil. There was a tumult of noise as they all shouted and swore vengeance at the trees. The more they did this, the tighter they were held. Soon all were breathing heavily, until they fell silent. Then, the only sounds to be heard were the sounds of sobs and moans.

"Death," pleaded Sally, "come quick!" Turning her head, she looked across as Thyme who had been lying silently. His lips moved as though he was in quiet conversation. "He has gone mad," Sally thought in despair. Love was about to die, or find its last breath in the realm of madness and insanity. She fell back, limp with desolation, tears and sweat dripping down her cheeks. She asked for oblivion, but nothing came. She wriggled her fingers and moved her shoulders. She felt herself passing into a world of dreams until... until she felt a hard slap on her cheek. Gasping with shock, she opened her eyes to see Thyme standing over her. "Quick!" he whispered. "The trees have given us ten minutes to leave. Let's get the others quickly before they squeeze us to death. Scrambling to her feet in shock, Sally saw Thyme darting this way and that, rousing everyone and dragging them to their feet. Finally, as the ten minutes drew to a close, the roots snapped shut and withdrew to their original positions.

They were safe!

"But how?" gasped Brindar.

"I found that I could talk to the trees," Thyme explained. I don't know how, but I found that they listened to me. I don't know why, but they seemed to like me."

"Babbling baboon!" snapped Basil. "Who talks to trees? Pah! I never heard such rot!"

"Then how are you standing here, you fat little piece of pork!" said Sally. She walked up to Basil and glared at him, her eyes flashing fire. They stood there, arms akimbo looking at each other. Suddenly Basil took a step back, flung his arms into the air and laughed. He laughed till the tears rolled down his cheeks. Sally looked at him, completely mystified. Finally, she could take it no more and poked him hard in the ribs.

"What the hell are you laughing for, you buffoon?" she snapped at him.

"The little lady defending her man!" chortled Basil.

Sally went pink in the face, and looked away.

"Silly buffoon," she muttered.

"Come on, let's move," said Percival. "Let's get away from this forested area. Maybe we should walk in the shade, but not sleep under the trees from now on."

They walked on. The wind was cool and walking was fun. The terror of the trees was soon forgotten; once again it turned into a fun walk in the park. Indeed, the day did not seem to end. The beautiful sun, the clouds became a little painful to look at. There was no change in the sky. Nothing moved. Nothing moved at all.

"Even the clouds are not moving," said Brindar suddenly. "This is weird. What is happening? We are in a strange place. Don't you think that the sky and the clouds look unreal? Almost like a painting?"

Startled, the others looked up. Then they all began to talk at once. Nervousness set in again as the tranquil mood suddenly evaporated. This was unreal. It was as though they were in a cardboard world. Were they in a painting? Was nothing real anymore?

Sindar stopped by a stream and knelt down. Dipping his hands into the water to get some to drink, he jumped back with an expression of disgust.

"The water tastes like oil!" he cried. "Like a thick oil!"

He stared at the others and suddenly started to cry.

"Damn, we are screwed! We shall die here with oil in our mouths. And we shall become part of a painting. This is exactly what they want, as revenge for us beating them at their own game..." He lay on the grass and beat the ground in despair. "There is no hope!" Then, he stopped and looked at Brindar in shock.

"What did you do that for?" he asked, holding his stinging cheek.

"There is always hope," said Brindar. "While there is life in us, there is hope. When we die, when the flame is extinguished, that is when there is nothing. There is no hope when we lose the flame in our hearts. As long as the fire burns, there is hope. We know that the Mrodics are evil. If we all take a vow now, to fight the Mrodics, we shall be imbued with a purpose that is stronger than life. That is when we shall find a way to escape this infernal place."

There was silence. Sindar staggered to his feet. "Let's move on," he said.

The sky darkened, and night fell. The wind blew through the trees telling tales of madness, despair, torture and death. It laughed at them -- a thin evil laugh. The sounds stayed with them even when they stopped their ears. They walked on, searching for direction, looking for a way out. Suddenly, the moon peeped out at them from between the trees. Its light seemed to reach down to them and fall at their feet. They looked at it in wonder; Rollo walked up to it as though mystified. He touched the light. It felt cool and solid to the touch. It calmed him; the light wrapped itself around his wrist and lifted him.

"Hey!" shouted Findar. "Catch him before he disappears!" He grabbed Rollo's ankles as Rollo was lifted high off the ground. Findar rose along with Rollo; then Brindar and Sindar grabbed Findar and soon they were all airborne. Last off the ground were Basil and Percival as they grabbed Thyme's ankles.

"Stop!" Basil and Percival looked down to see Trix and Jenna rushing towards them, swords in their raised hands. The two pigs closed their eyes, expecting any moment to be cut down mid-flight. But they did not feel the cold touch of the blade. They opened one eye each, only to see Jenna and Trix standing there, swords on the ground. They opened their third eye to shoot bolts of flame at the prisoners, but nothing happened.

"Quick! Grab them!" gasped Jenna as she jumped. Trix jumped with her and they grabbed onto Percival and Basil's ankles, pulling down hard. Yet, pull as they might, they found themselves being lifted higher and higher by the moonbeam, along with the rest of the group.

Up and up they went, into the clouds and up beyond them.

"What just happened?" rasped out Jenna. No one has ever escaped the Dungeons of Thron! Never!"

She looked down and closed her eyes. The world disappeared below her as she was pulled like the others into the inky black sky.

"This is the end," she thought. "We shall never be allowed to return."

Chapter 8

Escape From Mrod

It was dark. All they could feel was the brush of cold air as they swirled and whirled around in a daze. All conscious thought drained from their bodies; they were but a chain of connected beings flying upwards into the great void. Up, up, up they flew, twirling and twisting together like the strands of a giant rope. The moonbeam lit them up, bathing them in a silvery light, and when it seemed as if they could go no higher, they paused and twirled slowly about one point. Then they started to fall. Faster and faster they headed towards earth. Then, just when it appeared likely that they would crash to the ground with sickening consequences, their downward flight was arrested. An invisible force separated them and placed them gently on the ground.

They lay there for what seemed a long while, until conscious thought returned to each of them individually. As their eyes focussed, they realised they were outside the Dungeons of Thron, and at the pier of Mrod harbour. It was night and all was quiet. They could just about discern the hulk of a ship ahead of them.

The Raven, gasped Jenna. The two sisters looked at each other. This was the ship originally meant for them, before Azazel started to take them for journeys on The White Eagle.

"We cannot go back," whispered Trix. "We will be killed!"

"Unless we take them prisoner," whispered Jenna.

"Quick!" whispered Trix back. "We need to move fast."

The two sisters rose to their feet and began moving towards the rest of the group lying on the ground. As they approached Percival and Basil, who were closest to them, Trix whispered: "This should be easy."

As they bent down over the two figures lying supine on the ground, their expressions changed from triumph to shock. Percival and Basil suddenly opened their eyes and grabbed the sisters by their throats. Slowly, as if engaged in a perfectly synchronized dance, they rose, hands clutching throats, squeezing gently but hard. Jenna and Trix grasped the wrists of the two men, as they got to their feet; their breath came in short, painful gasps. As the hands tightened, the girls started to lose consciousness.

"Stop! Have you gone mad?!"

An agitated voice piped up behind them, and they turned quickly. Sally slapped them both hard on the face. Percival and Basil's eyes snapped, as though waking from a trance.

"Fools!" Sally hissed. "Without these two we cannot escape! We cannot take the ship. There will be magic in these ships that only these two can manage."

As Jenna and Trix sank to the ground, clutching their throats and gasping for air, Sally bent towards them and rasped out a question: "Will you take us on the ship? Quick! Or we shall kill you."

Hatred streamed through their eyes, but the sisters nodded assent.

"Yes, we will take you," said Jenna. "In any case, we cannot go home. But we have to move now. It will not be long before Threye and Azazel notice that you have escaped from the dungeon, and they will come after you."

"Yes," continued Trix. "Vengeance and murder will be uppermost in their minds. No one has escaped the dungeon before. How you did it is amazing! No one has ever won in the Game of Heads either, We simply don't know what happened. We will be blamed for not having been able to hold you back in the dungeon, and if we are caught we will be put to death."

Silent, like the night, the group boarded The Raven. It seemed as if the ship had been waiting for them; as they climbed on board it moved away almost as though it had a mind of its own. The Raven glided through the waters and soon they were out of the harbour and sailing on the open seas.

The new day in Mrod saw Threye and Azazel in deep conference. Threye's eyes flashed as he paced up and down his room, talking in his soft dangerous voice.

"They escaped from the dungeon and took The Raven. Jenna and Trix have gone with them. The two are henceforth banished!"

He paused: "When we catch The Little Birds, they shall be brought back to Mrod in chains. No more games for them to play. No more mazes. No more dungeons. Just a slow, painful death. I shall personally take care of Jenna and Trix."

Threye's voice trailed off as he looked at Azazel. "The laws of our land are strict. You know this. Trix is your wife but she has failed in her task. There is no room in Mrod for failure and deserters. Harden your heart. She must pay for her sins... and die."

The two looked at each other across the room. Neither spoke. Then Azazel nodded his head and said simply: "Yes."

"Good," smiled Threye. His eyes wore cold, cruel, implacable look. No one had bested him in over one thousand years, and hate filled every pore of his being. "Call in the rest."

As The Raven sailed away, a small group assembled in Threye's cabin. The cabin gleamed with a yellow light; yellow eyes seemed to be watching everyone assembled there. Azazel, Kale, Bessie and Dragor stood in silence, waiting for Threye to speak.

"The Little Birds have escaped the nest," said Threye. "This is unacceptable to us. I need to have them brought back. Snare them and bring them to me. Judgment will be pronounced, and their fate shall be decreed. The reward they get for their escape will be given to them. You are my chosen band. Go and bring them back to me."

Looking at Dragor and Bessie, he continued softly: "Dragor, you have done me proud in your time with me. I expect nothing short of exemplary performance from you. Bessie, this is your first major task. I know that you will not disappoint me."

His voice was soft and full of menace. His skin gleamed with a translucent white light, and his eyes sparked yellow. As he opened his third eye, he fixed them all to the spot. The eye moved from one to the other, searching, probing their souls for signs of any weakness, anything that would indicate that they were not with him heart and soul. As they stood there, they felt their souls being pried open, layer by layer, until all was bared to Threye's penetrating gaze. Then, finally, the eye closed, and they felt the life return to their bodies.

"Go forth!" concluded Threye softly.

Meanwhile, The Raven sailed swiftly on, its passenger's safe on board.

The days passed with Jenna and Trix holed up in their cabins, refusing to mingle with the rest of the crew, although they accepted the food that was given to them.

One night, a week after their escape, The Raven docked at a harbour.

Percival grunted and knocked at the door of the sisters' cabin.

"What's this place then?" he asked.

"What place?" replied Trix with irritation.

"We seem to have arrived at a harbour where everything is huge. Come and have a look. Is this one of your little tricks to have us re-captured? Well, it is simply not going to work.

Reluctantly, the two sisters left the cabin with Percival and stood stunned when they reached the deck.

"Where are we?" whispered Trix. "We have never seen this place before!"

"Well then, let's explore it," said a voice behind her.

Wheeling around, Trix saw Basil looking directly at her. He seemed to be noticing her for the very first time in his life. And as he gazed at her he thought he had never seen anyone as beautiful as Trix. Something of the gawking teenager seemed to come back to him as he mumbled.

"Cor... Shall we, then? Shall we walk together?"

"There seems to be no choice," smirked Trix, her eyes glimmering with amusement. This was indeed the first time she had smiled since that fateful evening in the dungeon.

They alighted and went ashore. The landscape was oddly, bare, reminding them of a desert. Yet there were trees and as they left the harbour they found themselves in a huge ground, surrounded by cliffs. Vegetation grew out of the cliff walls, vegetation that was low enough to grasp, and strong enough to allow them to climb. As they inched their way up the walls, the sun shone down on them mercilessly. The hard shrubs cut their hands, and blood trickled down their arms, mingling with the sweat.

Panting and wheezing, Brindar and Findar made it to the top first, followed by Percival and Basil and the rest of the group. The women came last.

As Percival looked down to note their progress, his eyes widened with shock.

A great, big, hairy, matted creature had got hold of Jenna, and another Trix. The two were pinned to the ground, with The Matted Giants' slobbering faces just inches from theirs.

Jenna and Trix closed their eyes. Spittle dripped off the giants' tongues as they licked their lips and drooled over the two girls. Their lust-inflamed faces drew closer and their fetid breath seemed to penetrate the very lungs of the two sisters lying powerless under them. Rage, impotent rage, shook their bodies as they struggled to escape the clutches of the monsters. This was something they had never experienced before. They had been used to power all their lives; tears of anger and frustration ran down their cheeks mingling with the dust below. And then the sun was blotted out as the giants fell on them, crushing the air from their lungs. They gasped in brief shock before passing into blissful oblivion.

With a roar of rage, Percival and Basil launched themselves from the top of the cliff onto the giants below. Years later, they often spoke of what possessed them to jump.

"A moment of madness," Percival would grin.

"Or clarity," Basil would retort.

Jump they did. The air whizzed past their ears as they flew to meet the earth below. The rest of the group stopped and stared as they saw the stout pair flying through the air towards the giants. A kind of madness propelled them on their downward path, and to the flying duo they seemed to accelerate faster than gravity would normally allow. They crashed into the giants, the impact knocking the breath from them. The giants fell on top of Jenna and Trix, crushing them. Roaring with rage, they stood up and, bending down, picked up the duo as they lay panting and gasping on the ground.

"Gor!" screamed Percival in shock. "What the hell!" The world seemed to move very fast indeed. Round and round they went, the scenery reduced to a blur. Then they were on the ground, where they lay, dizzy, with the sky revolving above them.

There was bedlam as the rest of the gang came crashing down on the giants. The air was filled with roars, as more of the hairy creatures joined in the fray, and the squeals of members of the gang as the giants made quick work of them. The skirmish was short and brutal. Percival and gang were clubbed to the ground and taken off to the village where they were put into a cage.

"Prisoners again! Damn! This is crap!" thought Percival glumly, as he wrinkled his nose in disgust at the stench surrounding the cage. The cage itself was large, its bars covered in sharp pointed plants. There were giants on every side. And absolutely no chance of escape.

"No privacy even," whispered Sally to Trix. "Are we expected to do our stuff in front of these men?"

"I hope not," whispered Jenna. "We'll have to do it when they are asleep. More importantly, how do we escape?"

They could see a cauldron in what seemed to be the centre of the village. From time to time, prisoners would be dragged, screaming, and flung into the boiling cauldron. What followed made them close their eyes and stop their ears. Still, they could hear the giants chomping on the boiled remains of the poor soul who had met his unhappy fate.

Whispers ran back and forth in the group as their agitation increased with each passing day. They had to escape! But how? Food came to them at regular intervals; they felt like throwing it away, but dared not. The leering eyes of the giants did not leave the women, who felt it was only a matter of time before they were taken by the giants for purposes other than to be eaten.

By the week's end they were all too depressed to even think about what to do. The food fattened them, making them all plump and oily.

"Looks like we are being fattened for the kill," said Thar glumly. "When they throw us into the cauldron there will be enough of us to eat. Maybe they will fry us in our own fat. We will be tasty enough..."

No one said anything; depression ran deep in the camp. The thought uppermost in everyone's mind was: who would be first?

The sun set behind the clouds. Sally looked at the giant leering at her.

"Disgusting fellow!" she thought. "If I could pluck his eyes out, I would!"

"Ouch!" she yelled as Jenna kicked her. "What did you do that for?" she asked angrily.

"Smile at him!" Jenna instructed.

"Are you mad, bitch?!" Sally almost screamed.

"No," replied Jenna calmly. "This is the thing to do. It may be the key to our escape. Now listen calmly."

Completely confused Sally just stared at her.

"If these giants are made to believe that we like them, maybe they will let one of us out for a bit of fun. As soon as that happens, the other will sneak out, grab the keys hanging from his belt and stick them into his eyes." So saying, she showed Sally some of the barbs that she had bitten off the bars of the cage.

"And if that does not work?" demanded Sally. "What then?"

"Then, we smile at two of them. Let them fight amongst themselves. In the confusion, we make our escape."

"Devious..." smirked Trix, her eyes lighting up. "I like it."

Looking at Sally, the two sisters said in unison, "It's the only solution. We cannot beat them by sheer force. We will have to use feminine guile."

Before waiting for an answer, Jenna whispered to Percival and soon the cage was buzzing with excitement. Thyme demurred, but was silenced with grim looks by the others. Basil rolled over to him and snarled: "Don't you bugger this up my friend. No time for jealousy here."

Morning came, and with it a beautiful sunrise that shone on Sally's face. It made her look even more beautiful than usual, and as she tossed her head in the morning rays, the light danced and played lovingly with the waves of hair that adorned her face. She lay on her stomach, face cupped in her hands, looking longingly at one of the giants. The ugly beast grinned back at her, and, slobbering with lust, approached the cage. Sally did not understand a word he said. Nor did he. Yet the language of love and desire was all that was needed to convey the message: He was to approach at night, when she would slip out of the cage and be united with him.

As the day wore on, the two exchanged glances from time to time. Thyme walked up and down the cage looking agitated. His brain told him that it was the right thing to do, but he hated the looks Sally was giving the accursed giant. He would willingly have dug his fingers into the giant's eyes and ripped them out, but he knew that he would probably have been eaten alive in return. With a burning feeling in his heart, he swallowed his pride and his jealousy. Sally had never looked so alluring as she did that day.

As day must give way to night, the sun passed into the shadows once again. It was the night of the new moon. The group looked up at the skies, silently thanking the heavens for the shadows into which they hoped to melt. They lay down and pretended to sleep. All but Thyme, who kept one jealous anxious eye open at all times.

The night grew still. Then, there was a small squeak. Silence again. Then the squeak gave way to a grating noise, and the gate swung open. Sally slipped out, giggling softly as the giant made mumbling sounds. She stood against the gate, stroking the giant's belly. His chest was too high for her to reach and she pulled at his chest hair, pulling his head down towards her.

His head bent, his dank, foul breath reached her nostrils in a thick blast of malodorous wind. His eyes shone and his teeth gleamed in the dark. And then there was a yell of pain, as the light in his eyes went out. Screaming in anger, the giant pulled away but before he could regain his senses, the other eye went out and he could not see. Trix had struck with lightning speed! As the great creature jumped around in agony, the group quickly exited the cage.

Fires were lit in the village as giants swarmed the yard. Howls of rage rent the night. The anger of the giants towards the lustful one was brutal: they clubbed him to the ground and shattered his skull. It was this mad rage that gave The Little Birds the time they needed to escape through the bushes towards the sea.

Guided by instinct, they ran as fast as they possibly could and went crashing over the walls of the short cliff that separated the village from the bay where The Raven was moored.

One by one they rolled down the cliff wall to land with painful grunts on the sandy shore below. Instinct was all that guided them as they rose swiftly and boarded the ship which pulled away a second before the first giant reached the shores.

Lying on the floor of the ship, feeling their bruises, they listened to the roars of anger and vengeance that soared high into the night sky.

"Where now?" asked Percival as soon as they had somewhat recovered.

"Home!" said Brindar.

"Yes," nodded Sindar. "To The Land of Ice And Snow we go. There we can rest at my father's village and prepare ourselves for the onslaught that shall follow. I feel it in my heart that the giants and Azazel will pursue us there. We have to recover our strength and prepare for the battles that shall follow us."

He looked around at the group, challenging them to come up with a better idea.

"What say ye?" Thar suddenly asked Jenna and Trix.

"We are with you," said Jenna. "You may think that you have been mistreated by my people. Yet we two now do not have a home. Threye will have us tortured and killed if we return home. I am sure of it. By now he would have discovered the little knife I gave Percival, and the two of us will be considered traitors. We are with you till the bitter end."

She looked at Percival and said: "It took a long time for me to forgive myself for giving you the knife with which you stabbed my father. It took longer for Trix to forgive me. Threye will know this. He will not forget. And he will not forgive."

"He could not have possibly known what I would use the knife for," said Percival. "Even I did not know. I did not know that it would be my knife wound that would give Sindar the opening to kill Esh. How could Threye not forgive you?"

"You don't know Threye," said Trix. "One day you will..."

Chapter 9

The Battle At The Land of Ice And Snow

As the Raven raced to the Land of Ice and Snow, Sally noticed that Percival and Jenna were becoming closer and closer. "Look at the two of them," she whispered to Thyme one day, as she watched them on the deck looking at the setting sun. The orange light lit their faces with a glow that only appears in the souls of people who are discovering true love for the first time.

"What about them?" replied Thyme. "Two folks having a chat are all I see."

"You are blind," snapped Sally in a huff as she went off to tell Basil who then told Trix, who then questioned Jenna about it. Jenna growled at Trix, but flushed deep red and looked away.

"You are in love with the pig?" asked Trix incredulously.

"I don't need to answer that," sniffed Jenna, blushing like a new rose.

As Jenna began to spend more and more time with Percival, Trix found herself spending a lot more time in Basil's company. To her surprise, she discovered that they were similar in many respects. Aggressive, fond of breaking rules, ruthless; and both had a fondness for toying with people. Trix discovered a kindred spirit in Basil, and the two of them found each other's company extremely pleasant.

As they reached the Land of Ice and Snow, scenes of joy and warm embracing filled the evening. Sindar the Elder was in tears as he held his son close. "I had almost given you up for good, though something in my heart told me you would return," he said.

As father and son embraced, the White Eagle sped onwards. Sailing alongside was another ship called the Black Dragon, captained by Dragor and Bessie. As the two ships went in search of the Raven, they pillaged and burned villages and towns along the way. Blood-lust raged in their veins, and as people kneeled and begged for mercy they laughed in the madness of their power and their strength. They had not felt like this in some time; memories of their defeat by the Little Birds from Mrod still stung.

As their ship sailed on, and as they focused more on killing and looting than on chasing, the gap between them and the Raven widened.

After the initial celebrations were over, Sindar the Elder declared one evening that they had no time to lose, and that they would need to prepare for battle. He was convinced there would be reprisals, and his only hope was that they would not be attacked before the winter.

"This," he said, "will be our strength."

Indeed, the days had begun to turn cold, and everyone was turfed out in the morning. This was particularly hard on Percival, who loved to sleep in. Indeed, he hated the cold; there was nothing that gave him more joy than wrapping himself up in his blankets and sleeping through till late in the morning. But alas! The covers were yanked off each morning, and if he protested there was the inevitable shock of cold, cold water as it was splashed onto his sleeping body.

"Oy!" he yelled the first time this happened. "That ain't fair... Brrr... It's so cold... I hate this! I hate this! I hate this! Why do we have to go?"

"Another bucket, Mr Percival?" Thar would enquire politely. "If you aren't quick, you'll miss breakfast and will have to run another ten rounds of the village."

"Naked," he added as he walked out the door.

"That Thar!" grumbled Percival sullenly as he changed quickly. "If I get my hands on him, I shall wring his neck." But wring his neck he did not. Instead, he huffed and puffed and cursed and cried his way around the village. He had to learn to climb trees, crawl through the stinking bogs, and learn how to fight. Worse, there was humiliation as he had to wrestle Jenna and was laid out on his back in less than a minute. He grunted and heaved, and only just managed to push her off his chest.

"Now with me, with me, with me!" trilled Trix, and the next minute he was laid out on his back again.

"Get off me, you witch!" yelled Percival.

"Or what, my future brother-in-law?" smirked Trix. "You'll smack me?"

"Whaaat?"

"Push me off, little brother," taunted Trix again.

"Witch!"

The training continued, and it was hard on them all. The only person who seemed to be able to skip training was Thyme. Thyme spent long hours walking in the Black Forest that ringed the village on the eastern side. From time to time, Trix would accompany him there. The two would come back from each visit quiet and withdrawn.

"How can they escape to walk in the woods?" grumbled Basil to Sally. Sally merely shook her head and turned away. Basil grumbled to Percival, and they grumbled to Jenna, who looked away. Finally, they grumbled to Thar, and to Brindar, until their grumblings reached Sindar the Elder, who merely said: "Let them be. Let them walk in the forest. It is good."

He paused, and added with a touch of asperity. "Do not gawks at me like two little schoolboys who have lost their lollypops!"

Finally, one night, Sindar announced: "The training is over. We will celebrate with dinner at my home."

The first snows had fallen on the ground, and it was starting to freeze. Trembling and shaking with cold, Percival and his friends arrived at Sindar's house. Dinner was a grand affair. The company was good, and boisterous, the food melted in their mouths, and the music set their souls on fire. Finally, Sindar rose and said: "I would like to offer a toast, but I fear that I may have left the last bottle of wine outside." Turning to Percival, he asked him to go and get it.

With a low moan, Percival walked outside and as he did so a fierce blast of air shut the door fast behind him. Before he could turn, he heard a low growl, and looking over his shoulder saw the largest, fiercest wolf imaginable. Yellow eyes glared at him, and the creature's tongue hung down over the sharpest, longest set of teeth Percival had ever seen. The wolf was huge, with matted black hair and a muscular body. It looked hungry, and as it pounced Percival set off with a yowl of terror. Round and round they went. Fast as the wolf was, Percival was faster. Fear motivated him and he flew over the icy ground with the sureness of one who had lived on ice all his life. Finally, however, stamina runs out before the will does and Percival could run no more. He turned to face the wolf, panting and coughing. Yet the instinct to live was strong within him, and as the wolf pounced Percival held it in a grip that was stronger than he had ever imagined. Fighting with desperation, he wrestled the wolf to the ground. As his hand gripped its throat, the animal seemed to melt and disappear into the ice.

Percival lay on the ground, stunned and exhausted. He only just managed to open his eyes when he heard the sound of clapping.

Sindar the Elder was standing over him, naked from the waist up, clapping and smiling. His eyes shone like two bright stars, and all that Percival could blearily ask was: "Don't you feel cold?" And then he fainted with exhaustion.

He came round to find himself surrounded by Lexters who smiled and raised their glasses to him in a toast. He stood up but was still too shaken to speak. As he looked around, he was knocked down by a charging smiling Jenna who smothered him in kisses, kisses that he returned with fervour. When he finally managed to stand up, he was looking into the eyes of Basil and Trix, who were both smirking and giggling.

"Witch!" he muttered.

"Sleep well tonight," said Sindar the Elder. "We will be attacked in two days. Tomorrow, I shall announce plans for our defence. Brindar will lead in the east, Sindar in the west. Thar and I shall retreat to the Icy Mountain."

Glancing at Percival, Jenna and the others, he announced: "Your roles shall be given to you tomorrow. Sleep well."

Meanwhile, the White Eagle and the Black Dragon continued their loot and pillage, the chase almost forgotten. Then, one morning, Azazel emerged onto the deck, his face drawn. He seemed nervous.

"We have forgotten our quest," he said. "Threye has reminded us of the purpose of our trip. Moreover, he has advised us against killing for the sake of killing. He has reminded me of the need to conserve our energy. We are guilty of wasting our time and energy, and of possibly letting the Little Birds get away. We are to make for the land of the Matted Giants who shall accompany us on our journey. From there, we shall make for the Land of Ice and Snow."

Saying this, Azazel retreated to emerge only when they landed on the shores of the Land of the Matted Giants, and again when they reached the Land of Ice and Snow.

Rumours gained ground on board the Black Dragon as the Kreechurs speculated about Azazel's absence.

"Been spanked by Threye has he?" they wondered.

"Yeah, got his buns whipped," someone quipped.

"He is going to be demoted," was the final consensus of the group as they neared the Land of Ice and Snow.

They arrived, finally. Three ships quietly waited by the shore as the dark night looked down at them, stars peeping through the shadows. The moon cast eerie shadows on the ships. Azazel emerged on deck and said: "We shall be moored here for two days. Two nights from now, on the night of the new moon, we shall attack."

"Who was that?!" he snapped suddenly, hearing a snigger coming from the Black Dragon. He looked across, his pupil-less eyes glowing white in the dark. Striding across deck, he searched amongst the suddenly cowering Kreechurs. Then, suddenly, his third eye opened and fire streamed from it turning the hapless Kreechur into a smoking pile of cinder.

"I hope the whispering from the Black Dragon will now stop," he hissed at Dragor. "Rally them around. Instill discipline in your group, or there shall be more deaths before we attack."

A shaken silence fell upon the group as Azazel returned to his cabin, to emerge only on the second day when the moon presented its dark face to the world.

It was quiet as only death can be. Azazel's eyes glowed in the dark as he slowly motioned the group forward. Like a long, ghostly shadow the crews of both ships alighted on the shores of the Land of Ice and Snow and made their way to the village where Thar and his companions lived.

The ice had set in, and the marauders were soon chilled to the bone. The night was quiet, and a pale moon gave a thin, shimmering light that was enough for them to see their way. Not a sound was heard, and the air seemed still, almost frozen. The cold rushed from the handles of their swords to their hands, and seeped its way into their bodies. The Kreechurs were the worst affected, not being used to cold of this nature, and not being very well equipped. Yet move forward they did, without complaint, for fear of being burned to a crisp in a flash of Azazel's eye.

Not a sound was uttered as they made their way to the village square. They approached Sindar's house. Dragor kicked it open and went inside.

"There's no one home!" he sneered to Azazel. "The Little Birds have flown."

"Stinking cowards," grinned Bessie. "Scared of our wrath and our vengeance, they chose to escape."

Azazel was quiet. He looked up at the sky. After what seemed a long while, he spoke: "A part of the group has escaped up into the mountains. I will follow them with my crew and hunt them down. They shall not live to regret this. Death shall come to them, and I shall make them hurt. Come Kale. We have work to do."

"What about us?" asked Dragor. "What shall we do?"

"Stay here with your crew, and the Giants. Secure the village. Kill anyone you see. Have no mercy. Then, burn down the village. Let it be razed to the ground, to be forgotten for all time to come."

His eyes glowed with vengeance as he made his way towards the Icy Mountain. The Mrodics followed, arrogant in their confidence that revenge was near at hand.

Dragor, Bessie and the Kreechurs stayed behind. Bessie kicked open the door to Brindar's home. The fireplace was still lit; the flames cast eerie shadows on her face. How she had changed. Gone was the innocent young girl who blushed when Percival looked at her. Gone was the shy bride who accompanied Percival on their honeymoon. That person was replaced by an almost murderous woman. Her arms were covered in tattoos, and she was fiercer than any of the Kreechurs who cowered before her in fear. This now was a creature that revelled in blood, death and torture. She looked around the cottage, and smirked: "The little cowards have run away." She noticed some wine and food, and remarked to Dragor: "Well, there is no harm in partaking of some of the refreshment while the Kreechurs keep watch outside. What do you say, my love?"

Dragor smiled, the gold in his teeth glinting in the firelight. Sitting beside Bessie, with his arms around her, he laughed a coarse laugh. "Well, we certainly deserve this."

Meanwhile, the Kreechurs huddled outside around a fire they had lit. The Giants sat some distance away, unaffected by the cold.

Teeth chattering, the Kreechurs cursed Bessie for making them sit outside whilst she ate and drank inside. They swore silently, not daring to voice the mutinous thoughts swirling around in their heads. Indeed, they were so preoccupied with their dark thoughts that they were totally unprepared for the bolt of fire that suddenly landed in their midst, burning three on the outer circle. Jumping up in panic, they looked around searching wildly for whoever was now firing fiery bullets at them, killing three of four Kreechurs instantly. Their piteous screams rent the midnight air, as their flesh sizzled. Dragor and Bessie came running out only to see their soldiers writhing in the agonies of death.

The Lexters and their friends swarmed the area, and the battle began in real earnest. Fires were burning around them, and the smell of burning flesh mingled with the crackle of the flames as it consumed all that came in its path. The Giants were up on their feet, roaring and charging. Suddenly, they stopped in their tracks. Trix and Thyme were approaching, Trix looked alluring. Her well-muscled and shapely legs looked inviting, and her waistline showed hints of promises to come. With a 'come hither' flick of her index finger, she beckoned the Giants to follow them into the Black Forest.

Maddened by lust, and seething with violent thoughts, the giants followed Trix and Thyme into the forest, crushing foliage underfoot and banging and hacking at the trees. The Forest stood there, ancient in its wisdom and implacable in its hate for all those who violated the spirit of the trees. Darkness engulfed them as soon as they entered; all they could hear was Trix's silvery laugh, urging them on. They crashed about, oblivious of the thickening air until they suddenly stopped, panting for breath. Despite the cold, they were sweating and breathing heavily. As they paused, almost doubled over, they did not notice the branches swooping low over them. Sap began to drip from the leaves, and onto the creatures, burning its way through their hair and skin. The Giants screamed in agony, thrashing wildly about. But the more they struggled, the more they were drawn in by some inexorable force. Slowly the sap dissolved skin and bone as, one by one, the Giants perished in that forest, the darkness blotting out the remaining light from their eyes. The breath went out of them, and the last of the Giants died there in the Black Forest, which stood immovable in its malice. The only two who had ever been allowed into the forest were Thyme and Trix, and as they bowed to the trees the trees seemed to thank them for the feast. Thus they were bound together, pig, Mrodic and forest; bound together in a silent pact, for eternity.

Back at the clearing, the battle raged on. Swords clashed as the Kreechurs fell one by one. Dragor and Bessie were the only ones who seemed to be able to hold their own in the battle, until finally Bessie and Percival came face-to-face. The fires played wildly on her face, as she looked at Percival with hatred in her eyes. They had not seen each other since that fateful night at The Black Pub. For what seemed to be a moment, they paused in the heat of battle, and looked at each other in the eye. Percival looked for signs of love in her eyes, but found none.

"Die, pig!" she screamed as they circled one another. "Die, so that I can then be free to marry Dragor." She spat in his face. Blinking, Percival managed to croak: "Why the hate? What did I ever do to you to warrant this hate?"

Without pausing, Bessie screamed: "You are weak, accursed man. And, now you die!" She jumped at him and knocked Percival to the ground. She stood over him, sword raised, poised to lop his head off. Percival lay on the ground, helpless in his anguish, and waited for death to come. Yet, that was not his day to die. As her sword started its descent, Bessie suddenly stumbled and fell, knocked down by a blow from Jenna. It was now Jenna's turn to stand over Bessie as she lay on the ice. The two women snarled at each other.

Teeth bared, Bessie sneered: "You shall die a miserable death, you traitorous bitch!" But then blackness came over her as Jenna clubbed her on the head. She was trussed up and hung on the nearest tree, as Jenna returned to the fray.

Elsewhere, Dragor and Basil were locked in a fierce battle. Trading blows, the two seemed evenly matched. They circled each other, panting, eyes locked, each willing the other to blink. Out of the corner of his eye, Dragor saw Bessie being clubbed to the ground. This was the opening Basil was looking for. Jumping at Dragor, he swung his sword. Dragor tried to duck and shield himself with his arm, as the sword came crashing down on him. Screaming with pain, blood gushing from his wound, Dragor turned and ran for his life, back to the shore where he scrambled aboard his ship and waited for the others to return.

The battle was soon over, and not a single Kreechur was left alive. Blood stained the ice red in some form of grotesque artistry. Mangled bodies, severed limbs, and blood filled the once pure white bed of ice and snow.

Percival and his friends gathered in Brindar's cabin, and they did not notice Micla slowly making his way to Bessie's trussed-up body. A Lexter, Micla was a mean, scrawny sort of fellow, shifty-eyed and miserable. Forever jealous of his brother, Zalyts, he had let the poison of envy eat away at his spirit. Yet it was he who slowly cut down Bessie's body; it was he who sought and found life in her unconscious body. Slowly, ever so slowly, he dragged Bessie to the shore. When he got there, he called out to Dragor in soft tones.

Elsewhere, the battle raged on. Up went the Mrodics, up they climbed, reaching the top just as dawn was breaking. Reaching the top, Azazel shouted:

"Come down and give yourselves up, you miserable Lexters. Give yourselves up or else I shall blast you from this earth!"

All that he got was a low laugh from Sindar the Elder, and as he laughed Azazel's temper erupted in a flame. He was tired, tired of the long journey and Threye's constant admonishments. He could not think clearly. And so he did not see the Silver Mirror being pointed at him as he opened his third eye and sent forth a blast of flame. The flame struck the mirror, and before Azazel knew what was happening, it had rebounded and knocked him off his feet. Slowly, ever so slowly, his body toppled over backwards and he started the long fall down to the valley below. Kale jumped after him, speeding to catch his body as it fell burning by his own flame.

There was sudden chaos amongst the Mrodics as they turned and ran for their lives. Unused as they were to resistance, their minds were blinded with panic. Several fell to their death in the valley below. The retreat was sudden and quick, and as they reached the bottom, Kale hissed: "Quick! Pick up Azazel and carry him back to the White Eagle."

They reached the sea where they found Micla standing on the shore. Looking at Kale, Micla was stunned by her power and her beauty, and as he gazed at her black flashing eyes, he dropped to his knees and begged to be allowed to serve her for the rest of his days.

"I shall be loyal to you," he swore.

Kale stood towering over him, black hair flying in the wind, her tight black outfit hugging her body. She was the vision of power and beauty that Micla had been searching for all his life.

She looked deep into his eyes, the eyes of a traitor, and spoke: "I do not like traitors, but I know that you will never betray me. Come with us, and let us see what Threye has to say to you. In the meantime, travel with Dragor. He seems to need someone to navigate his ship."

Turning back, she caught his throat and looked into his eyes. Her hand gripped his throat tightly, and her tongue grazed his lips, causing it to bleed. "If you even think of betraying me", she said, "I shall hunt you down, flay the skin from your back, and leave the wild dogs to feast on you." Shaking him, she walked away, with one command, "Follow me".

Micla crawled after her, his soul in her grasp forever.

She looked at the Red Dragon with a sneer in her eyes, and boarded the White Eagle.

The rout was complete. The two ships sailed slowly back to Mrod, leaving the ship of the Giants to be burned to cinders and washed away by the sea.

Chapter 10

Azazel Back In Mrod

Defeat was something they were not used to, and as Azazel was being carried back to his ship, unconscious, the retreating Mrodics were in despair. It was only the fierce will of Kale that kept them going until they were on board the ship.

"Set sail!" she cried. "We shall return to Mrod with speed. Azazel needs to heal, and our next move must be planned." Yet, brave as she was, there was in her heart a deep dread at the prospect of meeting Threye again. For all the soft silkiness of his manner, and his politeness, she knew there was nothing meek about him. He was old, very old, and had grown strong and evil through the years. During all the one thousand years of his life, he had schooled himself in the various dark arts, and had divested himself of every vestige of emotion remotely linked to kindness and mercy. Kale shuddered as she thought of meeting him. Threye would not be pleased.

Dawn was breaking as the ships left the shores of the Land of Ice and Snow. It was a bright cold dawn that greeted them. The sunlight shimmered on the cold waters, and the sky shone, a pale, silvery blue. Yet, the beauty of the morning sun was lost on the crew as they pulled away. Kale stood on deck, her mind filled with dark, sombre thoughts. As she stood, her black hair whipping across her strong white face, her beauty shining in the morning light, Micla's gaze came to rest on her face and he was transfixed, enchanted forever. From the moment he had seen her that morning, his heart had left him. He was now forever in Kale's possession. He was, in his mind, home. Her side is where he wanted to be for the rest of his life.

"Good morning to you!" he called out from the Red Dragon. The breeze picked up his voice and carried it across the gap between the two ships until it reached Kale. She looked at him curiously, and then gave the order for the two ships to pull up alongside. Looking across, she asked: "Who are you?"

"I am Micla, a former Lexter, and now forever bound to you. I saved one of your people last night and have brought her here. She was knocked down by a red-haired wench who is of your kind. I saw another one, a silver-haired one, lead some Giants into the Black Forest. She returned, but the Giants did not."

Kale looked across the ship, mystified. "You speak in a strange manner," she said. "Yet I hear from you that you betrayed your people, and that two of ours fought against us. The two shall be dealt with. We don't like those who betray us. Why should I trust you, and why shouldn't I kill you here and now?"

"I saved the wench from certain death," Micla replied. "I pulled her down from the tree and brought her to this ship. I hate my people. They have always looked down on me. They have always favoured my accursed brother and treated me with contempt. I shall never betray you. I am forever yours."

Kale looked at him intently, her eyes boring into him. For once in his life, Micla was able to meet someone else's gaze directly without the shiftiness that was an integral part of his character. Finally, she nodded and said: "You can join us."

She added: "Tell Dragor and Bessie, we shall speak this evening."

The ships sped on, and Azazel's body burned with fever. His soul was aflame; he did not eat or drink for three days. Shame, anger and mortification ran through his body, as his mind refused to accept the fact that he had been bested twice. He could not handle defeat. Conflicting emotions raged through his body, along with the fever that burned through him. As it began to subside, he recalled Trix's silver hair gleaming as she had danced and led the Giants to their doom. The memory caused him fresh agony, as he was confronted with the reality of her betrayal. He gnashed his teeth, and the fever returned anew.

Finally, on the dawn of the fourth morning, as he lay in his bed sweating, Azazel's fever left him, and he walked on to the deck. His face was cold and hard, as were his eyes.

"A council," he cried. "We shall soon return to Mrod, and Threye will not be pleased. I want a council meeting. We need to understand where we went wrong."

Ten minutes later, they were gathered in the Candle Room. Azazel and Kale sat with their eyes closed, as did the main lieutenants of the Mrodic council. Dragor, Bessie and Micla sat outside the circle. The Mrodics swayed to the music, eyes closed, in perfect sync with each other. Micla looked on curiously, wondering when the meeting would begin. Leaning across to Dragor, he whispered:

"Hey, when will they start the council meeting?"

"Shut up, you fool!" hissed Dragor. "The meeting has started, and we will be informed at the end. Shut up unless you want to be burned to a cinder."

He glared at Micla, eyes blazing. Micla retreated mortified and sullen.

Finally, Azazel opened his eyes and looked around. His gaze settled on Micla, penetrating and cruel. Micla shrank back in fear, knowing that he was indeed well and truly bound to the Mrodics.

"Is he the one?" asked Azazel.

"Yes," Kale replied.

Looking across at Micla, Azazel said: "We do not like traitors. You have betrayed your people once, and we find this abhorrent. If you betray us, your death at our hands will be long, lingering and painful."

Micla merely nodded. He looked around the room. The candles seemed to give off a threatening light and he realized he had never been so frightened in all his life.

The candle light burned him, without touching him. The dancing light played tricks on his soul, weaving its way into his innermost thoughts. Stammering, he said: "I... I...I w w will never betray you. I will be true to Kale as well. I swear this."

Azazel nodded and turning to the group said: "We were careless and overconfident. We underestimated the fighting spirit of our enemies. We frittered away our energy en route, engaging in useless massacre. This cannot happen again. We will see what Threye has to say to us, and what assignments we are given now. We shall be asked to declare war on these people and to kill them as quickly as we can. Now, until we get home I expect absolute harmony from all of you; absolute discipline."

The ships sailed on, and at dawn on the third day they arrived in Mrod. There was a message left at the pier from Threye, to rest that day. A council would be called the next day. Everyone dreaded the outcome. Threye would not be kind.

At sunrise, they made their way to Threye's house. Bessie and Dragor entered along with a distinctly nervous Micla. Azazel and Kale were already there, both looking downcast.

"Welcome, friends," said Threye smoothly. "You have had an interesting trip, I see. He paused and looked around at the group, his yellow-flecked eyes penetrating their very souls. The room was white, but was starting to glow with a yellowish hue. This was the Threye they had all learned to fear. His movements were soft and feline, his skin a silvery, translucent white.

Turning to Azazel, he asked, softly: "What, my Lord Azazel, have you to report? Have you done me proud? Nay, have you done yourself proud? Look into your heart and answer? Wanton violence during your chase sapped your energy, made you lose precious time, and made you careless and proud. Is this what you have learned all these years?"

"My Lord Threye, I have no excuse," said Azazel, looking down.

"Yes," hissed Threye. "You have no excuse, but there is one, one little thing that has redeemed you. You realized the errors of your ways before you landed on these shores."

"Yes, Lord Threye," answered Azazel. "Now I only ask one thing, to be allowed to go after the Little Birds and to crush them. I want to annihilate them, and erase the memory of their existence. My soul burns for vengeance, and retribution." Azazel's voice was fierce. Mortification, anger and wounded pride coursed through him; his body shook with it.

"You are not yet ready, Azazel," returned Threye. "Wheels have been set in motion and the world will change before vengeance can be had. The world will, and must, be mine, yet there are great battles to be fought. Old allies and foes will rise again, and we need to gather and strengthen our armies."

There was silence in the room. Threye seemed to have become larger, more menacing, as the power of this thought filled the room. His mind ruled the thoughts of all who were there, and their thoughts reflected only the mind of Threye. Thoughts of vengeance and violence. An angry energy radiated through the room. Yet, there was only one mind that dreamed of total domination of all he surveyed, and that was the mind of Threye. The defeat by the Little Birds rankled more than he would like to admit to himself. Defeat was not something he was used to; it was not something he liked. His mind went back over the one thousand years of his dominion. There was no such incident, no such record of defeat that he could recollect, and he burned with anger. The anger fuelled itself and grew larger and larger, and he swore to himself that he would gather the largest army ever known, and with it stamp the Little Birds off the face of the earth. Then, he would rule the world.

Threye's eyes snapped open, as Kale spoke: "Lord Threye, if I may interject... Lord Azazel was indeed disciplined in battle, as were we all. It is not due to carelessness that we suffered this defeat, but due to fatigue and an element of surprise. We fought bravely and would have been stronger were it not for Jenna and Trix's betrayal. Trix led the Giants into the forest of the Lexters, and Bessie was clubbed down by Jenna as she was about to kill Percival. She was trussed up in a tree and would still be a prisoner were it not for Micla here who saved her."

Her voice trailed off into a gargle, like water going down a drain, as Threye's eyes caught her own. "You were not careless?" he hissed. "Were it not for all the wasted energy and time subduing small peoples along the way, the Little Birds would not have had the time to build their strategy, or their fortifications. Yes, you saved Azazel, and this is what saves you now."

He closed his eyes. The air in the room was suffocating as they waited for Threye to continue.

"You shall all be here tomorrow, all but Azazel."

With that they were dismissed.

Kale, Micla, Bessie and Dragor made their way to Threye's house just as the rays of the morning sun were beginning to light up the night sky. As night gave way to the promise of a bright new day, they wondered what the day would bring them. They entered Threye's quarters, their faces reflecting the trepidation they felt. Threye opened the door and welcomed them in with a smooth graciousness that did nothing to allay their fears.

"Welcome, friends," he began, his body suffused with a faint, silvery luminosity. "Today is the first day of the rest of your lives. Today is a day of new beginnings; your lives shall change forever. You must listen carefully."

He paused and looked around at all of them.

"Bessie and Dragor, you two are the weakest links thanks to the indiscipline that you have displayed. Yet you are bound together, and shall be married. Bessie, your marriage to Percival is dissolved, and Percival knows of it. After you are married, I shall send you to the Island of the Trolls. The Trolls and I go back a long time in our history. If you are lucky, the Royal Couple shall tell you about it. They will resist your overtures, and may very well kill you. You, however, are to convince them to join hands with me one more time, in one last battle, in which we shall dominate the world and carve it up between us. You will then go back to the Giants, and shall recruit them. They will be thirsting for revenge, after their annihilation in the Black Forest. You shall be married here, in Mrod, by me, before you leave. Any questions?"

He looked at them, waiting for their response. There was silence.

"Good," he beamed. "It shall be done. You shall be married tomorrow, and then you shall depart. Preparations have already been made."

He turned to Kale and Micla, and spoke.

"The two of you shall also be bound together. You belong to each other in a way that even I, I must confess, did not anticipate. Yet there are ceremonies to be performed before you can be together. Each of you shall spend a week alone, and then you shall return to me. You shall return along with Azazel, at dawn, on the seventh day from today."

Bessie and Dragor were married that night. The wedding ceremony took place in a dark, gloomy, damp hall. Threye presided over the simple almost sombre ceremony. He was the only witness to the wedding, and as he pronounced them man and wife, he merely said: "The deed is done. Now you must both prepare to depart before dawn. I want your ship to pull out before the sun's rays even think about warming the earth for another day. Do not fail in this mission."

The Red Dragon pulled away from Mrod within an hour of the ceremony. Dragor and Bessie were grim-faced as they faced the Kreechurs who stood on board the deck. They felt as though they had failed in their mission. The rebuke rankled inside Dragor, and his pride was hurt. the desire for retribution burned inside him. Failure was new to him, and he did not take well to humiliation. He paced up and down, biting his lips in anger, until the blood flowed.

As he turned, the rays of the pre-dawn morning fell upon his face, and the dripping blood looked black, as it dripped down his chin. His eyes were red with anger, and his voice was full of a quiet menace. "We have an important mission to fulfill," said Dragor. "Threye seems to have lost faith in us, and this is something that I cannot tolerate. The glory of the Black Pub must not be allowed to dim. It must live on for eternity. When I am gone from this earth, Bessie and my sons will carry on the work that we do. Let them not say that their father and mother failed in their mission, and were weak. If there is any one amongst you who is faint of heart, step up now. If there is any one of you who is weak in body, step up now. It is better that the weak of heart die here, than continue further. There is no room for failure. There is no more room for weakness. Speak now, if ye want to return, or say with me, 'Glory Be to The Black Pub!'"

There was a roar as the Kreechurs echoed his cry. The Red Dragon pulled away on its voyage to the Land of the Trolls.

Back at Mrod, Kale and Micla were each taken to different locations. Micla, to his horror, was locked up in a cage that was covered with a green slimy cloth. He was, for all he could see and think, blinded. He felt himself being picked up and taken along a bumpy path. He cursed and fumed as his body bounced around the cage, but he dared not regret his fate. He felt Threye's eyes on him, and was convinced that Threye could read his innermost, his most secret thoughts. He cursed as the cage was thrown down, and then screamed in fear as he felt earth being thrown over it.

"Oh God," he screamed silently, "I am being buried alive!" He wept with a bitterness that ran through his body. He cursed and beat on the cage, trying his very best to escape. But escape there was none. Finally, covered with dirt, sweat and tears, he collapsed in a corner of the cage, convinced his life was over. Yet he did not go hungry. From time to time, food would mysteriously appear. He fell upon it like a raving lunatic, and spent the next two days counting the moments from one meal to the next. Finally, he lost all sense of time.

Somewhere on the third day, he felt something sliding all over his body. He had retained enough of his senses to be able to snatch at it. His hands grasped a smooth, scaly body, and he could feel a forked tongue flicking at his arm. Micla screamed in fresh panic. What new torture was this? Try as he might, he could not escape as more and more scaly bodies filled the cage. Tongues flicked at him, fangs bit into him, and beady eyes bored into his own. He was steadily being engulfed by a blurred sense of nothingness; eyes, fangs, tongues merged into one wholeness of sensation, until finally, one morning, he felt himself being stretched. His body seemed to be becoming smooth, slithery almost reptilian. His eyes were pulled sideways, and his nose flattened and the nostrils seemed to have become slits. He was dimly aware of profound changes taking place in his body, yet he was unable to control or measure what was happening. Visions of reptiles and snakes filled his mind, until finally an icy calmness overcame him. He felt himself entering a new centre. He seemed to have found a deep peace within himself.

Suddenly, the doors of the cage were flung open. Micla blinked. His eyes were pulled back, his body had a greenish hue, almost as though covered in scales, yet not so. His canines were sharp, his tongue forked. And as he walked towards Threye's house, his brain was cold, ice cold. A new self seem to have emerged from the cage, and his body twitched nervously. He was born again, and

The first person he saw as he entered was Kale. Her eyes were green, and there was a green tint in her hair. She smiled, to reveal sharp fangs that she could retract at will. She had changed. There was now a murderous coldness about her. She was, as she called herself, the Snake Queen.

"Welcome, Micla," said Threye in a gentle voice they had never heard before. "I trust that your temporary abode was not too uncomfortable?" His eyes were like slits in his white face as he looked at Micla keenly and waited for a reaction.

"I liked it," hissed Micla. He twisted his neck, this way and that, and as the foam gathered at the corners of his mouth, he flecked his tongue around. It seemed as though he relished the taste of the foam, and all that is distasteful to others. His eyes looked mad, almost deranged. There was no wickedness he was now not capable of.

"Capital! capital!" beamed Threye. "You are ready to go on a journey with Kale, to Percival's Land. But you shall not go alone. You will go with Erissa, my daughter. You shall capture the land, and once you have taken over you and Kale shall stay back to rule it, and to bend the people there to my will. Erissa will then go on to another mission."

Micla and Kale turned to see Threye's daughter standing behind them. She smiled. Like Threye, she too was silvery white, with silvery, white hair. Her three eyes were a deep, ruby red.

"Erissa will, tonight, be married to Azazel. They were destined to be together, and this shall happen tonight." Threye looked around at the group, and then turned to the entrance as the door swung open.

"Welcome, Lord Azazel!" he beamed. "You have arrived right on time."

Azazel bowed, and said: "What instructions do you have for me, Lord Threye?" His coal-black eyes gleamed as they alighted on Erissa. He had not seen her in years, and his mind went back to younger days when the two had frolicked together. With a sudden shock he realized that his young love for her had never gone away.

"Micla here, Kale, and Erissa will depart tomorrow morning for Percival's Land, where they will subdue the people to my will. The people will become part of the army that I intend to put together to destroy all those who oppose me. Erissa shall then go on to the Valley of the Kings."

He paused for effect, and his voice grew soft. "Tomorrow, after you and Erissa have been joined, you Lord Azazel shall enter the Dungeon of Thron. There you will endeavour to meet with Thron. If you succeed, Thron shall anoint you. If not, you shall die a painful death in the dungeons."

"Your will shall be done, Lord Threye," said Azazel, bowing.

"It is essential," continued Threye, "that you go through the trial in the dungeons. You have failed on your missions so far; you must redeem yourself in the dungeons. You must find yourself, or fall forever into the void from which you came. Is this something you are willing to do? Are you willing to take the risk? If you succeed, you shall receive powers beyond those you already have. Only Thron can give you these powers. If not, you shall fall. This is something you must volunteer for. You have no choice," Threye concluded, his voice quiet, yet silken. It was not the silkiness of a soft fabric but the silkiness of a deadly rope that tightens like a noose around the neck of a person condemned to die.

"Lord Threye," said Azazel. "I will go into the dungeons. I will brave the terrors of the dungeons, and I shall succeed." His voice was quiet, soft, and firm.

"Then it shall be done," replied Threye.

The next morning was grey and dull. A chilly wind blew through Mrod, as Azazel and Erissa hugged each other with a hunger that is felt only after years of waiting.

"We shall meet again," she whispered. Azazel walked straight towards a thorny bush in front of him. He turned and nodded to Erissa, and then disappeared into the bush which seemed to swallow him up whole.

"He has gone into the dungeons," whispered Threye. "The die is cast."

Threye walked with the remaining three to the shores of Mrod, where two ships awaited them. Kale and Micla boarded one called the Green Hawk, and Erissa, the Silver Vulture.

After the ships pulled away, Threye stood looking into the horizon a long while. His hair whipped about his face, his eyes gazed into the distance with an intensity that seemed to travel into the infinity of space.

His thoughts were dark, impenetrable, as he pondered the wheels that had been set in motion. The world would never be the same again. Not even he, Threye, could predict the outcome of what the future would bring. All that he knew was that the die had been cast.

Chapter 11

Departure From The Land Of Ice And Snow

Fatigue came over everyone at the Land of Ice and Snow as they watched the Mrodics and Kreechurs retreating in disarray. One by one, they collapsed onto the ice, oblivious of the cold. Thoughts of victory would come later; at that moment, the realization that they had pushed the Mrodics back was all they were conscious of. Not even the sight of Trix traipsing up singing, with Thyme behind her, was enough to rouse Percival and the rest of the group. Percival and Jenna lay there in the snow, looking up at the blue sky. They lay there in a daze, eyes unseeing, and minds blank. The events of the night had passed into the mists of time, and the memories of the battle seemed to be almost figments of their imagination. It was not until they heard Sindar the Elder's gentle voice that they dragged themselves p and staggered back to their cabins, lit fires, and collapsed into the warmth and comfort of a sleep well earned.

"A party! A party!" cried Brindar in the evening, as the group straggled towards Sindar's home, to which they had been summoned.

"A party?" groaned Basil. "How about some sleep instead?" His body ached, and felt sore all over. The memories of the battle were alive in his mind, and the battle scars were fresh. He had fought well. He was a far cry from the Pig who had left the shores of his home in search of Bessie and Percival. The bullying swagger had not left him, and never would, but a steeliness had entered his spirit. There was a strength that had come into him.

"Pooper!" trilled Trix, dancing alongside him. "Come on you old oaf! Don't be a party-pooper. Get some spirit into that old body of yours."

"Old?" snorted Basil. "You call me old? I am the one who fought Dragor and almost killed him. What did you do? You and Thyme, that lazy old bugger, just strolled along in the Black Forest. We fought!" He glared at her, and stood there arms akimbo, fire seeming to emanate from his body. He seemed to have forgotten his fatigue!

"Ah, but the Giants have not lived to tell the tale," retorted Thyme. "Unlike Dragor, who escaped, and unlike Bessie who..."

He paused, and stared. "Where is Bessie? How did she escape? Is she a miracle woman now?" he asked as they entered Sindar's house.

"No," replied a Lexter called Zalyts. "We have been betrayed by my brother, Micla. Micla helped her escape, and has defected over to the Mrodics."

"Now that you mention it, we should talk about this. The price of betrayal is death," said Sindar the Elder. "Let us talk first and then we shall celebrate."

He looked at the group gathered in the room with a degree of gravity that Percival found was a bit unwarranted. What about the party, he thought, and grumbled silently to himself. It had been some time since they had had something to celebrate. He had lost Bessie, had undergone fierce trials and tribulations, fought great battles, and had not had a decent cup of tea in ages. Surely they could wait until the next day to discuss Micla? His thoughts were soon interrupted as Sindar spoke.

"We have indeed won a great victory, but there is no time for relaxation. The Mrodics will regroup, and Threye will want his revenge. He will put together an army to crush us, and all those who support us. His anger will be terrible, and his thirst for revenge unquenchable. He will seek to extend his dominion, as he has done in the past. He will, in particular, want to vent his anger on Jenna and Trix."

"The two of you," he went on, looking at the sisters, "will now be treated as traitors and as outcasts. If you fall into Threye's hands, he will torture and kill you both. You know this. Your life is now with us."

There was silence in the room as Sindar the Elder continued.

"We have, in the meantime, a traitor amongst us. Micla. He is the one who helped Bessie escape, and the punishment for treason is death."

"I would like the honour of killing Micla to be mine, and mine alone," said Zalyts, with passion. His face was red, his eyes downcast. "Micla has brought shame on the family. We have been honourable people for generations, and his actions have tainted the family name. Micla is my brother, but the honour of killing him must be mine and mine alone."

"Granted," said Sindar the Elder. "You will have to be strong. You will be cursed and vilified by your family, even though you will have performed an act that is within the code of the Lexters."

"I am strong," replied Zalyts.

"Then let it be done," said Sindar. Looking at the motley crew around him, he smiled, breaking the tension, and said: "Let the revelry begin!"

It was a night to remember. Percival had never imagined there could be such feasting. The wine, the food seemed to be in endless supply. He had never, or so he imagined, eaten such food in his life, save at his own table. The wine almost matched the wine from his cellars. He was in a state of ecstasy.

The music and the dancing was the most heady he had ever experienced. Out of the corner of his eye, he could see Basil and Trix dancing; they seemed very close indeed. Sally and Thyme were together, looking happy. Sally was blushing, and Thyme's face was flushed. Not to be outdone, Percival jumped to his feet and pulled Jenna onto the floor. He was, at least in his imagination, the most skilful dancer that evening. In any case, he was certainly the most ardent lover among this group of people, and as the dancing continued late into the night, he pulled Jenna closer and closer until, at one point, he suddenly held her tight and kissed her. To his delight, he felt her return the kiss, her lips full and warm against his own. He felt her body press close to him, and as he felt her warmth, the joy of the moment hit him like a lightning bolt, transporting him to a place of happiness he never imagined could possibly exist.

Percival was in love again.

Sweating slightly, he pulled away from her and drew her to the table where they had been sitting. As she sat on her chair, Percival climbed up onto the table.

One leg slightly in front of the other, a hand on his heart, he cried out: "A song! A song!" As his sharp voice pierced the sound of the music, it faded and died away leaving the dancers momentarily stunned.

"A song! A song!" repeated Percival.

"Oh mercy!" cried Basil. "Please, not a song! Anything but a song! A battle, but not a song! I beg of you, please" He sank down on his knees, a beseeching look in his eyes.

Basil and Thyme stood transfixed in horror, their faces pale, their hands clapped over their ears, as Percival's voice rang out across the celebrations that had been so rudely interrupted. The words of his song have been buried in the sands of time, buried by everyone at the party, buried because they could not bear to remember Percival's shrill whistling singing voice. Only a few lines were preserved for posterity. Percival sang his little ditty:

"Azazel came, he saw, he was conquered,
A great defeat, he was served!

He ran away, tail between his legs,
For mercy, I did hear him beg!

The Giants were eaten in the Forest Black,
I know that they shall never come back.
The Forest wants more, but alas and alack,
The Giants shall never come back!

Dragor fought bravely, so did Bessie,
Both defeated, they ran to the sea."

At one point in his song, Percival standing on one foot, trying to look as heroic as he could brandished and swung his cup in the air. He paused, wondering how he had defeated Bessie, completely forgetting that Jenna had saved him. He paused, swayed, and fell over backwards, crashing onto the chairs behind him. Trix stood up, trying to see where he had disappeared, and then burst out laughing when Percival's loud snores came gently wafting up from under the table.

The celebration was saved, the merry mood restored as the feasting went on late into the night.

Early next morning, they were awakened by Sindar who accompanied the group down to the pier and spoke to them on board The Raven.

"The world will change," he said. "It will no longer be as it was, and all of you will play a part in shaping the future."

"Oooh," moaned Percival softly. His head was splitting. All he wanted to do was to crawl into his bed and disappear for the rest of his life. Playing a significant part in changing the world and the destiny of those who were to come was not something that remotely interested him now. Hot chocolate and a nice warm bed was what he was looking for at the moment. Through the fog of his hangover, and the piercing pain in his head, he could only just hear what Sindar was saying.

"The way will be dark, and there will be times when you doubt yourselves. There will also be times when you will doubt each other. Times when your enemies will seem strong, and times when you feel weak. For these times, you can call upon the power of the Rings I am about to present to you. These have the power of the Lexters, some of Azazel's powers, and something from the Cyffarwynds. These are the Shadow Rings. Wear them at all times. You are now the Brethren of the Shadow Rings."

Sindar the Elder looked at them, and with a final wave said: "Farewell for now. We shall meet again."

He turned and left. The Brethren boarded The Raven. The ship left the shores of the Land of Ice and Snow and Sindar the Elder was soon just a speck on the shoreline. He stood there silently and deep in thought, the cold wind whipping his hair across his face. The world would never be the same again, he knew. People would be destroyed, and a new world order would come to pass. Would Threye be vanquished? Or would he become stronger? Time would tell.

What would happen if Threye were to die? Good, then, would rule the world. But Sindar, who was wise beyond measure, knew that even if Threye were to be killed a new evil would soon arise.

How do you define good if there is no evil? God and the Devil, he thought, are twins joined at the hip. They are inseparable, condemned to be together always until the end of time, and condemned always to be in conflict with each other. One could not survive without the other. Forever at war, forever debating, their conflicting philosophies were entwined; the spectrum of good and evil ran along infinite shades of grey, impossible at times to separate.

His thoughts were heavy as he pondered the shape of the world to come. Good and evil were always dependent on the perspective from which you looked at things. Who then, of the twins, was the Devil? Who then, of the twins, was God? Were they at war with each other, or were they at play, forever in a dance, creating waves and patterns that the world fell into? Did the two, in their dance, and their play, look down at the universe and laugh?

Shaking his head, Sindar the Elder pushed these thoughts away and walked back to the village, to ready the villagers for battles ahead. There was work to be done. There would be time enough for philosophical debate. That time had not yet come.

Now was the time for war. His people had to prepare for the Time of the Long Strife.

Chapter 12

Percival Reaches Sangre

The Raven sailed away from the Land of Ice and Snow. The ship seemed to have a will of its own as it ploughed the ocean, sailing to a destination that was yet unknown.

On board, the Brethren, as they were now called, were too exhausted to care where they were going. They were on board the ship, and this is all they wanted to know. They slept, ate and slept again. The fires burned warm in their rooms, and they spent most of the first few days sleeping and resting. Their limbs were tired, their minds were exhausted, and the rest was refreshing.

Percival slept through. The after effects of the party seemed to have lasted unusually long. He had no idea that Rollo had carried him into his cabin. He snored. A few days later, he emerged from his cabin finally refreshed from his labours. He seemed to bear no after effects of the previous days, nor of his exertions during the celebrations. He walked up on deck, scratching his and asked of no one in particular. "Where are we going? By golly, I am hungry. Where's the food, and how did we get on the ship?"

The bemused looks of everyone present gave him the answer, and he turned to Jenna, a question in his eyes.

"The Raven will take us where she thinks we need to go," Jenna replied loftily.

"You have no idea then," Percival concluded.

"We don't need to know," retorted Trix. "The Raven knows where we need to go, and we will know in time. What would pigs like you know of these things anyway?"

"Witch!"

"Pig!"

They stood there glaring at each other, until finally Percival broke the silence. "Dammit, you witch, have you finished all the food on board? I knew it, you greedy woman...!"

"Stop it you two!" cried Sally. "You behave like little children sometimes. I must confess that we have no idea where we are going, and if it were not for Percival here I would not have thought to ask!"

The Lexters had, by this time, gathered around the little group; one by one they all confessed that they had no idea where they were headed. Finally, shaking his head, Brindar said: "We should just leave it up to the ship, and trust her. There is something mystical about the ship anyway. I felt it as soon as we stepped on board. As long as we trust her, we will be safe."

"See?" Jenna retorted with an arched smile as she walked away with Trix

"They look bloody smug don't they," said Basil. "Too clever by half!"

"Yes," smiled Sally with a twinkle in her eyes. "That's why you love the two sisters, you two." Looking at the men, she laughed. "Go on, admit it."

Glaring at her, the red flush coming to their cheeks, Basil and Percival walked away to the sound of laughter from the Lexters and Sally. Muttering and grumbling under their breath, they retreated to their cabins for the night.

It had been a long, strange journey from those simple times, when all that mattered was whether Basil or Percival would win Bessie's hand. None of the three of the original wanderers and past rivals could have imagined how their lives had changed. The evening before they were to arrive that their next destination saw Basil and Thyme standing at the top deck, looking out onto the waters as the sun went down in a fiery ball. Basil was not naturally a reflective old soul, but he had been stirred by recent events, the strange twists and turns that fate was taking them through.

The two friends stood there in silence, and then Thyme suddenly said, "Would you ever have believed that we would be here now, standing on the deck of this strange ship, as it takes us towards a land unknown to us? To adventures unknown? That Bessie would turn out this way, and that you and Percival would be allies?"

"No" replied Basil. "There is a strange magic in the air. The world is changing, and for some reason, we are part of this change. Life seemed so much simpler back in the day. Bessie was a sweet little thing. So very sweet. So very, very sweet."

He paused, and then continued in a manner that seemed almost wistful. "I wonder if I miss the old days. Damn! I was so close to getting Bessie... But, I think that none of us were fated to get her.. Who can believe that she would end up with tattoos on her body.. That sweet body of hers..." His voice trailed off, and he looked at the clouds as they danced with the sinking sun.

"Yeah", replied Thyme. "You would have married her, but then I would not have met Sally. So, from my side, I am happy in a way. Yet, I do miss the days, when we would sit under a tree in the garden, feeling the warmth of the sun as it filtered through the trees. Those were good days, and I wonder when we will experience those days again. I wonder if we will ever go home again, or if we will feel the same again."

There was no reply from Basil, and the two companions stood there in contemplative silence as the sea breeze signaled the end of the day.

The next evening, The Raven touched land. The afternoon sun was beginning to wane, and as the dying rays began to colour the earth a warm orange the Brethren disembarked to walk on shore for the first time in a week.

They entered a town that had been built up around the harbour. "This looks like a jolly place," Rollo remarked. "Indeed, I think it's a good place to spend a few days before we move on."

"Yes," whispered Thar. "But we should not tarry here for too long lest we tempt the Fates."

"Fates? What Fates?" snorted Rollo. "I tell you here that this does look like a jolly little town."

There was indeed something about the little town that seemed cheerful, friendly. Cobbled streets ringed by quaint brightly-painted cottages greeted their eyes, as they wandered about looking for a place to stay. The townsfolk were friendly, smiling and giving them directions to the closest inn.

"See," continued Rollo, "even their eyes smile, and when people smile with their eyes, it means they are an extremely hospitable and friendly people."

"I like it here," agreed Percival, looking around at the bright houses, and smiling at the townsfolk as they sat in their gardens sipping tea.

"Red tea," muttered Thar. "I have never seen red tea in my life!"

"Herbal tea, I presume," said Thyme, looking at the glass cups in people's hands. "Yes, the townsfolk seem very healthy," remarked Sally. "They all have nice red plump cheeks!"

After walking for about thirty minutes, they finally came to an inn. "The White Fang Inn," read Sindar looking up at the sign. "What a funny name for an inn." He knocked, and the door was opened by a plump, smiling lady dressed in a bright, blue dress.

"Welcome to Sangre," she beamed. "My name is Mrs Fangz. My husband and I run this inn. Welcome, welcome, welcome!"

"We are always happy to receive visitors," she added, walking towards the reception area. "I shall give you rooms right away. I hope you will be comfortable here."

Basil and Trix were assigned one room, as were Percival and Jenna. Mrs Fangz looked at the two pairs, and said with a smile. "Unusual couples, but well suited. Come with me." Ignoring the blushes of the men, she led the group to their rooms.

They were joined at dinner by Mr Fangz. Mr Fangz was as quiet as Mrs Fangz was talkative. Maps were handed out to the group and major attractions pointed out, while Mrs Fangz extolled the beauty of her hometown.

"You will enjoy your stay here," she beamed. "Mr Fangz and I will do everything we can to make your stay absolutely comfortable. But you must be tired, and I prattle on so. Forgive me, forgive me, forgive me. Please enjoy your first night in our hometown, and I shall serve you breakfast in the morning. Please don't bother waking up early. Enjoy your first night in our beautiful town..."

Mrs Fangz was up and bustling the next morning when the group convened for breakfast. Percival and Basil's eyes bulged when they saw the feast that was spread out in front of them. Eggs, sausages, bread, tea, juice, fruits -- all laid out in large quantities on a cheerful pink-and-white checked tablecloth. As they sat around the table and dug into the food, Mr Fangz came in to greet them.

"An honour, an honour indeed!" he beamed with delight. "Our mayor, Mr Benttwist has invited all of you for dinner at his home tonight. I am besides myself with joy. It is a rare honour to be invited to his home, and I shall be delighted to accompany you there."

Mr Fangz danced with joy as he spoke of the honour of being invited to Mr Benttwist's home. He did not notice that Percival and Basil were too busy eating to pay him much attention.

"Enjoy your day, my honoured guests," Mr Fangz continued, as he withdrew from their company.

"Greedy pig!" whispered Trix, poking Basil in the ribs. "Politeness always helps. One would think you starved on the ship!" She glared at him.

"No matter." said Sindar. "Let's explore the town."

Their day in town did nothing to dampen Rollo's enthusiasm, or Thar's reluctance to be seduced by the sunny charms of Sangre. They wandered about the streets, exploring some of the better-known attractions, until evening, when they made their way back to the inn to ready themselves for dinner at Mr. Benttwist's home.

"A rare honour, a rare honour," repeated Mr. Fangz rubbing his hands in glee as he walked with them to the house. The reticent host of the previous evening had been replaced by someone altogether more loquacious.

"Our host seems very friendly," whispered Sindar to Brindar as they brought up the rear of the group. "Yes, and a wee bit nervous," replied Brindar.

Mr. Benttwist's house was lavishly done up in black and red. The magnificent wooden table, the leather-backed chairs, the tapestry and heavy curtains all spoke of wealth, sophistication and power. Yet there was something dark about the house, something awfully dark and cold. It seemed as though they had entered the Halls Of Death. Sally shivered as they entered, wrapping her arms around herself.

"This place is spooky," she whispered to Thyme.

"Shhh!" hissed Thyme. "Don't offend our hosts."

When Mr. Benttwist finally arrived, they gasped in shock. For, hanging on his arm was a beautiful, slender young lady with white, alabaster skin and flaming red hair. Her nails were painted red, her dress a shimmering maroon. Mr. Benttwist too had white alabaster skin, but his hair was black, and slicked back. His clothes too were black.

The interiors of the house seemed to have been designed to reflect the colour preferences of the young couple.

"Welcome, my friends!" Mr Benttwist's voice was smooth, silky, urbane and without the slightest trace of warmth in it. "Allow me to introduce the love of my life, Christina Kilgore," he said, smiling widely, his teeth a sparkling white. Yet not a hint of the smile invaded his eyes.

The food and wine were of unsurpassed quality. Mr. Benttwist and Christina were excellent hosts. Yet there was a hint of menace in the air; it was if the guests were being silently evaluated. Mr. Benttwist seemed to have an inexhaustible supply of stories and anecdotes to tell, each more interesting than the other. And yet the sense of unease persisted. There was something about the two that chilled the visitors to the bone. They were all glad when the evening was over and it was time to return to the inn.

"That was one strange dinner," Basil said to Trix as they prepared for the night. "I do not have a good feeling about them folks, and I think that we will have some trouble before we leave this place."

"Yes, I think you are right," said Trix.

Night gives way to day, and the morning sun rose bright and beautiful dispelling some of the misgivings of the previous evening.

"Oh, what a beautiful morning," yawned Jenna as she lay in bed looking out at the blue sky. "Not as beautiful as you my dear," purred Percival, trying his best to sound every inch the gallant young lover as he watched her body move under the covers. He felt a stirring and slid into bed next to her.

When they finally arose and went down for breakfast, they found the rest of the group almost done and ready to go out.

"What a sweet pair of young lovers!" cooed Trix slyly, poking Percival in the ribs.

"Witch!" snapped Percival. "What about you and Basil? Hey? Hey?" He glared at her, eyes bulging in his head as he stood arms akimbo, ready to wrestle Trix to the ground.

"You gonna fight a lady?" came a lazy drawl from Thar.

Wheeling around, Percival snapped: "She's a witch!"

"Oooof!" he gasped as he went down. "Oooof..... Gerrofff me!" he yelled as he found himself flat on his back with Trix sitting on his belly. "She's squashed my breakfast, she has," he muttered. "Why is she always after my food?"

Trix got up, and with a silvery laugh said: "I am a lady, dear future brother-in-law. Treat me well."

"Let's go explore," laughed Sindar, as they left the inn.

They spent the next few days exploring Sangre. Everywhere they went they were greeted with friendly smiles and bright faces. They could go anywhere they wanted. Well, almost anywhere.

On the third day, while sitting at a coffee shop, Thar suddenly spoke. "Have you noticed how we don't seem to be allowed to go anywhere we want to go?"

"Thar, you are a suspicious old dog!" said Rollo, happily munching a sandwich. "This place has really good food!"

"You care for nothing but food," sniffed Thar. Turning his back to him, he continued to the others. "Think about it. We wanted to go to the Hanging Gardens, and we were headed off. We wanted to walk down White Street, and we were headed off. We wanted to walk down to the Wailing Wall, and we were headed off."

He paused, and added, with effect: "Think about it!"

There was silence as the others pondered what he had said. "Well, every place has some secret or other," said Rollo, still munching. "Don't make too much of it. This sandwich is incredible!"

"Tell you what," said Thyme. "The ladies have been invited to go to the Angel Bar this evening by Christina. Why don't we go exploring at night?"

"Not me!" said Percival. "If you don't mind, I will turn in early tonight."

"That's settled then," said Brindar. "Let's explore Sangre by night."

Later that evening, two groups set out from the White Fang Inn. The ladies, dressed to their skins in tight-fitting clothes, headed towards the Angel Bar; the gentlemen to explore.

It was dark. Dressed in black, the men blended into the shadows of the paved streets as they made their way to the forbidden areas of Sangre. All were high with anticipation, wondering what they would discover.

When they finally reached the walls of the Hanging Gardens, they found the gates locked. Disappointed, they turned to go back when suddenly Thar whispered: "I hear a sound! Quick, let's make out what we can before we turn back." Crawling around, they found a small opening through which they were able to peer inside. What they saw caused them to freeze with shock...

The gardens were populated by trees, strong trees, with thick trunks and wide branches. Each was weighed down by hanging bodies. A slow stench reached the group and they gagged. Yet try as they might they could not move, transfixed as they were by what they were witnessing.

Mr Benttwist stood in the centre of a circle of fire, holding a goblet filled with a red liquid. Raising it to his lips, he cried: "Bless this blood we drink. Bless this blood that gives us strength. Bless this blood that gives us power."

Raising the goblet to his lips, he drank deeply. The group around him raised their goblets and drank too. "Drain their blood, and strip the flesh from their bones. Drink and eat shall we. Power to the blood. Power to the flesh. With this eating, and with this drinking, we gain the power of these beings. We gain in strength. All Heil!"

Turning around, blood dribbling down his chin, Mr. Benttwist smiled. His teeth were white, pearly white, and sharp. The canines seemed to have grown into fangs, and his eyes seemed to pierce the walls that separated him from the group outside.

"Blimey!" croaked Thyme. "He can see us!" He quivered with fear as a slow sneer spread across Mr. Benttwist's face. He laughed, a soft, demonic laugh. Raising his hands, he seemed to pull the powers into himself. He stood still a few seconds, the light from the fire casting evil shadows, blood slowly trickling down his chin. Then he brought his arms down suddenly, and with his left hand on his hip, pointed directly at the group crouched outside.

The group found themselves unable to move. And then blackness came over them, as conscious thought faded from their minds.

Meanwhile the women were enjoying themselves in the Angel Bar, in the company of Christina who was dancing a slow, sinuous dance with a few men from the bar. The music was soft and hypnotic. Sally and Trix drank their red drinks from the small glasses they had been given. They found themselves throwing off their inhibitions and giving in to the music. They jumped onto the floor and danced, their bodies moving, their hair swinging in tune with the music. They smiled as they moved, as if in a trance.

They did not notice Jenna slipping away from the pub. Jenna was oblivious of Christina moving slowly towards Sally and Trix, oblivious of the deep kisses being exchanged between Christina and Sally, between Christina and Trix. Jenna was oblivious of the two women slowly slipping to the floor in a faint, of them being picked up by the men and taken away by Christina.

She was conscious only of a feeling in her gut, a vague sense of unease that told her to get back to the inn. The disquiet in her grew as she walked faster and faster, ignoring the smiles of the few people out on the streets at that late hour.

Jenna entered the inn and ran upstairs to her room. Percival was lying on the floor. Mr. and Mrs. Fangz were crouched over him, blood dripping down their chins. They looked up at her and smiled blood on their teeth and their chins.

"Come in, my dear," smiled Mrs. Fangz, slowly starting to get up. "Welcome!"

Jenna was conscious of nothing but the sight of Percival lying on the floor, blood oozing from his neck. He was white, as though all the blood had been drained from his body. His skin seemed a kind of shroud for his body. And then a slow, deep, wild anger coursed through her body and her mind focused on revenge.

Concentrating her anger deep in her heart, Jenna raised her hand and pointed it first at Mrs. Fangz, and then at Mr. Fangz. Her third eye opened, and a shaft of white flame flew from her pointed finger towards the approaching Mrs. Fangz. The flame hit her in the chest; the smile froze on her lips. Her body was flung back against the window in a charred heap. As she fell, dead, Mr. Fangz snarled and leapt at Jenna. He was conscious of fear mixed with anger in that snarl, and it was the fear that made him hesitate ever so slightly. The last thing he saw was the furious anger in Jenna's eyes as her third eye seemed to add to the white flame that was flowing from her fingertips.

Then his charred body was flung through the window, crashing onto the street below.

Had the lifeless eyes of Mrs. Fangz been able to see they would have witnessed Jenna crouch on the floor, sobbing slightly as she held Percival's lifeless body against her own.

Chapter 13

Azazel in The Dungeon

Threye walked back to his quarters, his mind filled with dark thoughts. He knew the future was unfolding before his eyes, and that he could control the final outcome. He knew that the world was at a turning point. For the first time in over a thousand years, he was not entirely in control and he was full of misgivings. This was new to him, and a nervous rage filled him. He paced up and down, and his mind was willed with thoughts. Thoughts that disturbed him; thoughts that prevented him from thinking calmly; thoughts that muddled him.

Anger, rage, hurt pride and an insane desire for power swept through his body and his mind as he sat in his room and contemplated the world. His mind wandered far, and as he spread his snares he gathered his allies about him. No one in the past had ever escaped Mrod; none had defeated his armies. Disbelief blinded his normally calm, clear, cruel thoughts. He would need allies before the end, and he was determined to stamp out the Little Birds. But the Birds had flown his carefully crafted cage, and were out in the world.

Jenna and Trix had betrayed him. Never in the history of Mrod had there been defectors, and thoughts of the pair filled him with a cold fury. He would stamp them out; he would obliterate them. The very memory of their existence would be blotted out from this world.

As he paced his room, the walls glowed yellow, yellow tinged with a shade of green. Was this the beginning of fear in Threye? The beginnings of jealous thought that would forever now be with him? Yes he needed allies, allies that would have to be coerced, seduced, controlled, but never trusted. He awaited the return of Azazel from the Dungeon of Thron. He and Erissa would be the keys to his future plans. Things would never be the same again. This was the only thing Threye was certain about.

The seeds of doubt were being planted in him as he paced up and down. Would he be at the centre of the universe once the current events had played their time out? Would he, he asked himself, and the first nagging seeds of doubt were being planted in his brain.

Meanwhile, after being swallowed up by the bush Azazel found himself in a beautiful garden. The ground was carpeted in soft, green grass, the pathways ringed with flowerbeds. The trees were laden with fruit. A gentle brook flowed by. Azazel had not expected anything quite so lovely, and he began to relax. He did not know where he was expected to go, but this garden seemed like a wonderful place to tarry for a while. As he plucked fruit from the trees, he reveled in their taste. He had never tasted anything quite so luscious, the flavour and fragrance of the fruit filled his mouth. He closed his eyes and smiled in satisfaction.

"This is not going to be so bad, after all," he mused. "The Dungeon used to be a fearful place in the past, but I think

I will not have such a difficult time. Maybe, its reputation is undeserved, after all."

He yawned and stretched out under a tree. His body went limp, and before he knew it he was dozing.

"I think I deserve this rest," he told himself before passing into the world where dreams acquire a life of their own.

Azazel slept soundly. His mind seemed to leave his body and depart to uncharted and undiscovered lands. Somewhere in the distance he saw Erissa sailing her ship The Silver Vulture towards lands he did not recognize. He pictured her turning to smile at him, and waved. He approached her as she stood on the top deck, and as she turned he took her in his arms and kissed her.

"It's been so long," he whispered sweeping her into his arms. He took her down to her cabin where he made love to her. As they lay naked in her bed, Erissa stroked his head. Everything seemed right with the world. Everything was in its place, in perfect harmony.

He stretched his naked body, and suddenly froze. His eyes snapped open and a thought flashed through his mind. Was he dreaming that he was with Erissa? Or was he dreaming that he was sitting in the garden surrounded by the grinning skulls of victims who had perished in the Game of Headz? It dawned on him that these were the skulls of creatures that he, Azazel, had killed. As the skulls glowed in the dark, they asked, grinning: "By what right did you partake of the fruit in the Garden of Skulls?"

"Did you seek permission from the dead souls that live here?"

"Did you approach with the required degree of humility?"

"We are dead; we cannot die again."

Yellow fires gleamed from their eye sockets, seeming to lick at his skin as the skulls crowded around him, chattering and giggling. Their teeth gnawned at him. He turned to run, but the skulls followed. They flew at him from every side, crawling along the ground, giggling, nipping, taunting. Their words crowded his mind, making it impossible for him to think. He was aware only of a wild sensation of terror, and he screamed.

The dead souls had come to seek retribution, and there was no escaping their mad, insane fury. Fear lent Azazel wings. He flew along the ground, gritting his teeth. Panting and sweating, he ran blindly, flailing at the skulls that were doggedly following him.

Then he tripped and fell, rolling on the grass, panting heavily.

"This is the end," he thought. "Maybe it is better to just die."

"And so, Azazel the Great is weak!"

"Esh?" stuttered Azazel. "Esh? But you are dead!" Azazel opened his eyes and saw Esh's head, its blazing red eyes boring right through to his skull.

"You will indeed die Azazel, if you want to. But only if you want to. Remember, young friend, you have become used to positions of power. What you believe to be your strength is a reflection of what your strength has been. But true strength is something you will find when you overcome adversity, fear, and perceived weakness. When you can reach deep into yourself and find courage, then only will you be truly brave. Fight, or die!"

Esh's skull went off into a cackle of laughter. "Die, Azazel... I shall find your flesh tasty indeed."

"Azazel shall die, Azazel shall die. His flesh is tasty. His flesh is sweet...." The skulls joined Esh in a wild chant. The air was filled with their chant, and the skulls bounced and danced together in a mad, frenzied dance.

Azazel, now desperate, looked deep into himself and screamed: "I am Azazel. Be gone, ye skulls, or I shall crush you!"

As he screamed with madness and with fear, something suddenly changed. His voice gained a certain conviction and strength. The more he believed, the stronger his voice became. The skulls paused and stopped, as though uncertain. When Azazel's voice burst through with a strength that even he didn't know he possessed, the skulls seemed to shatter and scatter in different directions.

Suddenly, there was silence. Azazel looked around and breathed in the solitude and peace that surrounded him. For the first time in his life he found the silence intensely beautiful. He was aware of the quiet rustling of the wind in the trees, and the touch of the grass. As he lay on the green carpeted earth, the sweat slowly lifted off his face. He had never felt more alive or more grateful to be alive than he did at that moment. He became aware of the brook bubbling in the background. The sound of the water was pure and refreshing, and he crawled towards it slowly.

Looking into the water, he saw his face looking back at him. He lowered his head, drank deep, and looked down again at his reflection. The surface of the water had been disturbed, the ripples turning his normally handsome face into something altogether ghoulish. His face seemed to have developed a grayish yellow colour. His eye sockets were hollow, and his teeth stood out like fangs. His lips were drawn back in a hungry smile, a tempting, taunting smile. He looked into his eyes and they seemed to hold him, drawing him into the water. Hypnotized, he felt himself being pulled with a strength he had no power to resist.

He fell face first into the water. It was cool and refreshing, and his body felt weightless, light. Giving himself up to the sensation, he allowed the water to take him where it willed. He let himself be taken over, and he went down... down....down...

The water itself seemed to change colour, become sort of reddish, and heavy.

Azazel suddenly found he could not breathe. He felt a hand gripping him by the ankles and pulling him down. He kicked angrily, yanking his foot this way and that. But the force pulling him down was stronger than he was, and he was looking at his mirror image. A malignant version of himself was pulling him down, further down, clawing at him.

Horror filled Azazel, but he realised it was not the horror of fear, it was the horror of being overpowered. He had always fancied himself strong. He realised now that there were beings in the world that were stronger than him.

Down he sank, to the bottom of the brook, choking with rage and helplessness. Yet he was powerless; there did not seem anything he could do to resist the malevolent force.

A last wave of lucidity swept through his mind, and he almost laughed to himself. There were beings that were more malignant than he was? He found that hard to believe. He, Azazel, was one of the strongest beings on earth; now his double seemed even stronger. He laughed soundlessly, even as he was drowning in the river of blood. He mocked the malignant being pulling him down, and his mind seemed to blaze with anger.

"You are but a shadow of me," said Azazel to Azazel. "You cannot exist without me."

Azazel smirked, and said: "I am you. Recognize me, and recognize you for who you are. You are pure evil, a force of nature that you do not know. Do you not know me? Do you not know yourself?"

Azazel looked at Azazel and said: "Yes, I recognize you. You are my true nature. Come back into me then, and let us rule forever."

Azazel laughed at Azazel, who laughed back at Azazel. Azazel laughed with Azazal, and suddenly Azazel laughed alone. The two had become one, and Azazel realised that he was now stronger than he had ever been before. He laughed and laughed and laughed. The madness in him gained strength. He sat up and looked within to find depths of evil that he had not encountered before.

"Welcome," said a soft voice suddenly.

Azazel looked up and found himself staring into the eyes of the most beautiful woman he had ever seen. Tall and slender, with skin that was not quite white and not quite brown. It glowed with a radiance that could only come from within. Her body radiated vitality, life, energy. Black hair streaked with green; green eyes that looked at him with mischief and promise. Azazel found himself looking into the eyes of Esmerelda.

"Welcome," she said again softly. Azazel was silent, not willing to trust what he was seeing. As his eyes left her, he realized that night had given way to day, and that he was now in a place that was considerably drier than the garden that he had been in the previous evening. The brook had disappeared, and the landscape was desert-like.

Esmerelda wore a light green cloak over a tight black dress. She moved with an almost ghostly grace.

"Come," she said. "We have to walk a bit before we reach the Palace of Thron." She walked lightly on the rapidly-growing bank of sand, and laughed when Azazel found his feet sinking into the sand.

"Hold my hand and walk with me." So saying, she offered him her hand and gently pulled him along. They walked this way, hand in hand, for a while before Azazel emerged from his stupor to ask:

"How long do we have before we reach the Palace of Thron? And what can I expect there?"

Smiling, Esmerelda merely said: "Patience, my dear friend. You don't even know my name. Wouldn't you like to know my name, and become better acquainted before we move on? Thron does not like it if his guests do not know their escorts. You must realise that very few people have ever reached the palace. The last was over a thousand years ago: a long, long time ago."

Pulling him down beside her, they sat under the shade of a tree that seemed to have magically sprouted from the ground for them to sit under.

"My name is Esmerelda," she said. "Do you know me? Have you heard of me? No? The last one of your kind who met me was Erissa." She smiled as she saw the shock on Azazel's face.

"Come, my dear Azazel. You have yet to learn complete mastery over yourself. This is a lesson you must learn before you can move forward." So saying, she flung her clothes off. Her naked skin gleamed in the light filtering through the shade of the tree. Her body gave off a musky odour, and she twined herself around Azazel. Involuntarily, Azazel felt his body reacting to hers and he stripped with an alacrity that was almost reprehensible. He yearned for her, and he almost whimpered as his body moved into hers. A thin film of sweat covered his body as it moved with an urgency and life of its own.

At the point of entry, Azazel opened his eyes and looked into Esmerelda's. Her expression had changed. No longer soft and alluring, it was cold, calculating and wicked. Her eyes played with, taunted him; they were strong and hypnotic. With a jerk, Azazel pulled himself away and with horror saw that her appearance had changed too. She was now an old crone, warts on her nose, long, sharp nails, and teeth like fangs. She giggled, and spittle drooled from her lips. Her withered body crawled towards him.

"Come into me, come into me," she cackled, her voice hoarse with lust.

"Stay away from me, you evil witch!" gasped Azazel, hastily covering his nakedness.

"You don't like me anymore?" Esmerelda croaked, her wrinkled hands offering him a withered breast.

"No!" screamed Azazel. "Stay away from me, you old hag!" His voice was thin with horror and disgust.

"Old?!" she screeched, changing back to the alluring woman who had greeted him just a short while earlier.

"Yes, I am old. They call me the Old One. Have you heard the name, you weak, measly man? You are weak, and you shall die!"

So saying, Esmerelda plucked a branch from the tree and hurled it at him. The javelin flew at blinding speed; Azazel had just enough time to duck before it landed.

He raised a hand, opened his third eye, and let forth a blast of hot fire. Laughing at his efforts, Esmerelda countered with a jet of water.

The battle went back and forth, neither seeming able to defeat the other, until suddenly Azazel, allowing his mind to quieten for a second. Memory of his powers flooded back into him, and he remembered that he had the power of invisibility. He disappeared.

"Where are you?" cooed Esmerelda. "Come out little Azazel, Esmerelda wants to play." Her voice was like a song, a warbling lullaby. She walked on bent knees, her body poised to lunge. She held a little knife in her hand, and sang: "Esmerelda is hungry, little Azazel. Won't you give her a taste of your heart, my dear? Just a teeny, weeny taste?"

All of a sudden, she was flung to the ground, her face pinned in the sand. Choking, she heard a grim voice above her saying: "Little Azazel has played the game. Come Esmerelda, let us go to Thron. He waits for us."

Taking the knife from her limp hand, Azazel continued: "Else little Azazel will have a little taste of your heart. Would you want that, my dear? And, a little souvenir of the same for Erissa would be nice."

Allowing her body to become completely limp, Esmerelda said in a small voice: "You have defeated me, Lord Azazel. I will take you to Thron."

They walked through the night and into the day, under the fierce sun, braving strong, dusty winds that cut their faces. Not one drop of water passed their parched lips, not one morsel of food. The sand swirled around their legs, making it difficult to move. At the end of the second day, the temperature dropped, and it started to freeze. The ground seemed to delight in chilling their feet, and sharp plants cut through their shoes. The wind blew little bits of ice into their faces, and, when it seemed like they could go on no more, a huge, dark shadow appeared before them in the night.

Staggering, they approached it and just as they were ready to drop with exhaustion a door swung open and they passed through the gates of the Palace of Thron.

Walking down the hallway, Azazel looked about him with curiosity. The ceiling was high, and bright. The hall was covered with hangings depicting scenes of happiness, mixed with those of extreme horror. On the walls were drawings of people being tortured in ways that were scarcely imaginable. As Azazel looked closely, he noticed that the paintings moved. Indeed, they were not paintings but people, creatures being tortured for the pleasure of Thron.

He approached the throne, and knelt.

"Arise, Lord Azazel," said a baby's voice. Azazel looked up in surprise to see a baby on the throne. Esmerelda was standing beside the throne, looking at Azazel with eyes that were deep with the knowledge of time. It was impossible to penetrate the thoughts that were hidden so craftily behind the veil of her eyes. He looked back at Thron, at the baby's body, and then into the eyes of Time. Indeed, he fell right into the eyes of Thron. His body was cast into a maelstrom. Blurred visions flew past him, as he went back in time. He saw his childhood, his growing years, Trix and Erissa. He saw Threye, and the escape of the Little Birds from the dungeons. His mind was a mass of confusion, as he realised that there was no escape from the dungeons unless Thron himself willed it. Just as there was no entry into the palace unless Thron allowed it...

And then his body was thrown back into the whirlpool, twisting, turning, blurred visions flashing by with an intensity that shook him. He saw the changing of the world order; he saw that he would play a significant role in things to come. Yet he could not see clearly what his role would be, or how things would end.

As his body was flung back onto the floor, he found himself looking into the black impenetrable eyes of a young man. He realised that the eyes had no pupils; they were dark pits without a soul.

"Welcome," the young man said. "I am Thron. You are privileged indeed, Lord Azazel, to have entered my palace and to have been given a brief glimpse of what has happened; what will be. You saw the Little Birds, I see. Yes, they escaped by my will. Nothing here happens that is not of my wanting. You will have to leave the dungeons with Esmerelda by your side. She shall be your companion. Yes, you know her as the Old One, the Witch of the Dungeon. She shall be by your side on your future journeys."

Thron looked at Azazel, divining his thoughts, and continued: "Esmerelda will not be your lover. This is not for you. You shall stay with Erissa. Esmerelda will be my emissary in the world, and your companion."

Thron stood in front of Azazel, and said in a deep voice:

"Arise Azazel, Lord of Chaos. Go forth into the world as my emissary."

Thron had now changed into an old man, his forked tongue escaping from his lips as though savouring what was to come. His black eyes, those impenetrable pits that seemed to hold all knowledge, all power, did not change. There was a deep well of malice in those eyes, deep power that held no pity, no feeling but that of dark intent.

As Azazel found himself being cast back into the whirlpool, he had a last brief glimpse of the young baby sitting on the throne, a baby with deep black eyes.

Then his body twisted and twirled, and all memory left him.

He found himself standing in front of Threye, Esmerelda by his side. It seemed as though he had been there all the while. He had only a dim recollection of what had just transpired.

Had he entered the Dungeon of Thron, or had it all been just a dream? The only thing that made him believe that this had been no dream was Esmerelda by his side.

"Go forth, Azazel!" said Threye, a smile in his eyes. "You know what is to be done."

The next morning, two ships left the shores of Mrod bound for the Valley of the Kings. Azazel was on board The White Eagle; Esmerelda commanded her ship, The Emerald Shadow.

The die was cast; pieces were being put in place. Threye smiled to himself as he stood on the shore watching the ships disappear in the distance.

Chapter 14

Escape From Sangre

Sally woke up in the dark, her head throbbing. Crawling about on all fours, she bumped into warm bodies, bodies that moaned in pain, cursing her for her clumsiness. She felt blood trickling down her head, into her mouth, and she whimpered in fear and pain.

Finally, exhausted, she sat back against a wall and started to cry. It was cold and damp, and a foul, putrid smell came from somewhere. She sniffed. Was this the smell of rotting bodies? Was this something else? She smelled decay, death and fear. Sally drew her arms about herself and shivered.

"We will die in here," she moaned, her mind wandering to the future she had hoped to have with Thyme but now would never. A future with children playing about their feet in the garden, on bright sunny mornings. A future where she and Thyme would grow old together. She closed her eyes and tried to imagine this future, but it seemed far away, remote, and somehow unreal. Why couldn't life be simple, she thought? Why did it have to be so complicated, with so many trials?

A finger poked her in the ribs, and she started. She looked into a pair of bright eyes.

"What ails thee, child?" asked a kindly voice.

Sally merely whimpered, and the voice continued: "You are hurt, and you are scared that you will never get out of here. And you will never experience having children. Am I right?"

"How do you know? And who are you?" blurted out Sally, wrapping her arms tight about her, more scared than ever. Out of the blue, there came this strange voice. It was somehow eerie, and Sally did not want anything more from the voice.

A small light came on and Sally found herself looking into the wizened face of an old woman. White hair flowed in abundant waves about her shoulders, and a peaceful energy radiated from her body. Her eyes were lively.

"You can call me Mama Kuko," the old lady said. "I come from the land of Lavonia. We are known as healers. However, this is not the time to be talking about me or my history, don't you agree? This is the time for action, the time to escape, or things could turn out very badly for you and your friends."

Taking Sally's hand she said firmly: "Come my dear. Let's wake your friends, and move quickly. The world is changing, and changing fast. There is no time to lose."

Scarcely waiting for Sally to recover, Mama Kuko woke Trix and the rest of the Lexters. There was a commotion. The other prisoners began to stir. There was a sudden mumbling and rumbling that took on its own momentum and shape. The commotion roused the attention of the guards who looking in only to be greeted by Mama Kuko wailing and beating her chest, complaining that she was being beaten to a pulp by the hungry, growling prisoners.

Grumbling under their breath, the guards opened the doors of the prison. "If the Medicine Woman is beaten to a pulp, then she will be of no use to Mr. Benttwist. Why does this sort of thing have to happen under our watch? Mr. Benttwist will not be pleased. No he won't!"

Cursing softly, they opened the doors and were mowed down by the rapidly advancing group of Lexters led by the massive bulk of Rollo. Not for the first time did Brindar silently commend Rollo for his heft.

Screaming and charging, the group managed to confuse the guards. Any chance of a recovery was thwarted by bolts of fire emanating from Trix, and Thyme's high-pitched squeals. Indeed, Thyme seemed to have discovered a weapon in his voice, his desire to break loose unleashing an unbearable whistling scream.

Then there was a mad rush as the rest of the prisoners ran out in a scramble to escape. Several guards were trampled underfoot as the Brethren made good their escape.

"Quick!" yelled Trix, "to the inn!"

"Run in the shadows!" shouted Thar. "We are not out of danger yet."

Dawn was breaking, yet the dark had not given way to day. As the sun stretched wide its sleepy arms to pierce the night with its brilliant fingers, the Brethren ran swiftly in the fast-disappearing shadows, to the safety of the inn.

As they burst into the room, they were struck by the silence that greeted them. There was no one at the reception, no smells of breakfast cooking or tea brewing on the pot.

Basil sniffed, and said: "Something's wrong. I smell it in the air. Let's go and find Jenna and Percival. They are the only two who are not here." Not waiting for a response, he led the charge up the stairs and ran through the doors to find Jenna sitting on the floor, weeping, next to the lifeless body of Percival.

Trix looked at Jenna, and then at the open window behind her, her eyes taking in the room with a sweep. She noted the dead bodies of Mr. and Mrs. Fangz against the wall. She rushed to the window and looked down at the pool of blood below.

"What happened here?" she demanded, her voice tense. Meanwhile, Mama Kuko had dropped to her knees besides Percival, staring at his white face and feeling his stiff body.

"He needs medical attention immediately," she said. "We will need to escape this island and get him back to Lavonia. My countrymen, Dhanvan and Zywie, have the special skills to treat him, and to remove the poison. Both Percival and Jenna will need to be treated, for body and soul. We will need to move fast or else he will move into the shadows and will be beyond our help."

"What happened here?" repeated Trix. Jenna quickly narrated the scene of the previous evening when she had found and killed Mr. and Mrs. Fangz as they were drinking Percival's blood.

"Yes," muttered Mama Kuko. "These people inject a strange poison with their teeth. It sucks the soul out of the victim through the blood as they drink it. Blood is their main source of food and energy. Deprived of it for too long they waste away."

Jenna looked at her and continued: "As I sat there with the dead bodies of Mr. and Mrs. Fangz around me, and Percival lying here on the floor, I suddenly heard the door crash open. Before I had time to react I was flung to the ground and Christina's body was pinning mine to the ground. Her mouth was open. I could see her fangs grow; her tongue too grew long and sharp. Her mouth reeked of a foul odour. Her eyes were sharp and cruel. She laughed, a mad laugh, and as she picked a knife from her belt, no doubt to stab me, I heaved with all my strength. She flew over my head.

We scrambled to our feet and faced each other, panting. 'Little Jenna wants to play then', she snarled. Her voice was filled with hate and fury. 'Little Jenna killed my friends and now she must die!' she went on."

"With that, she charged at me. I sidestepped and clubbed her on the head. She stumbled and I grabbed her arm and twisted the knife away from her. I could see the rage in her face as she pulled another knife from her belt and stabbed at me. We went back and forth, until, finally, I managed to stab her thigh. As she screamed in pain, I let forth a blast, a weak blast, but it was enough to topple her. It hit her on the shoulder. She was standing next to the window. The last thing I saw was her toppling through it and onto the street below. I think she is dead. As she fell, I dropped to the floor. I recovered only moments before you crashed through the door."

"Come," said Sindar. "We have no time to lose." He had been standing by the window and was watching the street from where he stood. There was chaos as the recently freed prisoners ran this way and that in a mad rush to escape. They picked up anything they could lay their hands on, to beat the people and guards rushing to recapture them.

"Let us take advantage of the confusion," Sindar said, "and make good our escape. Rollo, pick up Percival and carry him. We shall shield you as we make our way back to The Raven."

Slipping quickly down the stairs, they made their way out into the street. "Don't carry that knife onto the ship," said Mama Kuko to Jenna, noticing her pick it up as she left the room.

Then, as they ran along, she seemed to have a change of heart. "On second thoughts, carry it with you. You may need it before the end is up."

They ran, trying their best not to be noticed. But it was impossible. Brindar and Basil, who were leading the charge, hacked their way through the crowds with a vigour borne out of desperation. Sally and Thyme flanked Rollo who carried Percival on his massive shoulders. The two sisters brought up the rear, along with Thar. All had one thing on their mind: to make it safely to Lavonia.

Desperation is a strange thing; it can blind you. Not a single member of the group paused to consider where exactly they were going, or indeed whether Lavonia was the answer to their hopes for a reprieve. It could very well have been a place of horror and danger. At that moment, nothing mattered but to escape.

They reached the pier and found themselves face-to-face with Mr. Benttwist, his normally suave face mottled and purple with rage.

"Stop," he screamed, "or you shall die!" His hand brandished what looked like a sword, and he seemed ready to strike the first member of the advancing group. It was at that moment that Thyme chose to let forth a piercing scream, as he broke rank and charged at Mr. Benttwist. He ran blindly, with no clue as to how he would attack his assailant. His anger lent him force.

Mr. Benttwist paused, his hand held high, sword in the air, as the scream burst through his eardrums and into his brain. Then, suddenly, Thyme seemed to disappear from sight. He had slipped and crashed into Mr. Benttwist's knees, toppling him. Mr. Benttwist rolled over Thyme's back, and was flung high into the air. As he descended, his sword stabbed him in the leg. He fell to the ground in an ugly heap and, before he could recover his breath, Rollo stamped on his chest, knocking the breath out of him. He lay there on the ground, wheezing, blood beginning to ooze out of his mouth. His blood was greenish-yellow in colour, and gave off a foul odour.

Hearing his screams, the rest of Mr. Benttwist's group stood frozen. This was the breakthrough the Brethren were waiting for. There was no time to stand and wonder at the strange nature of the blood that was oozing from his mouth. They hacked their way through the guards, leaving no one alive. The rout was complete, and no mercy was shown. No mercy could be shown. They ran along the pier. Miraculously, The Raven appeared before them in the morning sun, like a welcome apparition.

Gasping, they boarded the ship, collapsing one by one onto the deck in exhaustion. Mama Kuko walked up to the front of the ship, stroking her sides and whispering. The Raven left the shores of Sangre, headed for Lavonia.

They had escaped. It was nothing short of a miracle, that they managed to escape so easily. There are times when the Fates are kind. They keep you alive, to allow you to live another day. The Day of Death and Reckoning may not be far, but to the desperate, the smallest reprieve feels like manna from Heaven, and that is all that matters at that time.

The Brethren lay sprawled on the deck for the better part of a day and-a-half. Their adventures had exhausted them in ways they had not imagined possible. Finally, after dinner on the second day of their escape, Sally, who was seated next to Mama Kuko, said: "Mama Kuko, please tell us your story, and how you came to be captive on Sangre."

Mama Kuko smiled, and said: "Well child, if you like I will tell you my story. But I will try to be brief as I sense that all of you are still tired from your recent adventures, though this time the fatigue is more in the mind than in the body."

"I am from Lavonia," she continued. "We are an island that very few people know about, as it is hidden from sight. Only few are allowed entry onto the island. Threye has searched for Lavonia these past few centuries, but his eyes cannot pierce the veil that hides the island.

You, Jenna and Trix, will be the first of your kind ever to set foot on the shores of Lavonia."

"We leave our island only under exceptional circumstances. We are healers; this is what we do. You will find that Lavonia is exceptionally beautiful and calm. I am rare amongst my kind, inasmuch as I have always had a desire to travel. So, one morning, I took my ship and set sail to explore the world a bit. After sailing for a month, I came to the shores of the Valley of Kings. When I landed, it seemed as though I had been sent here by providence. There was a stillness about the place, as though it had been visited by the plague, or some other illness, as indeed it was. The people were suffering from a strange disease that attacked both their hearts and their minds. They were quite simply wasting away in their beds. None was more ill than the king himself. Regus is his name; his wife's name is Regina."

"I was taken to the palace and granted an audience with the king. As he lay there in his bed, frail and seemingly close to death, he asked me to heal his people before I healed him. I was given a room in the palace, and I set about the task. It took all of six months, but at the end of a hard struggle I finally managed to cure the people of their deadly disease. I then turned my attention to the king, working at his bedside for the next two months. He recovered, and as he sat up in bed, his eyes bursting with the energy of a life renewed, I fainted by his bedside with exhaustion. I regained consciousness only a week later, and was feted by the entire population of the land."

"I asked the king for leave to return to Lavonia, but he begged me to stay. And I did. I stayed at the palace for three whole months, all the while soaking up the people's adulation until it completely went to my head. I began to think I was the best healer of all time. A short while later, a delegation from Sangre visited the king. When they heard about the wonders that I had performed, they fell to their knees and begged the king to let me travel to their land as a terrible sickness had afflicted the people there. The king was reluctant to let me go, but I insisted, promising him that I would be back in less than a month."

"That was my folly, and result of my new-found vanity." She sighed, and went on. "The hallmark of a healer is the quality of humility and service. This is something that I had violated. When I went on board the ship I was full of vanity and demanded a comfortable cabin for myself. Frugal quarters was no longer a condition that I would accept."

"We left the shores of the Valley of Kings and travelled to Sangre. The food on board the ship was magnificent. The spreads laid out, the wines served, were something I would not have believed had they not been served to me."

"One evening, after dinner, and having drunk a bit too much, I went to my cabin and flung myself on the bed.

I did not care to undress, or to lock my door. I slept the sleep of the dead, and did not awaken until I found myself in a room in an area of Sangre they call the Wailing Wall. It was called this because this is where they came to hear the wailing of prisoners being taken to the Hanging Gardens or other places where the blood was drained from their bodies. My head hurt, and as I rubbed my stiff neck I felt two puncture marks."

"I knew then that I had been taken prisoner, something made possible only by my own stupidity and vanity. My powers had left me; had I not met you I doubt I would have had the strength to escape."

She looked at Jenna and concluded her story by merely saying: "When you and your friend are cured, so shall I be."

There was a pensive silence in the room. Mama Kuko rose and said: "I must rest now. In two days we shall be in Lavonia. I shall remain in my cabin until then."

"Wow!" muttered Thyme as Mama Kuko withdrew. "Strange bird indeed... Ow!!" he squealed when Sally kicked him sharply on the shins.

"Have some respect!" she said tartly.

In two days, The Raven was enveloped in a thick mist. As the ship sailed through it, members of the crew stretched and yawned.

"God, I'm sleepy!" said Brindar. "I think I shall have a little shut-eye."

"Good idea," echoed the others one by one. Sleep came to them like a refreshing breeze. It gently caressed them as they slept. The Brethren slept a dreamless sleep, dead to the world and to themselves. Little did they know it, but the period of healing had begun. Sleep is indeed a wondrous thing. Little understood, and often not appreciated enough, it has the magical ability to heal body and heart. They had been through some fierce adventures, and were more tired in body and soul than they had realized.

Later, when they awoke, they found themselves moored on the shores of the most beautiful land they had ever seen. Mossy green grass carpeted the ground; the trees were laden with fruit and flowers. A waterfall could be seen in the distance, and a bubbling brook seemed to gambol and dance its way to the sea. Everywhere there was a sense of peace, of wellbeing, of a hidden wisdom.

As they set foot on the shores of Lavonia for the very first time, a deep, comforting voice said: "Welcome to Lavonia. My name is Dhanvan, and this is my spouse, Zywie. Here you shall rest and heal. You are amongst the very few who have been permitted to come to Lavonia. We hope you enjoy your stay. It shall be our honour to serve you and to help you become whole again."

They looked at Dhanvan, a tall man with a flowing white beard and long, white hair. Despite the age that seemed to be reflected in his beard, his eyes were young and bursting with compassionate energy. His wife, Zywie, was tall, slender, with black hair and eyes flecked with orange. She too was the epitome of warmth, healing and comfort. The Brethren knew immediately that they had come to a place of comfort, safety and healing. Their hearts were at peace.

Meanwhile, far away in Sangre, Mr. Benttwist and Christina raged, cursed, and pledged eternal revenge.

"I will have them one day!" swore Mr. Benttwist. His voice was hoarse, and little drops of green blood flecked his mouth. His chest hurt, and he found it difficult to breathe.

"And so you shall," said a voice inside him. "Join me, Threye, and my Mrodic forces in a war against these filthy vermin, these Little Birds. Let us slaughter them and drink their blood."

"Yes," said Mr. Benttwist to the voice inside him. Threye had reached out to him. He did not know how. He did not care to wonder how Threye had got inside him, and was slowly starting to control his mind. All that he was conscious of, was a bling rage, and a thirst for revenge.

Looking at Christina, he said: "We shall join forces with Threye, and we shall have our revenge."

She smiled a smile full of wicked rage, a look of madness creeping into her red eyes. Her mind was occupied by thoughts of Jenna. She too, wanted blood, and she was oblivious of everything else.

Mr. Benttwist threw back his head and laughed, an evil, gurgling laugh, the laugh of an insane man.

Chapter 15

Cured In Lavonia. Return Home

"Welcome," said Dhanvan as he led them to their temporary homes. "I hope you will be comfortable, and that you will enjoy your stay here. This is a place of healing and rest. Your journeys will continue, and you will have difficult times ahead. In the meantime, rest, recoup, heal your bodies and your spirit."

Zywie nodded, smiled, and said: "Your friends Jenna and Percival need special healing and will be taken to a place where this can be done. They will be back in ten days; by that time I hope that you will all have recovered."

Turning to Mama Kuko, she added: "Mama, you must come with me. Your spirit is heavy and your mind has shadows that need to be cleansed. Indeed, you were in great danger of passing into the shadows. I hope that you can be healed. Come!" With that, she held Mama Kuko's hand and led her away.

While walking away, she turned her head, and smilingly said, "Have some fun as well. Good food, sleep and laughter never did harm anyone. We may look grave, but we definitely enjoy a chuckle."

Percival and Jenna went with Dhanvan and the rest of the group settled down to rest. They lay in the shade of the trees, a sense of peace and wellbeing pervading them. Their bodies relaxed as they looked up at the sunlight filtering through the trees. Soft and inviting, the sun's rays entered their eyes and seeped into their bodies, inviting them to relax and forget their recent adventures. They became aware of the softness of the ground and the feel of the grass under their bodies. All was well with the world; everything was in harmony. They felt the tension flowing out of them like a poisonous sap slowly leaving their bodies. One by one they closed their eyes and allowed themselves to sleep.

Jenna and Percival, meanwhile, travelled through Lavonia for three days and three nights. As they went, Jenna marvelled at the scenery around them. She had grown up in the green land of Mrod, yet here there was a difference. The green of Mrod was not comforting; the leaves there were sharp, dark green and mottled. They seemed to echo Mrod's angry spirit. Here she saw nature in a whole new way, a nature that was calm, healing and gentle. Her soul relaxed and she smiled inside of her as she walked to a destination that was yet unknown.

On the morning of the third day, they passed below a waterfall and into a wooded valley. They arrived at a hut where Dhanvan stopped, saying: "We have arrived at our destination. Rest today. The healing process shall begin tomorrow."

The morning dawned bright and bursting with life. Dhanvan arrived with his assistants, and said: "We shall start with the cleansing waters." The two were taken to a refreshing stream. As Jenna took off her clothes, she tried to imagine the feel of the water flowing over her naked body and shivered with anticipation. She put a toe in the water, then allowed herself to sink to the bottom. As she lay with her head back, she prepared to relax her mind and her body. She sighed, as the cool water washed over her, cleansing her, calming her. The waters entered every pore of her being, and she relaxed completely.

In a few minutes however, the water turned from cool to hot. It soon became almost unbearable and burned her skin. Bubbles rose to the surface, swirling as if they sought to escape. Anger seemed to be in the bubbles, and fury in the waves of the water. The calm bliss had turned to agony, and the waters seemed to sear her skin, burning it, scorching it.

Near her, Percival whimpered in agony. Jenna twisted this way and that, begging to be allowed to jump out of the water. Yet she seemed to be bound; the more she struggled, the more her skin burned. "Aaaiiyeeee", she screamed. "I am burning, burning." She opened her eyes in an agony of frustrated rage, her mouth screaming obscenities and threats. Flexing her muscles, Jenna tried to pull herself and Percival out of the waters, but she was powerless. There was no escape from the burning, scorching waters. The torture seemed to go on for hours. Hours.

Finally, she collapsed back into the water exhausted and closed her eyes. Her mind went blank as she gave herself up to the sensation of the water swirling around her body. She drifted, mindless, into a world unknown.

Then, almost imperceptibly, the water seemed to change again. It began to cool, and her body tingled with a pleasant healing sensation. Jenna sighed in almost animalistic pleasure, as her body stretched out in the water welcoming it and allowing it to flow over it. The waters had become welcoming again. They had become her friend, allowing her mind to soften and to welcome new sensations. Miraculously, their skins bore no signs of the burning water. Everything was calm. Everything was good. All was well with the world again.

Too soon, almost too soon it seemed, she found herself out of the stream. Casting a last longing look at the waters, she allowed herself to be led back to her bed. Dhanvan smiled his eyes gentle and warm.

"Good," he said, "the moment you stopped fighting and welcomed the water, you allowed it to cleanse you. We are all creatures of Nature. When we fight it, torment it, we kill Nature. Something of ourselves dies as well. Yet, when we soften, when we welcome Nature, we allow it to strengthen and purify us. It heals us, and makes us stronger. We appreciate the world that we live in, and learn respect. Tomorrow we shall put your body through the strengthening mud. Sleep well till then."

Jenna flung herself on her bed and looked over at Percival. He seemed to be moving slowly, and then suddenly he opened his eyes. He peered at her confusedly, and then she was on top of him, kissing him everywhere.

"You're back!" she cried in joy.

"Where am I?" he asked.

"Let's just say that you are in a place of healing," said Dhanvan, coming back to them. "Heal yourself. Let us help to heal you. We shall talk a little bit about your adventures then. For now, rest. Your body and your soul still need to be healed. Sleep well, for tomorrow we start the next phase. This will take two days, and you must rest."

They were woken up early the next morning and as they proceeded in the morning sun they arrived at what seemed to be a marsh. Walking became more and more difficult, and soon both of them were huffing and puffing their way along the swampy pass. The squelching mud rose to their ankles, and then slowly to their knees. As they sank deeper and deeper into the mud, the panic in their bodies rose, swirling and curling and catching in their throats like a spiky ball. They were now neck-deep in the mud and could barely move. As they twisted their bodies this way and that, they found their strength flagging until, finally, they stopped trying. Meanwhile, the sun bore down on them its gentle rays seeming to have turned into something harsh, something that appeared to have a mind of its own, a mind designed to hurt. Flies rose from the mud and flew around their sweaty faces. The maddening buzz went on forever, as the flies crept into their noses and into their mouths, sticking in their throats. "What sort of cure is this?", asked Jenna to herself. "This is more like torture than a cure." She, of the Mrodic race, who had lived victoriously and often viciously, could not begin to imagine what torture and pain felt like. As she was cursing and crying, a voice inside her head intoned, "The path to Heaven is through Hell. The path to redemption is paved with burning stones. Only when you go through the pain, will you be reborn, and you will feel bliss. Be strong, not weak. Yielding is not always a sign of weakness."

It all seemed too much, and then suddenly Jenna remembered the stream.

"Don't fight it," she yelled to Percival. "Don't fight it, but don't let it defeat you either..."

"What?" screamed back Percival, his face red with anger, fear and desperation. The flies continued to irritate his body and his mind. He tried to thrash his arms about, but they were held fast in the mud. Suddenly, his body went limp. His head drooped, and he closed his eyes. His tongue lolled out of his mouth, and was soon covered in flies. For all purposes it appeared as if Percival had indeed died.

Day gave way to night, and the mud appeared to freeze. The flies still stuck to their faces and eyes; their little legs even seemed to penetrate their skin. Jenna pushed her mind away from what was happening, and appeared to pass into a zone of complete indifference. When it seemed as though he would finally collapse, Percival's face suddenly snapped and he looked across at Jenna with a clear, penetrating look in his eyes.

"It's time!" he said suddenly.

"Time?" she stuttered with shock, her face almost completely covered with flies. "Time for what?"

"It is time for these flies to fall off and die. They are a pestilence and a nuisance but they cannot be part of me.

They can penetrate my skin, but they cannot penetrate my mind any more. It is time." His face was radiant, and his eyes were clear. There was a new found strength in them, and peace. Was he about to give up his life, and die, she wondered?

Dawn was breaking, and as the sun's rays began to warm the cold air of the night the marshy swamp seemed to melt and they found that they could move. The flies slowly dropped from them and died, their black bodies mingling with the brown mud that now appeared fluid. As Percival and Jenna reached the shore, they were greeted by a smiling Dhanvan, who gripped them both by the hand and helped them on shore.

"Rest today," he said. "Tomorrow you start the last phase of your healing."

Tired, the two slept through the day in each other's arms. Watching them sleep, Dhanvan thought: "They are each other's strength, incomprehensible though this may seem. As long as they are together, they will be impossible to defeat. They will spread light." He looked at them for a while, and then turned away allowing them the privacy of their rest together.

The next day was cold, windy and wet. The mood was hostile and bleak. Percival and Jenna shivered as they were led down the path; they wondered what the day would bring. After walking for around ten minutes, they came to a fork in the road and were led down separate paths.

At the fork, they were held back by Dhanvan, who said: "This is where the two of you go your separate ways. If you cannot find your way back to each other, you will be lost to yourselves forever. It is your task to find each other. If not, you are lost. This is the final step. May your hearts guide you well."

The unhappy pair looked at each other, tears welling up in their eyes. They could not speak. Unspoken promises hung on their lips as they stood looking at one another. Would they meet again? Or would they be lost to each other forever? Would they lose their souls in the process? Dark thoughts weighed on their minds and bore down on their hearts as they turned abruptly away from each other and proceeded down their respective paths.

As they walked, the path seemed to get narrower, until suddenly it grew dark and the air was still and heavy. Both Jenna and Percival stood in the dark, wondering what to do.

Percival steeled himself and continued walking. He bumped his head, stumbled and fell and tried to tell himself that there was no reason to panic. He told himself that if he could survive the swamp, he could survive anything. He recalled his adventures and assured himself that he could brave anything. Hours passed, and he still could not see. He was alone with his thoughts, thoughts that bumped and swirled around until they were a confusing tangled mass and he could not think clearly. Moments of panic crept into his heart, and he sat down panting. He could feel the sweat pour down his face and freeze. What was he to do? Where was he to go? Would his past be a guide to the future? Was there anything in the past that would guide his footsteps as he stumbled this way and that?

Meanwhile Jenna stepped into the shadows boldly, walking quickly and with precision. She had never been scared of the dark and was confident that her vision would guide her well. She opened her third eye, expecting the blaze of fire to offer her some light and burn any obstacles that crossed her path. But there was nothing. No light, no fire, nothing but a cold beam of darkness. She sat down confused. This was certainly not something she had expected. A blaze of light yes, but a beam of darkness?! What was this? It was completely beyond her comprehension. She stumbled about in confusion, a frustrated rage slowly building up inside her. Her mind was numb with fear and anger, fear that she would lose Percival forever, and anger with herself for not being able to find her way. Her mind went back to the times they had had together, how she had thrown him over the side of the ship, and how love had crept up on her silently, quietly, like a shadow in the night. Yet now, she of the Mrodics, felt utterly helpless.

Hours passed. Percival and Jenna staggered about on their respective paths. Their fear of losing each other mingled with another fear: that they would starve and die in the dark, their flesh and bones stripped clean by the rats and insects that would inevitably find their way to the rotting flesh. All hope seemed lost as, ultimately, each sat down weeping quietly in the dense darkness surrounding them.

Their hearts went out to each other. Percival recalled how he had been able to identify Jenna by touch. Jenna remembered how Percival smelled. It struck them both that they had not quite lost all their senses, and with a fresh sense of anticipation they rose and walked on. As long as there was life left in their bodies, they knew that there was still hope that they would find each other again.

As she walked, Jenna sniffed around energetically. She would smell out Percival, even if she could not see him. Then, suddenly, she smelled a beloved smell. She took a few tentative steps forward, and whispered: "Percy?" A hand reached out and touched her face, and a voice whispered back: "Jenna?"

Tentative though their voices were, they knew that they had found each other and that whatever trials they would have to undergo they would have each other. They fell into each other's arms, weeping and holding the other close. The moment was sweet; it was something that stayed with them until the end of their lives.

Slowly, ever so slowly, the darkness lifted and light filtered down on them like a soothing balm. It gave them energy, and as they looked around they saw that they were sitting on a mossy clump, surrounded by trees and flowers. Indeed, nature seemed to blossom as the two sat looking into each other's eyes.

Soon enough, Dhanvan came by with a gentle smile in his eyes. "Come!" he said. "It is time to rest before you start the journey back to your friends tomorrow."

As the sun set on the evening of the third day back to camp, they saw the evening fires being lit and their friends sitting around laughing. They noticed that the group seemed larger than before.

Trix was the first to spot them, and as she bounded up to greet the pair, she poked Percival in the ribs, and chortled: "You have put on weight, I see... Getting a little flabby, eh?"

"Witch!" retorted Percival.

Joy, it would appear, had been let loose and it was a while before Percival was able to extricate himself from the arms of his companions. Looking over at the newcomers, he exclaimed: "Bardor! Noir! What are you two doing here?!"

"It's a long story, my friend," said Basil. "It's a long story. You have no idea what has been going on. It seems.... ooof!" he stopped as Thyme jabbed him in the ribs.

"Let Bardor and Noir tell the tale," Thyme said.

Percival looked at the pair. Friends? he wondered. Yes, they were friends now. How life had changed from the time they had shoved him face down in the muck outside Corky's Top Hat Shop. They were friends now, companions who had laughed and drunk together, companions who had braved adventures together, and who had looked into the eyes of death.

A sudden wave of nostalgia swept through him, and he turned to Bardor with tears in his eyes. Holding him by the arms, he said: "Tell me my friend, what news do you bring of home?"

Bardor sighed and said: "The news is not good. For a long time after you left, people wondered what had become of the three of you. Although there was no news, we thought time would bring you back, along with Bessie. But you know how it is. People get on with their lives, and whilst we kept an ear out for news of you, we continued with our daily business.

"One day, a month ago, a beautiful woman with three eyes landed on our shores. She walked up to Porky's Inn and asked for food and lodging. She was undertaking a long journey, she said, and hoped to pass a few days in our land.

"In the beginning she was well liked, as she regaled people with tales of her adventures. Some of the young ladies especially were drawn to her, Blanche in particular. She and Blanche were often seen walking arm-in-arm, and she seemed to spend a lot of time in the lane where Bessie lived. Then, one day, she moved into Bessie's home, and made it her permanent abode. Worse, Blanche moved in with her, and as the days passed, we noticed a change in Blanche. She had always been fair and beautiful, but now her white skin acquired a pasty look and her eyes became vacant and hollow. They resembled a bottomless pool, a pool of hell.

"Strange things also started to happen at Bessie's house, which, at times, glowed with a yellow light. Blanche started to get more people to go there, and they all seemed to be in a trance. They began to change too. Some acquired tattoos; some took on a mean, hungry look. There was clearly something amiss.

"One day Erissa, as she called herself, walked up to the main square, stood at a podium and announced that she was taking over the land. She had to continue on her travels, but Blanche would be regent. When Porky tried to protest, she opened her third eye and burned him to the ground."

"At that point," butted in Noir, "Blanche laughed an unearthly, evil laugh. All those who opposed her, she said, would die. Where was that sweet young girl? Who was this maniacal creature there in her stead?

"Brandishing weapons, Blanche immediately declared that from that very moment Erissa would continue on her journey and she would be in charge.

"That night, a small band of us gathered in the shadows of what was left of Porky's Inn. We determined not to give in. We formed a group and called ourselves 'Percy's Bards'. Bardor is our leader, and we started a small campaign against Blanche. But she seemed to have been given strange powers by Erissa. She could, by her touch, cause living things to rot and die at will; people shrank from her in horror and in fear. The stench of decay seemed to follow her around. She wore tattered black clothes. She was a true manifestation of death and decay."

"Soon enough," continued Bardor, "we had gathered a small and loyal band, but orders for our capture and death had already been announced. We knew this was not the time to fight, and so, one dark night, we made our escape. We set sail without knowing where we were headed.

"After sailing for a few days, we were overcome by strange vapours, and when we awoke we found ourselves here. We saw Basil kissing Trix and almost attacked him for being the enemy, but something stopped us. And so, here we are!"

Percival looked at Trix who had turned bright red. "Sunset Red," he whispered to her, winking an eye.

"Shut up!" she snarled back.

"Witch!"

At that point, Dhanvan rose and signalled that it was time to sleep.

"There will be enough time tomorrow to plan the next step," he said.

Sleep? How would it come to Basil, Thyme and Percival who now knew that their homeland was not theirs anymore? Where do you go if your home is taken away from you?

Troubled thoughts flashed through their dreams all night, mingling with dreams of the others. And so it was three pale, drawn pigs who awoke the next morning with anger and determination in their eyes.

Chapter 16

Battles In Percy's Land

Sunrise.

This is normally such a beautiful time of the day, when the first rays of dawn break the dark of night. As the light peeps over the horizon, a person sitting quietly under a tree can feel the cool morning breeze. A keen ear hears the first warbling sound of the birds. Peace reigns, and in that magical hour, when the slanted light sends its cool rays towards the dawn sky, all is well with the world.

Yet, the joys of morning were lost on our heroes. The morning found them in a sombre mood. The news about home had disturbed them; they longed to return to deal with the unexpected threat. Breakfast was had in silence. Even Percival and Basil, who had the heartiest appetites of the lot, did not comment on the elaborate feast that was laid out in front of them. Not one burp passed their lips. Appetites

"Thank-you, Dhanvan. Thank-you, Zywie," said Percival. "Without you I would have been lost. Now I have my life back, I will make best use of the time that is left to me in this world." Percival felt alive. He felt electricity passing through is veins, and he felt he could take on the world. He had come a long, long way from the rather careless and thoughtless young pig who had swung down from the chandelier to get his love, Bessie.

"You did it all yourself," said Zywie. "Dhanvan and I only helped. However, your journey back would not have been possible without your willingness to return."

Turning to look at Jenna, she smiled and said: "Your love for Jenna certainly helped. Love is a powerful force indeed. Love builds, it strengthens, it spreads. Hate, on the other hand, eventually weakens the soul and destroys it from the inside. You too, have come a long way. I could not have imagined you doing this a year ago."

Percival and Jenna bowed, and bid the two of them farewell. "I hope we meet again," said Percival as they left.

Farewells were spoken and as they were about to board The Raven, Mama Kuko arrived.

"You cannot leave without saying goodbye to me!" she said. "I too will be going on one last journey back to the Valley of Kings. There is work there that needs to be done."

"Fare thee well, Mama Kuko," said Dhanvan looking troubled. "May your journey take you back home."

Mama Kuko smiled and boarded her ship, as did the others. They bid a final farewell to Lavonia.

The journey was quiet and uneventful. The seas were quiet, the sky was bright. White clouds sailed gently in the sky, and everything seemed peaceful. Was it the quiet before the storm. Basil, Thyme and Percival often paced the decks in silence, wondering about the fate of their homeland. Never in their wildest dreams had they imagined that their home would be desecrated. Anger grew in them slowly. It burned, and the fires of revenge rages inside them.

They arrived on the shores of Percival's Land in the dead of night. There was a hint of menace in the air, and a sense of decay. The once-green avenues were now desolate; armed guards strutted about chewing tobacco and spitting it on the streets.

Percival, Basil and Thyme hissed under their breaths with barely controlled rage.

"Shh!" whispered Thar. "Control yourselves! There will be time enough to plot our revenge. That time is not now."

They crawled along until they came to the hill near Percival's house. This seemed to be the only place in town that had not been affected by the desecration around them. Armed guards stood at the gates leading to the house.

"A distraction," whispered Sally. "I will walk up to them. Brindar, Sindar, you creep up behind them and finish them off."

"Kill?!" whispered Thyme, his voice anguished. "I know them; they cannot be evil!"

"Stop being a sentimental fool!" snapped Sally. "They have crossed over. Their souls have been corrupted. They will kill you in an instant. This is not the time to hesitate, to be weak!"

Thyme was silenced by her look. Sally stepped out of the shadows and sauntered up to the guards, stroking her hair and smiling at them winningly.

"Where's a girl to get a drink in these strange parts?" she asked. "I have a thirst that needs quenching." The guards leered, leaning towards her, spittle dripping from their mouths. Their breath stank, and it took all of Sally's resolve to stop herself from taking a step back and covering her face. Smiling at them, she said: "C'mon boys..."

The guards continued leering, and took their hands off their weapons. This was the last thing they did. The Lexters, who had crawled up behind them, jerked their heads back and slit their throats.

Dragging the bodies into the bushes, the group ran quickly up the pathway to Percival's house. Mortimer opened the door, for Percival had given his special knock. Master and manservant hugged each other, tears of joy rolling down their cheeks.

"Quick, master, come inside, you and your friends," he stuttered. "Times are not good these days. The old town has changed, and the stench of evil fills the air. Blanche rules; and where she goes death seems to follow. Her once-pretty face now has the whiteness of death and decay. What should we do?"

There was silence. Then Thar spoke: "Where does Blanche live? What is the size of her army, if she has one? Are there any weak points? Tell us quickly, we have very little time to lose."

Mortimer blubbered for a bit, tears rolling down his cheeks. Jenna got up to sit by him. Laying a calming hand on his arm, she said: "Speak."

Mortimer looked at her, wiped the tears from his eyes, and asked: "Are you Percival's young lady then? What happened to Bessie? She who was so nice and sweet?"

"Bessie has gone over to the other side," said Percival quietly. "There is nothing between us except hate and enmity. Now answer the questions that Thar has asked."

Nodding silently, Mortimer spoke of when Erissa was in the town; how she had corrupted most of the people here, how Blanche had moved into Bessie's home. The town has changed, he declared unhappily. The old days when there was so much song and laughter have gone. He was beginning to babble incoherently, when Trix suddenly got up, poked him in the ribs, and laughed: "Don't worry Mortimer old friend! We will set things right." She laughed her silvery laugh and sat down again looking contented. Mortimer and Percival looked at her aghast. They had never seen anyone poke Mortimer in the ribs. He was much to dignified for that; even his incoherent babbling did nothing to erase this image from their minds. Then Brindar spoke:

"We need a plan," he said.

"Yes," Thar agreed. "However, we shall have to move quickly, in silence, and in the dead of night. A stealth attack is what is needed. We do not have the numbers to launch an all-out frontal attack. There must be some way we can discover and attack their point of weakness."

"Point of weakness," Mortimer moaned. "They are invulnerable. They are invincible. All is lost!" His chins jiggled as tears once more rolled down his ample cheeks. He sat there, looking the very picture of defeat and despair.

"Think, man!" growled Sindar. "Tell us everything you remember. Surely you go out every now and then? What do you see?"

Slowly but surely, over the next few hours, they prised information out of Mortimer. It was like trying to extract oil from a rock, and there were times when even Percival stamped his foot in frustration. But, gradually, Mortimer forgot his fear and began responding to the questions that were being asked of him. He welcomed the prospect of getting rid of Blanche, once universally loved now hated and feared. Yes, even her followers feared her.

Finally, at dawn, they had most of the information they needed. Basil stretched, yawned sleepily, and, scratching his underarms, yelled: "Mortimer, breakfast!" He rubbed his hands in anticipation of a hot breakfast of rolls, eggs, fruit, tea and a range of assorted goodies.

Silence reigned, a silence broken only by the sound of Basil and Percival chomping at their food. At long last they were satisfied. They leaned back, stretching and yawning sleepily.

"Mortimer, off you go," said Percival. Have a look at the situation around Bessie's house. We need to know how many guards she has stationed there, and how heavily the door is barricaded. I am off for a hot bath and some sleep..."

"Don't forget to check whether there is any way we can scale the wall," said Thar.

Sleep came to all of them, and it was deep and dreamless. By the time they awoke, the sun was beginning to set over the trees. Mortimer had made them some tea.

Indeed, he had been busy; gone was the blubbering mass of the previous night. Standing before them now was a butler bubbling with excitement.

The Lexters stood around sheets of detailed drawings he had made, nodding and muttering under their breath. Finally, Brindar looked up and said: "We move in tonight, after dinner. We will have to resort to stealth. Thar, Sindar, Jenna and Trix shall take the lead. Sally, Thyme and I will watch the sides. Rollo, Basil and Percival shall make up the rear."

"Why should I make up the rear?" protested Percival with some indignation.

"You are not exactly stealthy!" Thar replied.

"Moreover," said Sally sweetly, "you and your muscles will be required for the big fight, when they counter-attack."

"Muscles?" chortled Trix. "Put him in a tree and tell him to jump. His weight will do the rest... unless the tree falls under it!"

"Witch!" glared Percival, looking at her with some heat.

"Don't worry dear," smiled Jenna. "You'll be just fine." She laid a comforting hand on Percival's arm and smiled at him.

And then it was time to go. Dressed in black, they made their way through the shadows of the night. They moved slowly until they came to Bessie's house.

"Blanche takes a short nap after dinner," whispered Jenna. "That's when her guard is down, remember. Let's position ourselves."

"Bring down the guards, and then let Rollo charge the door," whispered Sindar.

Brindar looked at Sally and Thyme. "Once the forward group goes through, we attack from the sides and scale the walls. Ready, on my signal."

They waited in the shadows, each minute dragging on for hours. Their nerves were taut, as they struggled for patience. Jenna and Trix fidgeted, itching for battle. Then, suddenly, Thar gave the signal. They moved silently, almost invisible, to come up behind the guards. One by one, the guards were overcome and gently lowered to the ground.

Thar gave the signal to Brindar. Sally and Thyme moved quietly, attacking the guards along the sides of the building. Then they started to climb. Rollo charged, broke down the door, and then all hell broke loose.

When Blanche was awoken from her slumber, her initial reaction was one of disbelief. That someone could attack her little fortress was something that had never crossed her mind. She sat paralysed as her guards and lieutenants waited for a signal. It was too late; the incoming group was soon upon them slashing and burning (fire blazing from the two sisters). They died like moths being burned by a flame. Then Blanche smiled. Her face did not light up when she smiled. It was as though a crack had appeared in a ball of alabaster. Her teeth and gums glowed white. It was not the white of gentleness and purity. It was the white of death and decay.

Her hand reached out just as one of the Lexters advanced, sword held aloft. She held his arm, seemingly in self-defense. He screamed as his arm seemed to decay and fall off. The Lexter's face turned ashen and he fell down dead, decay spreading through his body like a rapidly mutating virus.

Blanche stalked the advancing Lexters, who scattered out of her way taking care only to hack at the now emboldened guards. Things would have turned were it not for sudden reinforcements in the form of Percival, Basil, Sally and Thyme.

Blanche hissed, moving towards the door. As she turned, Jenna raised her arm, closed her eyes and let forth a burst of flame that leapt through Blanche's dress and burned her leg. Blanche screamed: "You will pay for this, you witch!" she spat out, her voice hoarse with rage and malice.

And then she was gone, disappearing down the stairway and vanishing into thin air.

The battle was over as suddenly as it had begun. None of the guards were spared. Soon the town's lights were on in celebration.

"There shall be retribution," marked Bardor. "This is not over by half."

"Yes," Percival agreed. "We shall prepare the next step tomorrow. But tonight, we celebrate."

The town turned into a carnival, as people celebrated their freedom from Blanche and her supporters. Indeed, they seemed to forget that she had only disappeared, and had not been eliminated. But all that did not matter in the sheer joy of the moment.

At long last, the sun peeped shyly into the wee hours of the morning spreading its golden blue rays and bringing a new vigour to the townspeople. Corky shook Percival by the hand as the two looked at each other for a long while, lost in each other's thoughts.

While Corky was admiring the changes that had taken place in Percival, Percival was thinking of that fateful day when he had stepped into Corky's Top Hat Shop to buy a hat to woo Bessie. The day history changed.

Suddenly they both said together:

"Do you remember the day I stepped in to buy a hat?" asked Percival.

"Do you remember the day you stepped in to buy a hat?" queried Corky.

Bursting into laughter, they hugged one another in a rare spirit of camaraderie. The Top Hat Shop had been burned down, but Corky vowed to rebuild it and set up a secret room for members of Percy's Bards.

By the time the sun had shifted to its noonday position, the euphoria of the night was beginning to wane. Sindar said:"

I think the time has come for us to go our own ways for a while. Threye will mark this as another defeat, and will seek vengeance. His mind seeks domination over the world and he will brook no defiance. He will muster his armies and come to crush us all. I do not know what will happen; whether there will be a grand battle or many small ones, or both. But matters are coming to a head, and we must act."

There was a sudden silence as the levity of the past few hours drained away. The sound of mumbling could be heard as everyone wondered what was to be done next. The fact that Blanche had not been destroyed hit them with full force.

"We need to split into various groups, go to our homes and prepare ourselves for what is to come," continued

Sindar. "I propose that we go back to the Land of Ice and Snow. I also propose that Sally and Thyme return to Sally's Island, and that Bardor and Noir stay here to build reinforcements."

"And what shall we do?" enquired Basil politely. "Shall the rest of us go on holiday?"

"Quiet," hissed Trix, "let him speak."

They looked at Sindar expectantly, and Sindar looked back at them. Then Zalyts said: "I have heard of the Warlocks, fierce creatures who bear an ancient grudge against Threye. If the four of you can find them and persuade them to join our cause, our forces shall be strengthened and we will defeat Threye. Without them it will be difficult."

"And where do they live?" asked Trix.

"I do not know." said Zalyts, "though I have heard that Dhanvan has access to directions, and that he provides the information only when absolutely needed. You shall have to communicate with him in spirit, not in person. If he agrees, his spirit will guide you to the Warlocks. He himself will not accompany you there."

Stamping with impatience, Percival said: "Sure, sure, all this is very nice. But what do we do?"

"We sail tomorrow morning," said Brindar. "All of us, to our appointed destinations. There is no time to lose. Percival, your ship will know exactly where to go. Let us now spend the day preparing fortifications as there will be reprisals to come."

The next morning the friends rose early and bid their farewells, amidst scenes of sorrow and promises of undying friendship.

"We shall, in times of need, communicate through our rings," said Thar. "Fare thee well. We shall meet before the end."

And then they were gone. Bardor and Noir stood on the shores watching the ships sail into the horizon. Things suddenly seemed empty, and the wind seemed to blow with an ill will. They shivered as the chill touched their bones, and stood for a long while in seeming indecision. Suddenly, Bardor shook his head and said: "It is time to go and prepare for the retaliation that will come."

Over the next two days they built reinforcements around the town. Bardor walked around with an energy that did not seem to flag. "Build, build, build," he exhorted everyone. "We cannot be too safe."

At the end of the third day, he knew nothing more could be done. The town was safe. It was surrounded by barricades. Bardor was satisfied they could now hold out against any attack.

At the stroke of midnight, at the end of the third day, two ships pulled silently up on the northern shores.

Mr. Benttwist, Christina Kilgore and friends emerged from one, Kale and Micla from the other. As they came ashore, a dark shape rose from the sands to greet them.

"Welcome!" said a hoarse voice. "Welcome to my home. I have been waiting for you. It is time to reclaim what is ours -- mine."

"We are here," said Kale, "to assist you in reclaiming the town and to rebuild an army to crush The Little Birds."

"We are here for vengeance," said Mr. Benttwist.

"Vengeance alone is not enough," said Kale. "An army has to be built, and build one we shall. The time will come to annihilate each one of these miserable creatures. But that time is not now. The time will come when Threye's reign is once again complete, his dominion total. But we will need to work towards it."

She looked around her and asked: "Are we clear?" Not waiting for an answer, she then turned to Blanche and said: "Let's go. The time to reclaim the town is now!"

Chapter 17

Bessie And Dragor With the Trolls

As night descended, Bessie and Dragor stood on the deck of the ship, The Red Dragon. The stars were coming out in an inky blue sky. They stood, arms entwined, feeling the cool breeze on their faces. Then their lips locked in a passionate kiss. Life was good indeed, far away from everything, from wars, from battles, from strife. This was their time together, and they imagined themselves in their own little cocoon, wrapped up nicely, complete in themselves.

Leaning against Dragor, Bessie sighed contentedly and said: "I wish this trip could last forever."

"Yes indeed," said Dragor, pulling her close. "It would be perfect. We could sail away together into the sunset, never to return to anything. Ever"

Bessie sighed again and looked up at him, a deep love filling her eyes. How could she ever have believed she were in love with Percival? What a fool she had been! A shadow flitted across her face when she thought of Percival and the last battle at the Land of Ice and Snow. She had almost had him there, were it not for that bitch Jenna. Percival had fought a good fight. But Jenna? She would get her!

Dark thoughts interrupted her romantic ones, and the intrusion would not be dismissed easily. Bessie pulled away from Dragor and looked up at the skies. Silver dots in an inky blackness. She felt the enormity of the infinite universe, and wondered if she and Dragor would find a home eventually, in the vast nothingness of night.

Suddenly, a shadow loomed before them and the ship thudded to a halt. They seemed to have run into some sandbars.

Dragor commanded the Kreechurs to stay on board the ship; he and Bessie would explore. The goal of their mission came back to them: to arrive at the Island of the Trolls, to convince the trolls to join Threye's army, to join in the battle to crush the Little Birds. Indeed, they had quite forgotten their mission.

Dragor and Bessie climbed up a small, hilly slope and arrived at a wooded patch of land. The going was tough; the trees did not allow them much place to walk. Finally, they sensed some light in the distance.

"Stop!" commanded Dragor as his ear caught the sound of rhythmic drumming coming from nearby. The beat penetrated the night, the rhythm steady and hypnotic. Dragor and Bessie were drawn to the sound, almost against their will. They crept closer and closer, their minds held fast, until they came to a clearing in the woods. There, in the centre of the clearing, dancing slowly around a fire was a circle of trolls. They were dancing slowly to the rhythm of the drums, as though in a trance. The fire cast eerie shadows on their faces, making them look cruel in the firelight. Their stony faces took on expressions that

Bessie had never dreamed possible. She stood transfixed, watching the creatures dance. Then, almost involuntarily, her body started to move to the sound of the drums, slowly at first, then with greater abandon. Watching her, Dragor found himself drawn into her rhythm. There in the woods, the two moved freely to the sound of the drums. They felt completely alone, their bodies moving in unison. The universe seemed to stand still. Nothing else existed, nothing but the rhythm of the drums. Indeed, they seemed to have discovered a new rhythm in each other, filled with a power they did not know existed. As they danced it was as though they mirrored the rhythm of the cosmos; they felt like they would touch the skies. They felt as though they were dancing amidst the stars that twinkled around their faces. The dark night pulsated with the drum beats, and the waves they created with their movements. Darkness enveloped them, a deep darkness that came with a suddenness that caught them unawares. It seemed to be a part of the dance, and the dance a part of the darkness; and they were an integral part of both.

Hours passed, or so they thought. They lost all sense of time. All that existed now was the dark. Even the drumming eventually fell silent. They had no idea how long the darkness enveloped them; then suddenly there was a bright light. It seemed to elbow its way through the dark. From a mere pinhole it became a shaft of light with an iridescent glow. It fought the dark, and as it did so it gradually dispelled the shadows to become brighter and brighter. The light hurt their eyeballs!

Suddenly Bessie and Dragor found themselves lying on the ground in a courtyard, surrounded by trolls of every shape and colour. There was not a shred of kindness on their faces, yet no trace of malice either. The faces looking down at them seemed completely devoid of expression; cold, hard eyes penetrated their own. Then the implacable circle parted and they found themselves looking at what appeared to be the leaders of the group.

Looking around in confusion, Dragor stuttered: "What? How?! I thought that trolls are turned to stone in the daylight? But you are all moving!"

"Don't let fairytales fool you, Dragor," said the woman harshly. "We were never turned to stone, and shall never be turned to stone. We know where you come from, and we know who sent you. What we do not know is why and how you dared come to our island."

"Please," whispered Bessie. "Please don't kill us. We will tell you. But first, how do you know our names?". She was terrified, and her voice trembled with terror. Her lip quivered as she spoke, and she stammered out her plea.

The man laughed. His laugh was harsh. It hurt their ears. "There is much that we know, little Bessie. But first, some refreshments are in order. The two of you should eat and bathe first. We must not forget our duty as hosts."

Sometime later, Bessie and Dragor found themselves in what seemed to be a throne room. A man and a woman were seated on thrones; they realised they were in the presence of the troll king and queen.

"Kneel!" ordered a troll pushing them to their knees. Bessie and Dragor felt the incredible power that resided in the bodies of the trolls, as they were forced to their knees.

The Troll King and Queen were slim, and had fine features. There was a natural elegance in their stony expressions, like they were born into nobility. Indeed, they were from a long line of kings and queens. The look in their eyes was one of immeasurable cruelty. No expression crossed their faces as they looked down that the pair kneeling before them.

"Speak," said the Troll King finally. Gynt was he; this was the name by which he was commonly known. His red features seemed to glow with an inner fire, an iridescent ruddy hue emanating from his black face.

"Speak, and tell us your story," he continued.

"Tell it well," said his wife, she who was known as Huldra. "Tell it well or this shall be your last day alive."

And so Bessie and Dragor told their tale. When they came to the part of Threye and their mission to bring the trolls into his army, the troll king exploded, a red flame seeming to burst from his body.

"Join Threye?!" he spat. "Join that traitorous creature? His word is worthless and he cannot be trusted."

"Begging your pardon," broke in Bessie timidly, her voice quavering as she anticipated a heavy fist crashing down on her head. She closed her eyes and winced as she spoke, her body tense with fear.

"You would hear the story would you?" asked the Troll King. "Well, listen then to a tale of betrayal."

He paused, sat back, and seemed to collect his thoughts. His face was inscrutable.

"Threye is very old," he began. "Threye is amongst the oldest beings on this planet. He emerged from the Dungeon of Thron as a young man, over two thousand years ago. No one had seen him before, and he walked along the pathways of his country, Mrod, with the look of one who knew exactly what he needed to do. At that time Mrod was ruled by Valafar, an intensely cruel and powerful overlord. Valafar ruled over the lands and the oceans, yet did not have dominion over more than half the world. He was proud and brooked no disobedience, no rivalry. Indeed, none had the courage to face him until the day Threye emerged from the dungeons. Threye walked to Valafar's home, knocked on the door, and announced himself as the new ruler of Mrod. He gave Valafar the option of submitting or suffering the consequences."

"Valafar laughed at the young Threye and spat in his face. Threye merely smiled and opened his mouth. His tongue shot out and touched Valafar on the cheek, burning it. The two fought. It was a fierce battle that raged for seven days and seven nights. Not once did Threye lose his smile; at the end of the seventh day he impaled Valafar's head on a pole and walked around Mrod proclaiming himself ruler. And so it has been since."

"In the first few hundred years, there was peace. Then things started to change as peace became increasingly defined as peace on Threye's terms. He became quieter, more sinister, and gradually began to reveal his powers. Even as more and more people subjected themselves to his will, there were others who resisted. He came to us once, to seek an alliance. There was a race of people, he said, who were proving troublesome. He spoke to us in honeyed tones and pleaded for our help. He promised us half the spoils, and some more. It was to be an important battle, he said, as these people were determined to disturb the peace. He wanted to build an era of peace and harmony, one that could exist only under his benevolent leadership. But since he had asked for our assistance, he was prepared to be generous."

"We agreed," said the Troll Queen. "We agreed without thinking, and prepared for the grand battle. We are a warlike race; battle is in our blood. We take no prisoners. We exterminate our enemy, yet if we have one other quality it is this, that we honour our word. And so, our army met with Threye's at the appointed place."

"It was a dark night, and it had started to rain. The air was damp and chilly. Our men stood waiting for instructions. Then I saw the people we were supposed to annihilate. They looked harmless enough, and I wondered why Threye was having such a hard time with them. I looked across at him as he walked towards me, and he smiled. There was evil and malice in that smile. His face was otherwise expressionless. I wondered at his intent. Threye came up to me and said: 'When I shoot the fire from my arm, that is when we attack.'"

"He took a deep breath, and waited. The time seemed to pass very slowly. Threye was calm, almost at peace with himself. His tongue flicked in and out of his mouth, almost in anticipation."

"Suddenly an old man emerged from one the houses. He had a regal bearing but seemed anxious. He stood in the doorway, and as I looked across at him I saw a flame arch and weave its way towards him. The flame curved and twisted. As it approached the old man there seemed to be a snake's head at the tip of the flame. The mouth of the flaming snake opened wide; the fangs were long and sharp. The snake head seemed almost greedy, and the man was paralysed. As we watched, the snake engulfed the old man. Then it was replaced by black smoke. When the smoke cleared there was no sign of the old man. Nothing remained, not even ashes."

"'Now!' said Threye almost inaudibly. 'Now!' He moved, and almost in a trance we moved with him. The battle was short and brutal. Not a single creature was spared. The dwellings were flattened. All through the battle Threye stood still, smiling, directing the battle with his mind. He remained untouched by everything that went on around him, yet I felt as though the destruction gave him considerable joy."

"The battle went on through the night. By morning it was over. As the rays of the sun began to spread out, I approached Threye and asked him which part of the land we would get."

"Threye laughed in my face and told me not to be a fool.' Did you fulfil your part of the bargain?' he asked. 'No. It was me and me alone who directed the battle. You and your army were weak. You were unable to attack any part independently. You and the rest of the trolls are weak. Begone!'"

"I roared with rage and ordered my army to attack. We charged, but as we did so we were caught in a whirlpool of air. We were twisted this way and that. We were lifted high into the air and brought down hard on the ground. Laughing, Threye said: 'You are weak. Begone, or I shall order the winds to take you to lands far away. I shall banish you to a place beyond the boundaries of this world.'"

"We retreated to our island, and have had no contact with Threye since. Yet we have not forgiven; nor have we forgotten."

The Troll Queen got up off her throne and approaching Bessie asked: "Tell me my dear. Why should we support Threye again?"

Bessie looked up at the Troll Queen, her face turning white. Her mind was blank with panic; she could not think. Her mouth hung open stupidly. She was transfixed by the look in the queen's eyes as she conjured up images of herself being killed and tossed like a rag over the edges of the island.

"Please, if I may speak," she heard her voice as though from a distance. "There is a land that Threye hates. You could capture this land first. That would strengthen you. If you would then support us in the battle with Threye, we would be exceedingly grateful. Else Threye will kill the two of us."

"And where is this land that you want conquered?" asked the Queen.

Dragor, gradually gaining confidence, spoke of the Land of Ice and Snow, the last battle there, the annihilation of the Matted Giants, and their burning desire for revenge. The more he spoke, the more he felt the trolls were paying attention.

Finally the Troll King spoke.

"Threye desires this land?" he asked.

"Yes," blurted out Dragor. "But if you take over the land first, then you have territorial rights over it. I shall tell Threye that you took it over, on pain of death to me."

The royal couple looked at the two petrified beings in front of them. Fear was alien to Dragor, but even he felt a deep fear just looking at the trolls. There was no unnecessary evil in their faces, but there was a deep implacable malice that was tangible. The royal couple seemed to be in communication with each other, a wordless communication. Finally, they looked at Dragor and Bessie, and the King spoke.

"Let the deaths roll. Let the world feel the pain of Gynt and Huldra again. Yes, we shall battle with you and we shall conquer. But remember, if you betray us your death shall be inevitable. Indeed, it shall be long-drawn-out and exceedingly painful. You shall cry for death, and I shall hold it back at my pleasure. And then, when I am bored of your pain and your tears, I shall allow you to die. Are we clear?."

Silently, with terror gripping their throats in a vice-like grip, the two of them nodded.

Huldra looked at them, and said, in a cold. cold voice, "Then, let it be done". There was silence, and then she began to sing softly. Her voice was soft, evil, hurting and, Dragor and Bessie knew they were trapped between Threye and the Trolls.

Chapter 18

The Valley Of The Kings

Erissa stood on the deck of her ship, the Silver Vulture, her mind preoccupied with thoughts of Threye, her father. She had never known him to go to the lengths that he was going to destroy a bunch of upstarts. In her mind, the Little Birds were just that -- a bunch of upstarts who had managed, through a mixture of good fortune, low trickery, and the betrayal of two women, to cheat death. Yet, her mind was sore with the fact of their escape and the betrayal of Jenna and Trix. Never in her mind, did the thought even enter, that maybe the two had not intended to defect to the other side. It did not cross her mind, that the fear of reprisals on their return was the real driving force behind the two women's initial defection. Love had crept up on them silently, like a ghost at night. There was no room for forgiveness or mercy in Erissa's heart. A slow anger seethed inside her.

They had escaped from the dungeons, they had defeated an army sent to destroy them at the Land of Ice and Snow, and had escaped from Sangre. For the life of her, Erissa could not understand how Threye had managed to have this series of defeats inflicted on him, especially since the Little Birds did not possess any special magic, nor did they have spectacular fighting skills. What then was the secret of their success so far? Threye must have been unusually worried, else he would not have sent Bessie and Dragor to importune with the trolls. Nor would she have been sent to the Valley of Kings. And what of Azazel? What would become of him now that he had emerged as the Lord of Chaos? He was only the second in the remembered history of Mrod to have emerged from the Dungeon of Thron. The first had been her father. It had marked the start of Threye's long reign as Lord of Mrod. Was he about to be usurped by Azazel?

Erissa's mind was troubled as they neared the shores of the Valley of Kings. With whom would her loyalty lie should Azazel decide to usurp the crown? With her husband? Or with her father? Was Threye playing a larger game here?

Erissa sighed as they approached the shore. She alighted and began her walk up to the king's palace.

It was Mama Kuko, Erissa discovered, who was the favoured one at the palace. This was her second trip to the Valley of Kings, and when she arrived she was given a royal welcome. She had been put up at the palace, and walked freely amongst the townspeople. Wherever she went, she was treated like a royal guest. She had, after all, healed the people the last time she was here, and they treated her with love and respect. She was clearly the king's favourite.

Although Erissa was welcomed, she was clearly unable to get the king's attention. She did intend to melt him over time, and being overlooked was not something she was used to. This is not something that was to her liking. But she was a patient woman and knew how to bide her time.

Erissa spent the next few days in the town, smiling at people and studying their nature. She walked up and down the cobbled streets, sitting in cafes, relaxing. There were times when she would sit in the evening sun, her eyes closed, her red hair gently blowing in the breeze. Many a young gallant would find his heart skipping at the sight. Yet none dared approach her. There was something beautiful, strong and mysterious about Erissa; yet something also told them she was not to be approached in the normal, happy, carefree way young men are wont to use. Instead, they would sit around waiting for Erissa to notice them.

One evening, Mama Kuko, chancing upon Erissa, walked up to her with a friendly greeting. She sat down, and started to talk with Erissa, asking her about herself, and telling her about The Valley Of The Kings. As the sun's rays dipped behind the horizon, the two women forgot about the passage of time as they spoke and spoke. It was the first time that each was seeing the other as anything but a rival to the affections of the king and his people. They spoke, and a bond was created between the two.

From then on the two women became engrossed in their conversations and often took long walks in the town. They seemed inseparable, like two sisters who have been together since childhood. Yet, Erissa was Threye's daughter. No matter how much she may cloak it, she cannot change her true nature.

As they were sitting in a street-side cafe one day, a woman came running up the road. She was distraught; her daughter, May, she claimed, had been possessed of a strange affliction. She kept screaming about the arrival of a new lord, a lord who would bring chaos to the land. As she screamed she would tear her hair out. Moreover, the woman, who's husband appeared to have gone into shock and so seemed incapable of doing anything.

"May I come with you?" Erissa asked Mama Kuko who instantly got ready to go visit the girl.

"Come along," said Mama Kuko. "However, remember, healing is something that can consume one's body and spirit. It is something that you do only with pure love and compassion."

As Erissa approached May, the young girl seemed to become even more hysterical, screaming about an evil trinity that was approaching.

"Chaos! He is coming!" she screamed. "Chaos! With the Old One, and she with the Sly Mind shall divide the land. Get away from me! Get away from me!"

She stood up and spat at the ground. Mama Kuko held her by the arms and cooed gently. But despite her best efforts, May would not be calmed. Soon enough, her father came along. He looked like a ghost. His chest was sunken in, his eyes were hollow. His mouth drooled spittle. Approaching Erissa, he sank to his knees. He seemed to fall as his arms went around Erissa's feet. He seemed to have lost his mind completely. As Erissa bent to gently pick him up, she found that his soul had left his body. He was dead.

Mama Kuko was disturbed. This was not what she expected. Erissa and she walked back to the palace in silence, each alone with her thoughts. The next few days, as she struggled with May, Mama Kuko returned late in the evenings, almost too exhausted to eat. She would immediately go up to her room and lie down. Erissa would bring her food, massage her feet and temples, and help her sleep. The old woman warmed to Erissa again.

One morning, when she arrived at May's house, she found her seemingly healed with Erissa sitting beside her, smiling. Mama Kuko was stunned to see the change in May. She looked deep into her eyes, trying to see what was behind the smile. She wondered what was in her soul. She noticed that the expression in May's eyes did not vary although she stood there a long while waiting for a change. There was nothing. Mama Kuko sighed and stood up.

"May does not seem to be healed," she said.

"But she is!" her mother replied. "We are ecstatic with what Erissa has done for us. She came early in the morning with some herbs, prepared a drink, and suddenly there was a change in May. She seemed to calm down and began to smile. She looked up and Erissa hugged her and they spoke. I am so happy..."

Mama Kuko glared at Erissa and asked, with some asperity: "Of what did you speak may I ask? Of what?"

"Oh nothing much," purred Erissa. "She merely asked where she had been over the last few days, and I assured her that she had been here. She was not convinced for a while, but as we spoke she realised that she had not, in fact, left home for some time. She now has a deep need to go on a holiday, on a trip to cleanse her soul. I tried to convince her that there was nothing to cleanse, and that she was pure..."

"What of the Evil Trinity?" demanded Mama Kuko. Shaking Erissa, she repeated: "What of it?!"

"Oh there is no Evil Trinity," said May shyly. "I was mistaken. I must have been led astray by my father, which is why he died. The Trinity is a holy one, and once I am back from my trip I shall worship it and shall create a following for this Trinity."

Try as she may, Mama Kuko could not change the mind of May or her mother. They seemed to be completely taken up by Erissa, almost as though they were under some sort of a spell.

Turning on her heel, she walked off in a huff with Erissa running after her.

They walked back to the palace quickly. As they neared, Erissa suddenly appeared breathless and in some sort of pain. She doubled up, clutching Mama Kuko's coat. She gasped: "Mama, I love you very much. I was only trying to help. Please believe me."

Falling to her knees, she seemed to be weeping. Her grip on Mama Kuko's coat was strong and the older woman was forced to stand still, looking down at the weeping girl. Finally, her face softened and she pulled Erissa to her feet. Hugging her, she said: "I love you like a younger sister. I know that you were only trying to help."

And so it was that they walked arm-in-arm into the palace.

Yet, a shadow had been cast between the two women. They began to spend more time apart. As Mama Kuko withdrew, she began to spend more time alone going for long exploratory walks into the countryside. There was soon a vacuum at the palace. Mama Kuko was not available like she once was to give King Regus counsel and to discuss topics of deep philosophy. He found himself turning more and more to Erissa, who willingly filled the void. She found no sympathy with Queen Regina, however. The queen found her company distasteful and kept her distance. Her instinct warned her against the beautiful woman, and she spoke with a few ministers who all seemed to have taken a deep instinctive dislike to Erissa.

As Mama Kuko's walks took her further and further afield, Erissa began taking over the king's mind. She wove tales of deep magic into her discussions with him. She spoke of faraway lands, great alliances and territorial expansion. Slowly, the king started thinking about armies, military manoeuvres, alliances with powerful friends.

One day, Mama Kuko invited Erissa for a walk. They strolled far into the country. Mama Kuko appeared troubled.

"You are a cunning woman, Erissa!" she said at last. "I have no idea how and when you planted the seeds of military grand alliances and glory in the mind of the king, but that is all he dreams of these days. Tell me, of whom do you speak? Who is this powerful ally, and who makes up The Trinity?"

Erissa looked at Mama Kuko and smiled. "I speak of Threye," she said. "He is my father and is the most powerful living being in the history of this planet."

"Yes, I thought so," replied Mama Kuko. "I felt that you were close to Threye. I knew you to be a Mrodic the moment you set foot on this land."

"Then why didn't you expose me?" asked Erissa.

"I don't know," said Mama Kuko. "Maybe, I fooled myself. Maybe, I let the conversations we had, allow me to believe that you were a bit different. Maybe, I was just fooling myself, and maybe I am a sentimental old fool."

"You are no fool, Mama Kuko," replied Erissa with a sardonic smile. "There is more to you than you realize. You are not the same Healer who came here long ago. You have changed since those days, and one day you will let yourself recognize the power of that change. And then, the world shall turn once again."

"I am going to withdraw," replied Mama Kuko. Her eyes were blazing, and there was anger in the eyes. Erissa looked deep, and saw deep anger. Then, she looked closer, and she recognized the seeds of something else. Mama Kuko was about to change, and she smiled inwardly. "We are becoming soul sisters, she thought to herself."

"We have reached the Grey Hills", said Mama Kuko. "I am going to sit and meditate in the deepest cave here, the Grey Cave of Meditation. I shall remain deep in my meditation and vapours till the time is right for me to emerge. Then you shall see me again. Yes, I know that

Azazel and the Old One are making their way to the valley, and this shall be one of the places from where Threye shall form one of his armies. Tell me, you, Azazel and the Old One are the Trinity of whom May spoke, is it not?"

Erissa merely smiled and looked deep into Mama Kuko's eyes. The expression in her eyes changed. Gone was the friendly, almost seductive look of an attractive young woman. Gone was the allure of beauty. All that there was was the emptiness of a deep evil, a mind designed to ensnare people, a mind designed to poison, to manipulate. A mind that was remorseless and merciless. As Mama Kuko looked into Erissa's eyes, she found herself looking into long years of malice, cruelty and a black humour. Eyes that spoke of love for her father and her husband; eyes that loved all things evil. The eyes were like magnets drawing Mama Kuko deep into her, capturing her mind.

Shaking her head, Mama Kuko took a step back. With a slight smile, she whispered: "I see. You are powerful yes, but not powerful enough yet. The time will come."

She turned and walked into the Grey Hills. Erissa watched her retreating back. She smiled.

"The seeds have been planted," she murmured to herself. Then she turned to go. As she walked back to the palace, a small wisp of smoke emerged from the hills. Mama Kuko had begun her meditations.

Back at the palace, Erissa found the king waiting for her. He could not bear to be away from the young woman, indeed a distance had sprung up between him and his wife. He fancied himself a conqueror and was impatient to build an army and expand his kingdom.

"When do we leave?" he asked looking at Erissa. He thought she had never looked so beautiful, so alluring. He longed to touch her.

"We shall start immediately," replied Erissa. "But first you must build a team of people who are committed to you. In the town there is a young girl called May who shall rally the faithful amongst the townspeople. You, my king, must speak to your wife and your ministers, and identify all those who are truly loyal to you. The rest must be banished. A chain is only as strong as its weakest link. If you allow the naysayers to remain in your retinue, they will weaken your cause." She was sitting close to the king; he could smell the subtle perfume of her body. As she looked into his eyes, he felt a deep pull.

As they parted, Erissa kissed him on either cheek. She then kissed him close to his mouth, and whispered: "You are married, and so am I. When the day comes we can be together. Forever. Till then, be patient."

Everything seemed to stand still. Erissa began slowly caressing and kissing his face and throat. Her tongue flicked from time to time. The king held his breath in an agony of pleasure and anticipation. All that he knew was that he wanted Erissa, that he had to be patient, and that he wanted Erissa...

Everything fell away; the world did not exist except for her smell and touch. Regus now belonged heart and soul to Erissa, and was ready to do her every bidding.

Morning came at last. The king summoned his wife and his ministers to his chambers. The queen's face was stony as she listened to his plan. Her expressionless eyes gazed at her husband and Erissa sitting close to one another. The king spoke animatedly, ambition and lust for conquest filling his eyes with a new glitter. This was not the man she had married, but instinct held her back. When he asked about her loyalty, she merely bowed.

"We shall follow you, my lord," she said, and withdrew.

Regina then called a meeting of her faithful followers, and said:

"We must leave. We must leave tonight under cover of darkness. Evil is afoot and we cannot fight this alone. Like my husband, we must seek allies."

"Where shall we go?" asked Prismus, one of her ministers.

"I do not know," answered Regina. "But I do remember Mama Kuko talking of a band of unlikely foes of this evil that is brewing. The Brethren of the Shadow Rings, she called them. Their leader is an unlikely hero named Percival. Let us go in search of him and his followers. We shall try the land where his search for a bride began. We must leave tonight."

"Aye," said Googol. "I have long been the chief commander of our king, and I fear that a mindless ambition and greed has overtaken him. Let us indeed leave tonight. I shall prepare a good ship for our departure."

"Which ship is this?" asked a sly voice.

"Never you mind Eel!" said Googol. "Never ye mind. I shall lead all those who are faithful at the stroke of midnight. But remember, not a word."

"Aye," said Eel silkily, as he withdrew. Googol looked troubled. After a while he said: "We will leave an hour before the appointed hour. I fear that Eel is about to betray us."

As the clock struck 11 that night, the Black Shadow pulled silently out of the harbour of the Valley of Kings. Regina stood on deck, watching her home recede into the shadows. She knew that the world was changing. Her home would never be the same again. She swore that if she ever set foot on its shores she would weed out all evil and would never be forced to leave it again like a skulking coward. If she returned, she would reign over a free land.

At exactly 12, Eel was seen waiting at the harbour along with a small force that had been given to him by Erissa. They waited in vain for Regina. They waited through the night, and when he returned in the morning, Erissa's wrath was terrible to behold.

She caught his wrist, and her eyes bore into his own. He felt a white shaft of pain speed through his body.

"You have failed me once," Erissa hissed. "You shall not fail me again or I shall burn you to cinders. Are you clear?"

"Yes," gasped Eel, wincing in pain. "I shall not fail you. I swear."

"Do you swear loyalty?" she hissed again.

"Yes, I swear loyalty," Eel whispered.

"Complete and total loyalty?" she asked yet again.

"Complete and total loyalty," he swore.

Erissa looked deep into his eyes and slowly released her grip. The mark of her fingers was burned into his wrist.

Looking at it, she said: "My mark is on you for all time. You belong to me now."

There was much to be done. Erissa went into town with Eel and found May at home. Giving instructions, she told the two to gather all who would be faithful and to identify all those who would hesitate.

"I do not want anyone who is faithful to the queen to remain free for long," she said.

"Shall we round them up and imprison them?" asked May.

"No. The time to deal with them will come," Erissa replied.

By the time Azazel and the Old One neared the shores of the Valley of Kings, a small army had already gathered. It grew in strength as more and more people swore loyalty to Erissa, and to Threye.

As their ship pulled into harbour, Azazel and Esmerelda emerged, Azazel looking exactly the same outwardly. Yet there was something different about him. A wild aura seemed to surround his body, an aura that moved and had a life of its own.

The Lord of Chaos had arrived on the shores of the Valley of Kings.

Erissa embraced Azazel and said simply: "We are ready."

He smiled down at her, saying: "We shall now wait for instructions from Threye. The die has been cast."

Chapter 19

The End Of The Black Pub

Home: such a sweet word. As their ship approached, Sally's heart was flying. She stood on deck talking incessantly of home. She longed to see her parents again, and her friends. She longed to go for parties...

Yet in her heart Sally knew she would be here only for a short time. Until the next move. She didn't know what that next move would be. Everything had flowed from one step to the other. The fact that Threye was gathering an army to destroy them was not something she had thought deeply about. They were indeed fighting back the forces of evil, but only as a response. They had not seriously thought about counter-attack; nor had they believed there would ever be a concerted attack on them.

As the ship approached, she stood by Thyme, who was unusually contemplative. Their lives had changed so much since that fateful day when he and Basil had shoved Percival into the muck. Events had moved swiftly. None of them were the same, spoiled pigs of old. He wondered if they would ever fit back into their home. Since that fateful shove, they had had only snatches of respite from the never ending roll of battles, fights, dangers, escapes. Yet, there was drama in all this, he thought. There was much that was good. They had found new friends. He had found Sally.

"Ah, Sally, Sally, Sally.....", he thought, looking at her with love and affection. "What would my life be without her? Nothing.."

He hugged and kissed her with affection, and looking at her surprised face, he blurted, "You know, I am so happy that we shoved Percival into the muck, and messed up his top-hat. Damn, right, yeah, baby! Without that, I never would have met you..". He bussed her again, and seemed all set to take her right there and then. But, that would have to wait, as the ship pulled into the harbour.

Sally was home again!

It was so good to be home and Sally squealed with delight when her parents opened the door and enveloped her in their arms. Her cares and worries melted away when she saw their faces. Life was good again, and she could now relax. The days of fearing for her life were over, for now. She and Thyme could lie in bed till late morning; make love in her room in the filtered light of the morning sun. They could eat to their heart's content. They could watch soft rolls of fat gently form around their waists and laugh about it. Indeed, they could laugh again, and it felt good.

And yet, this is sometimes not enough especially for those who have become used to battle and adventure. About a fortnight later, Sally and Thyme ventured out into town where they noticed wild celebrations taking place.

"That's odd!" said Sally. "There is no festival at this time of year. I wonder what the festivities are about."

Try as she might, she could get no one to satisfy her curiosity.

"Be happy," said everyone.

"Life is short. Enjoy it," they said.

"They really seem to be celebrating life itself," remarked Thyme in surprise.

Back home that night, a mystified Sally asked her parents what the celebrations were about.

"Why are you so surprised, my dear?" replied her father. "Do I detect a tone of disapproval? You have changed, child. Your experiences seem to have made you dour. Get out, enjoy life! You are young."

"Dad's gone mad," Sally whispered to Thyme later that night. "This is bizarre. I can' understand what'u happening. We must get to the bottom of it tomorrow."

"Yes," said Thyme. "I would not call your father mad, but I am a bit surprised by his attitude. This is not the old man I know, and I am curious too. Let us explore."

With the dawning of the new day came a new arrival. A ship docked into harbour and out of it emerged a regal looking woman and her retinue. It was Regina. As she walked into town she was stunned and pleased by the celebrations.

"This seems a happy sort of place," she murmured to herself. Turning to her followers, she said: "We shall make this our resting place for a while. Then we will make enquiries about this Percival, of whom I have heard much."

Word about Regina's arrival spread fast and soon Sally was on her doorstep. "Why are you making enquiries about Percival?" she demanded. "What business do you have with him?"

"And who are you?" asked Regina haughtily.

"I am Sally, and this is Thyme my husband," replied Sally with equal haughtiness. "Thyme and I are Percival's companions and we would like to know your business with him."

The two women stared at each other for a while. Then Regina said: "Come inside and tell me about your adventures."

Sally walked into the house, followed closely by Thyme. With an eye on the courtiers standing behind Regina's chair, she told her story. She noticed, with interest, Regina's reaction to the names Mama Kuko and Erissa. When her story was done, she demanded to know once again why Regina was seeking out Percival.

A few hours later, the two women walked into town leaving the men behind.

"You have a jolly town," remarked Regina. "I have not seen such celebrations in my time. Our people are a happy people. We celebrate events and we celebrate our festivals, but we have never seen celebrations such as these!"

"It is unnatural," muttered Sally. "Something must have happened to make people this way. I just cannot seem to get to the bottom of it."

She stamped her foot in frustration as she stood in the middle of the town square, arms akimbo, glaring at the festivities going on around her. People were dancing with abandon, quite oblivious to her discomfiture and anger.

"Come, let's try and get a better view of what's happening," said Regina finally. They walked into a nearby restaurant and as they climbed up to a balcony, Sally said: "I am sure there is mischief at work here. I cannot believe that all this festivity is natural. The devil himself must have put something into the water." Regina looked at her thoughtfully, then looked back over the dancing crowds.

Suddenly there was a clash of cymbals and the sound of a bugle rose over the music. A motley procession entered the centre of the square, led by a bald, distinguished looking man.

"People of the town, rejoice!" the man cried. "I welcome each and every one of you to the celebrations. Life is a song; we must sing and dance to its music. Drink to life! Drink to music! Drink to passion!"

As the procession made its way around town its members handed out drinks to the people who screamed back: "To life, to music, to passion!!"

"The Kreechurs of The Black Pub!" burst out Sally. "And that must be Mortimer, Dragor's right-hand man. I knew it! There is mischief at work. Do not have the drink!"

"Ladies..." called out Mortimer. "Drink!"

"No!" screamed back Sally. "We shall not drink this foul brew!" A Kreechur approached menacingly, but before he could react Sally rushed him and, holding him by the throat, pushed him over the railings onto the street below. She watched as he tumbled over, almost in slow motion, breaking his neck as he landed. Mortimer yelled: "Arrest that woman! Both of them! Disturbers of the revelry! Disturbers of the peace! Arrest them and bring them to The Black Pub for justice."

"Arrest them!" screamed the crowd as pandemonium broke out. "Arrest them, arrest them, arrest them..." The crowd chanted slowly, almost in a hysterical trance. They danced around, and chanted, "Arrest them, arrest them, arrest them...". Round and round went the people in their mad dance, and the chant grew louder and louder. A strange rhythm was being established in the mad, dancing, chanting crowd. They knew not who was to be arrested and why. It mattered not. All that they were conscious of, was their chant and the wild dance.

"Quick, run!" ordered Regina. The two women dodged the crowds grabbing at a pair of carving knives on a barbecue stand as they ran, and slashing wildly. They sped through the narrow lanes, the Kreechurs in hot pursuit.

Then suddenly they were back at Regina's quarters. They managed to slip inside without being spotted. Outside, they could hear the Kreechurs howling with impotent rage, vowing vengeance and a painful death if the two were ever caught.

They stayed indoors for the next two days, not daring to even turn on the lights. They felt they were being watched all the time. Furtive peeks out of the window confirmed this.

"What shall we do?" asked Sally at last. "We cannot stay here like this forever."

"No," whispered Regina. "I cannot go out, and neither can my people. They will be instantly recognised."

There was silence, then Thyme said: "I am a master of disguise."

"Since when?" asked Sally in surprise. "You have kept this a secret from me?"

"I learnt it during my time with the Lexters. Thar also taught me the art of moving around in silence," he said, ignoring the look of enquiry in Sally's eyes.

"I will go out in disguise and I will explore the city. I will be gone a few days. In this time I will find out where Mortimer sits. If indeed it is The Black Pub I will check out the lay of the land. I will discover the best way to attack the pub. I will also find out who in town is ready to help us. I will return with a plan that we will have to execute without delay, quickly, and ruthlessly. They outnumber us, so strategy and speed will be our only allies."

"And so will cunning," he added after a slight pause.

He then asked: "Are we all agreed?"

They nodded in silent assent. Looking around, Thyme said: "Good! I shall go and prepare myself."

He asked for some black clothes, a bit of white powder, a lock of Regina's hair, a knife, and some polish. An hour later, he emerged a vagabond. He shuffled; his hand was in a bandage, a red stain in the middle of it. Everything about him spoke of a man down on his luck, a beaten man.

"Wish me luck," he grunted in a deep voice. And then he was gone.

For the next few days there was nothing to be done. Sally was sullen, withdrawn. She could not believe that Thyme had hidden something from her. This was a gift she had never dreamed he had. She had believed him to be a sweet, amiable sort of chap, someone who could be relied on to stroke her hair when needed, and to love her. But also someone who needed protection at all times. Things were different now. Yet there was something alluring, something indefinably exciting about this discovery. Sally found herself getting warm; her face flushed. She sighed with desire and waited for Thyme to come back with an impatience that was more urgent than she had felt before.

Thyme returned on the fourth day, at night. There was blood on his shirt and he had a look of urgency about him.

"We will have to move fast!" he said. "We must make out move between four and five in the morning. This is the time the Kreechurs are asleep, and so is Mortimer. At midnight they seem to gain a sort of mysterious energy, and The Black Pub changes. The lights change, the paintings on the wall changes. Even Mortimer's face and aspect change. Indeed, he seems to age. His teeth become sharp, his face lean, a magnetic look comes into his eyes. Any guest at The Black Pub is immediately mesmerised and captured, disappearing in a puff of smoke. An hour later all that is left of him is a pool of blood which the Kreechurs are quick to clean up. Mortimer stands, blood on his face and a look of delirious ecstasy in his eyes. He then sinks into a chair and his face slowly returns to normal. I could see he was tired. Then he sleeps. When he sleeps the rest of the Kreechurs sleep too."

"There is a window that they leave open, for air I suppose. This is our only attack route. At about 5 in the morning they begin to stir, so we will have to be through by then. There is only one way leading to The Black Pub that is unguarded: a small path that cuts across West Street. The path is a winding one, with grim-looking buildings on either side. I never saw anyone go in or out of these buildings, but I sense there is always someone inside, looking out. We shall have to creep along the path quietly. Wear black, but carry mirrors. I don't know why I say this, but this is what we must do."

"I will need a day to gather small sharp knives for all of you. And mirrors. I know where to get them. I will be back." And with that he was gone.

Two days later, Thyme was back. It was almost 11 at night. He said: "We must act now. There is no more time to lose."

They dressed in silence and left The Black Pub in single file, blending in with the shadows as best they could. The night was cloudy. A cool breeze was starting to blow. Regina shivered.

"This is indeed the night for an assassination," she thought. She only hoped the assassination would not be hers.

After what seemed an age, they finally reached The Black Pub. Thyme signaled for them to stop.

"We will wait," he whispered. "I shall go on ahead. When I give the signal, you will have to follow me through that," he said pointing to a small window.

Taking a wicked-looking knife out of his trousers, he crept along the walls silently. There was an air of purposeful resolution about him. Sally was struck once again by the new Thyme she was witnessing. She stood in the shadows, waiting for his signal. Then, in the moonlight, she saw him slowly raise his knife and draw it across his throat. The knife gleamed faintly. Thyme disappeared through the window.

"Now!" whispered Sally to Regina and ran quietly across the last steps to the window. She followed Thyme inside. Regina and the rest of the group followed close on her heels. As they entered the main room of The Black Pub, they saw Thyme standing over Mortimer, a pool of blood on the floor, steam rising from the knife blade.

"Quick!" whispered Thyme. "Let us act fast and slit the throat of every Kreechur we can find. Be ruthless. Leave no one alive." With that he waded into the semi-unconscious

Kreechurs, cutting their throats as he went. After a moment's hesitation, Googol followed him and soon the room was thick with the blood of dead Kreechurs.

The first rays of the sun entering The Black Pub revealed a scene of death and destruction. Regina said: "It seems that it is time to go."

"I have one more thing to do," said Thyme. He kicked away the dead bodies lying across Mortimer, pulled another knife from his trousers and, kneeling, severed Mortimer's head from his body. He then deposited the head into a sack that he pulled out of a deep pocket in his jacket. The knife sizzled and melted away.

"What happens next?" asked Googol.

"We return home," said Thyme. "We lie low for a few days. The townspeople will not get their daily grog, and I fancy there will be much unhappiness."

"Unhappiness?" asked Sally in surprise.

"Yes, the effects of what they have been drinking will take seven to ten days to wear off. They will react. They will tear each other's hair out. They will scream and shout. They will behave irrationally. After a while they will cry and beg for more of what they were given. Only once this stage is past will they slowly return to normal. But remember, they will never be the same again and this will be the everlasting tragedy of what has happened. They will always feel somewhat empty. Like something is missing from their lives. I do not know what will follow from this; time alone will tell. Now, let us lie low and wait for the chaos to pass."

The next days passed slowly. Now that the excitement of killing Mortimer had passed, Thyme seemed to have reverted to his old self. Sally could not help but feel a bit disappointed. Was this change only temporary? She looked at him closely for some sign of the Thyme who had taken charge and had led the attack on The Black Pub.

Ten days were soon over. One day Thyme said: "Wake up! It'lI time to go to the square." Rubbing the sleep out of her eyes, Sally looked at him blearily and asked: "What, what, what... Time for what?"

"It is time for us to go to the town square. The people have calmed down and now we need to let them know what happened. Get dressed and follow me."

Later, at the village square, Thyme called for attention.

"Listen up all ye good folk. I know you have been suffering these past few days. But you have now been cured. You were being drugged by this man from The Black Pub." With a dramatic flourish, he uncovered Mortimer's head and held it up for everyone to see. The gasp went through the crowd.

"There is only one thing left to be done," Thyme said.

"What's that?" shouted the crowd.

"The Black Pub must be burned to the ground and places like this must never be allowed to spoil the good name of your land again. Follow me."

He turned and the crowd followed him obediently. When they reached The Black Pub, an old man walked out of it with a little pouch in his hand. He handed Thyme some white powder.

Thyme called out to the crowd to stand back.

He flung Mortimer's head into window of the pub and then, flinging the powder in, cried: "Let The Black Pub burn!"

The old man threw a flaming brand into the window. There was a loud explosion. White flame burst through the window and snaked up the walls and roof of the pub, working its way around the building and setting off little explosions as it went. In about an hour, the pub was reduced to ash. There was nothing left of it. Just a memory.

Chapter 20

The Second Battle At The Land Of Ice And Snow

Sally and Thyme were making their way back to her parents' house when they bumped into some old friends. It was Thar and they realised in shock that he was limping. His clothes were torn, his body covered in bruises.

Indeed, all the Lexters looked bedraggled, tired and hungry, and bore signs of recent strife.

Turning to Thar, Sally said: "Tell me what happened! We did not expect to see you in this state."

He nodded at Brindar and Sindar, before saying:

"When we got home there was much rejoicing at our return. We spent a few days celebrating and exchanging tales of our adventures. One day, Sindar The Elder called us in for council.

'There will be reprisals,' he said. 'I cannot see very far, but they will come soon and we shall have to be prepared. We have spent the last few days making merry; during these days our enemies have been preparing their next move. I sense that Threye is gathering his allies. His malice is deep. It has been a long time since any one group of people has managed to defy him in the way that you have done. He seeks nothing more than total destruction, and total domination. We must prepare.'"

"His words chilled us, more so because we knew them to be true. We had been full of joy over our recent triumphs, and events had tired us out. We needed a respite, and we needed to celebrate. We had. We also knew that an enemy as implacable as Threye does not wait for us to celebrate. He moves, he marshals his resources, and he manipulates others to join his cause."

"From that day on, we did nothing but prepare for the attack. We did not know where it would come from, or when. We just knew it was inevitable. Sindar The Elder's words had put a chill in our hearts and we sensed that this attack would be different from the previous one. We had come round to the belief that we had won the last battle with Azazel more by luck than by anything else. Our spirits were low. We began to build fortifications, and to train. Much of the euphoria that we had come home with dissipated, and we were anxious. Maybe this was the cause of our undoing, I don't know. But our bodies felt feeble and weak, and our minds did not have the same spirit of adventure that we normally have."

"At last, the fortifications were done and we gathered for a meeting. Sindar addressed us, and as he spoke it struck us once again that the world as we knew it was about to change. Sindar spoke of a few months of strife, but, strangely, he did not seem depressed in the manner that the rest of us were. 'Drink,' he said. 'Lift your spirits. Dark though the night may be, the sun will rise again. Even if we are destroyed, we shall rise again like the phoenix.'"

"As we retired for the night, we contemplated his words. We were unable to sleep; we felt no peace. Walking around our home, I looked at the guards at their watch. They seemed fidgety and worried."

"My mind was disturbed, but I must have slept for I was suddenly awakened by a very loud noise. It was as though the world was coming to an end! There was the smell of fire; loud, guttural voices were all around us."

"I rushed outside and was confronted by a sight that I never thought I would see in my entire life. Dragor and Bessie were back, but they were not alone. As they whooped in joy, I could see that the lust for blood and revenge was upon them. They seemed to be drunk with a murderous frenzy. They were accompanied by a group of stone-like creatures, cruel and implacable. Our weapons did not seem to affect these people at all. They seemed impervious to pain. As I ran out, I saw their blades gleaming cruelly in the fire, as they hacked and killed."

"In the distance was the sound of crackling flames. Brindar came running up screaming that the giants were burning The Black Forest. There was madness everywhere as we saw our homes go up in flames, and our friends, wives and children mowed down without mercy. My mind went blank as I stood there paralyzed. I could not believe what was happening. Things would have been worse for me had it not been for Rollo, who, charging forward, sent Bessie flying through one of the huts as she was about to cut me down with her sword."

"Stunned, I looked around and saw my wife running, gathering together women and children and pushing them towards the shadows. That was when my mind snapped and I realized that I could not just stand there forever. Charging towards Dragor, I rammed him with my shoulder as he was beginning to chase the women and children. Brimming with rage, I hacked at him wildly, forcing him to retreat. Then, just as I was about to pass the blade of my sword across his throat, I saw a figure advancing. This had to be the king of the trolls. I had only enough time to register that his features were finely carved, enhancing the look of cold, implacable cruelty on his face. I retreated, and bumped into Brindar."

"That is when I urged Thar to retreat," said Brindar. "There was nothing else we could do. We remembered that we had built ourselves a place where we could shelter in the event of an attack. The Dark Hollow is what we called it, and that is where we went. Everything seemed to be lost. Slowly, fighting off the trolls as best we could, we moved towards The Dark Hollow and one by one disappeared into the ground right before the trolls' eyes."

Sindar spoke: "As we sat there, we could hear howls of victory mixed with howls of rage. They had won, but they had not achieved their objective of total annihilation. Then the sounds died down and we could hear them speak."

"'The miserable creatures have been defeated,' said the Troll King. 'This land is now ours, ours for the keeping. We shall not give it up to Threye. We shall support him in his further battles, and the lands that we capture will be ours. This, Dragor, is the message that you will convey to Threye.'"

"'Yes your highness,' we heard Dragor say. 'But what of the Black Forest?'"

"'It has been burned down,' said another voice that we surmised could only have been the voice of a giant. 'The Black Forest is no more, and we have avenged those who died the last time.' A crude guttural laugh followed this statement, and then there was silence."

"Crouching in the hollow, we heard them celebrate and our hearts burned in agony. We wept for the loss of our homes. Why? We asked ourselves. We had done nothing to harm anyone. We had not set out to threaten Threye or anyone else. We lay there on the ground and wept."

There was silence in the room. Thyme stoked the fire that was starting to die. Shivering a little he asked: "What happened next?"

"What happened next," continued Thar, "is that Sindar the Elder, after hearing us weep and moan for a bit, stood up and addressed us firmly. I would even call him a bit harsh. Where was our spirit? he asked us. Where did it go? Was one setback going to defeat us? Threye had suffered minor setbacks at our hands, and all that it had done was enrage him and make him gather together his allies. We now had to plan the next steps."

"We looked at him, as he stood there, his face lit by the burning fires. The fires seemed to dance around his face, lighting it, and giving it a strength that we had not seen before. This was a new, determined Sindar, and he seemed to us to be stronger and fiercer than we had ever known him."

"The Black Forest could not be destroyed easily, he told us. For one, its roots lay deep in the earth. Trees set on fire by the giants would resonate deep within the earth and their shoots would be strong and hard and full of hate. Moreover, seeds that had fallen onto the giants hairy coats would be carried to the lands of the giants. The memory of the fire would be imprinted on the seeds, and in the land of the giants new trees would spring up that would overcome the giants and destroy them. The seeds of the giants' destruction had been written into the very trees and forest they sought to destroy."

"The trolls are a different matter altogether; they cannot be defeated so easily. Only the Four Winds, acting in unison, can be harnessed to help destroy them."

Looking at us, he continued: "I shall travel to The Icy Plains. There I shall meditate with a select few. If I am successful, I shall return in seven days. If not, then you shall never see me again. If I am not back by the evening of the eighth day, you must leave. I shall take Rollo and others with me."

"Rollo?" burst out Thyme in surprise. "Why didn't he take you, Sindar?" he asked.

"I don't know," said Sindar. "The ways of my father are mysterious sometimes. He has told me that when I am ready he will initiate me into some of his mysteries and pass some of his powers on to me."

He continued: "So we waited for seven days. We didn't know when or how my father left. We woke up in the morning and found him, Rollo, and two others gone. Thar's wife was one of the four who went with him; Zalyts the other. The rest of us stayed where we were, speaking in whispers. Most of the time was spent in contemplation. We were ashamed of ourselves for letting our hearts and spirits sink. Yet there was nothing to be done but to wait. We crept out one by one to forage for food and bring back news of what was happening. We were quiet, very quiet. The trolls had taken over our homes, and devastation was rampant. The heaviness that we felt in our hearts was slowly turning to hate, and a desire for revenge. Yet the path to this revenge was dark and we could not see the way. We sat there in The Dark Hollow, and waited."

"On the eighth day, in the afternoon, Sindar The Elder returned. Rollo, Chandra -- Thar's wife -- Zalyts, and another woman walked into the hollow. Indu was her name. Rollo had met her in The Icy Plains, and married her. She came from a long line of moon maidens, and seemed to have a deep connection with Chandra. We were stunned by her luminescent beauty. How could Rollo, a big, bumbling fellow, attract someone with so much grace and beauty? Our questions remained unanswered for Sindar was not forthcoming about his visit to The Icy Plains."

"He merely said that the days and nights had been extremely cold, and that the winds howled. They had sat there together, naked. On the fourth day, Indu seemed to descend on a moonbeam, and as she walked the earth she went up to Rollo and held his hand. She then meditated with the rest of the group. On the seventh day, they managed to harness the winds and gain their promise of help. They spoke of the Lord of Chaos, the trolls, and the need to defend the earth lest it be destroyed completely."

He paused and looked at the group. Sally, Thyme, Regina everyone sat eyes wide, mouths open looking at the Lexters. They had not, in their wildest imagination, expected to hear such a tale. After a pause, Regina begged them to continue.

"While my own story seems tame in comparison, I shall be glad to tell you my story at the end of yours," she said.

Thar nodded, and continued.

Sindar The Elder then spoke to us. 'Brindar, Sindar, Thar. The three of you must leave the Hollow, and the land we live in. You must take your ship and go. I shall come to the shores with you to see you off. The Icy Petrel will know where to steer you. I shall stay here with Chandra, Zalyts, Rollo and Indu. We shall meet up in due course, in Mrod.'"

"'In Mrod?'" we gasped. 'Yes, in Mrod,' he said. 'The die has been cast; we shall meet in Mrod when the time is right. You must go in search of your friends, and you must gather your forces. You will need to free two lands before the final battle is fought in Mrod. There is nothing to be done but seek the destruction, if indeed possible, of Threye. And there is no other way but to meet him in his own land and defeat him there. Otherwise this saga will continue and we shall all be destroyed.'"

"Stunned as we were by his words, and worried, we were nevertheless cheered. They gave us the strength to continue. 'You have not used your rings', he added. 'You will have to take recourse to them before the end. You shall see the power of the rings when they are used. Singly, each is strong. Together, they shall wield a strength that will be hard for anyone, or anything, to withstand.'"

"That night, we crept out of the hollow and made our way to the shore. The area was guarded by a giant and a troll, both pacing up and down, looking for signs of intruders. As we walked down slowly to the shoreline, we saw the giant scratching his body. He seemed to be in pain as he walked. His features were contorted. The troll, on the other hand, was stoic in his guard. Someone slipped on the rocks, sending a pile of them hurtling down. The troll stiffened and his nose twitched. We realized that he was sniffing us out. Then suddenly he charged, and before I knew what was happening he was upon me. I had not expected such a burst of speed. As his bulk came bearing down on us, I tumbled and fell backwards. The stars went out. All I could see was the dark shadow of the troll against the night, and the greenish glow of his eyes. I closed my eyes and raised my hand in defense. This is the night I die, I thought. But do I want to die? No, I shall escape. I shall live to fight another day. The thoughts rushed through my head in a confused frenzy, and a rage filled my body along with a strong desire to live. I raised my hand, fist clenched, and, to my surprise, a flame burst from it straight into the troll's eyes. He was blinded and thrown backwards by the blast."

"That's when I picked up Thar and yelled, 'Run'!" said Brindar. "We ran towards the ship and jumped into it.

The giant was too caught up in the throes of agony to do anything to stop us. We were off."

"That was the last we saw of Sindar The Elder," said Thar. "We left about fourteen days ago. We didn't know where we were headed. We encountered rough seas and bad weather all along the way. Although we cursed the weather, we were thankful we did not encounter anything worse than bad weather. Finally, we landed on your shores and now we are here with you. Our tale is done, and a sorry tale it is."

"What happened to you all since we parted?" he asked.

Regina began her story, with many interjections from the Lexters. They had not realized they were in the company of a queen, and they bowed to her in respect. They started when they heard about Erissa, and were curious about the disappearance of Mama Kuko.

"I don't like it," said Brindar. "Nothing good can come of her disappearance. Yet, we can do nothing about it. We shall have to wait and see what happens."

They nodded through the tale of Sally and Thyme, and when Thyme narrated his part Thar clapped him on the shoulder and laughed in approval.

"That's the way to go, my friend!" he said.

"And why wasn't I told of this?" demanded Sally.

"Oh I had sworn him to secrecy," replied Thar. "I had my reasons, and they shall stay with me. All I can say is it was for the best."

"What is to be done now?" enquired Regina. "We cannot sit here idly forever."

"I agree," said Googol. "We need action. We need a plan. Shall we embark on an expedition against Erissa?"

"No," said Sindar. "Erissa is too strong for us. We must wait."

"Wait for what?" demanded Sally impatiently.

"We must wait for Percival," said Thar. "We will meet Percival here. That is when we shall have forces strong enough to venture forth. Till then, we wait."

The Lexters nodded in assent. There was nothing to be done but wait.

A new council had to be elected. People needed to get back to work. There was much to keep them busy, and the time flew by.

Two weeks went by. Then, one morning, just as the sun was beginning to rise, two black ships sailed into harbour. One was The Raven. Percival, Jenna, Trix and Basil emerged from the ship and walked into town. Percival looked about him. His mind was filled with memories of his honeymoon with Bessie. He saw the familiar places he and Bessie had visited. Those days were gone now; the innocence that Bessie seemed to possess then was only a faint image in his mind. Yes, the world had indeed changed since those days. His world had changed. He had changed.

In those days he had walked the streets with Bessie's hand in his. Now he walked hand-in-hand with Jenna.

They knocked on Sally's door. It was opened by a sleepy Thyme, who, catching sight of them, whooped in joy, jumped up and hugged them all.

"Come in!" he said. "Welcome! We have been waiting for you."

Chapter 21

The Valley Is Reclaimed. Or Not?

Laughter and rejoicing. Two words that seemed to have disappeared from the lexicon of The Little Birds, as Threye called them. Where indeed had the simple days gone? When Percival and Bessie first set foot on the shores of The Exotic Island, as newly-weds. A lot had happened since that fateful night Bessie had disappeared in The Black Pub. They had stumbled onto a world of evil and magic. They had changed, and as they sat in Sally's living room exchanging stories, the past was but a distant memory. All they were conscious of was a feeling of warmth, camaraderie, and the comfort of knowing that they had formed true bonds of friendship; bonds they knew would stand the test of time. They were a motley crew, creatures from different lands who had come together by accident and stayed together through their shared belief in the dignity of life and their desire to preserve all that was good in the world.

As they sat sipping tea and eating breakfast there was a knock on the door. Jenna opened it. "Welcome," she said as a group of forbidding looking people walked into the room. Tall, lean, strongly built with fine features, they were a good looking bunch. Their eyes spoke of strange powers, of an ancient knowledge, of battles won, and of deep suffering. There was pride in their eyes, yet a glint too that spoke of extreme ruthlessness when required.

They looked down at the group sitting in stunned silence.

"My name is Abramelin," said the leader. He was tall and pale and had long black hair that tumbled down to his shoulders.

"And you can call me Tamsin," said she who seemed to be his wife. Stunningly beautiful, with long black hair like Abramelin, she was lithe, almost serpentine. Her eyes were black and set deep in the hollows of her face.

The silence in the room was palpable.

"Who are you?" asked Thyme finally. His eyes were wide and his voice was little more than a whisper.

"We are Warlocks," replied Abramelin. "We have an old history with Threye. Would you like to hear our story?"

"Yes," said Sally, her voice sounding a bit stronger. Turning to Percival, she addressed him: "We would also like to know how you met them, and what our next move is. So far we seem to be going from crisis to crisis. This has to stop. We cannot always live on the run."

"That is why we are here," said Abramelin. "Now, if I may get a cup of tea, I shall tell you our story and whence we came."

Accepting a cup, he sat down. He looked deep into its contents as though lost in another world. When he spoke his voice seemed to come from far away.

"This is a story that goes back a thousand years. It relates to the time when Threye had just taken over Mrod and was beginning to wage war with other lands. He had revealed his true nature, and his powers were young and strong. He had taken over most of what we know and was advancing further and further. His lust for power knew no bounds, and his desire to increase those powers remained unsatiated."

"He was already well versed in magic. He had heard of The Wizards, the Cyffarwynds, as they are called, and wanted their powers for himself. The Wizards are powerful indeed, more powerful than Threye. But they do not participate in the affairs of this world. And they shall not do so until the hour is very dark indeed. We were appointed guardians of their lands, and were all sworn to guard them forever."

"We knew of the coming of Threye, and were prepared for battle. He attacked swiftly, at night, with the large army he had amassed. Yet he was defeated and forced to retreat. He came again, and again. Each time, he was sent back. Finally, his forces were decimated and he was captured. Our armies brought him to us, and he stood before Tamsin and me, head hanging low."

"We were stunned," said Tamsin. "He seemed so small and fragile. This all together powerful enemy we had been fighting seemed weak. He did not seem to have any courage in him. Why were people so scared of this weakling? All strength seemed to have drained from him. He was weak, or so we thought, and for the first time something like pity found its way to my heart. He begged to be taken before The Wizards, to ask for their forgiveness. Still, we were skeptical. Everything told us he ought to be killed, but something in him seemed to beg for forgiveness. We were forbidden to take him to The Wizards, yet in a moment of weakness we betrayed our oath and took him beyond The Misty Gates."

"As soon as Threye stepped foot in The Misty Realm, and came face-to-face with The Wizards, his demeanor changed. He seemed to grow in strength as he leapt towards The Wizards. His body exuded a yellow aura; his eyes gleamed. The Wizards sat motionless. They seemed to be asleep, drowsy, and we realized our blunder. Threye moved towards them in an arc. At the very moment he landed before them, they opened their eyes and looked straight at him. He froze mid-flight and we heard him scream in agony. As he writhed and contorted in pain, he was enveloped in yellow flames. At that point, The Wizards looked at us and we heard them speak in our heads."

"The voices in our heads were agonizing!" said Lucifer. "The Wizards reminded us that we had broken our oath, and that we would be condemned to lifetimes of wandering until Threye had been exterminated. With that, they disappeared. Everything vanished except for Threye, lying on the ground, his body scarred and burned by the flames. He had turned an iridescent white, his yellow-and-green eyes leered at us, his tongue flicked in and out. 'Oath-breakers', he called us, and then he laughed. His laugh was pure evil. He knew that even now he had gained a victory. A victory that was least expected. The

Wizards had gone and there was no one left to challenge him. No one except us. I leapt forward to sever his head from his body, but he simply melted away. In our moment of weakness, he had tricked and defeated us."

"The Wizards have since retreated to invisible lands. The time has come to resume our battle with Threye," Lucifer concluded.

The sun outside the room was shining, but the air inside was dark and heavy. The weight of history seemed to hang in the air. Once again, the group was seized with the feeling that the world was about to change. Regina stood up and said: "We should go out and get some fresh air. Maybe we will hear Percival's story better when we are out in the sun."

"Good idea," said Brindar. "Let's go. The sun on our backs shall do us good. It has been long since we sat, allowing the sun to give us warmth."

As they walked down the street, Percival was struck again by how much he had changed since he first walked these streets. He looked at Jenna strolling beside him. He was not the same smug and satisfied person he had been in those innocent days. He smiled as he recalled how he used to strut the streets with the arrogance of inherited wealth and lineage. He was not the dashing hero he had fancied himself to be in his imagination, yet there was something strong about him now, something that could be fierce in battle, yet tender in love. He had discovered powers of resilience in himself, and he had learned that he could take the rough days with the good. He had discovered a humility in himself, a humility he had never dreamed he would ever possess.

Percival sighed, took a deep breath, and clasped Jenna's hand tightly in his own.

"Come," he said to the group. "Let us sit here. This is the restaurant where Bessie and I had our last meal together before she disappeared with Dragor."

Looking around, he laughed and continued. "Those days are gone. In a sense, it is fitting that we sit here. That was the last meal we had together, before my world changed forever. It was after that meal that I began my hunt for Bessie. Maybe after this one we shall hunt for Threye. We shall turn from being the hunted to being the hunters."

"But first," laughed Thar. "Tell us what happened to you. You've heard our story, tell us yours."

"Oh let me, let me, let me," interjected Trix with a gleeful laugh. "This is one story I must tell. Hee! Hee! Hee!"

"What's so funny?" asked Brindar.

"Wait, and prepare to be entertained," laughed Jenna.

"You too?" said Percival indignantly. "You have allied with the witch?!"

"We started off in The Raven," began Trix, still giggling. "We sailed for a few days, not really knowing where we were headed. To be honest, it was fun. We lay on the deck in the sun, gazed at the stars and moon at night, and let the cool breeze fan our skin. Oh yes! Those were good days."

"Here we were, our lives in mortal danger," said Sindar with wonder, "and there you were enjoying the sunset!"

"Some people seem to have all the luck in the world", growled Brindar. "They laze around, sunning themselves, possibly having a massage, while the others fight to save the world. Ahem!"

"Anyway," continued Trix, ignoring him, "one day we arrived on the shores of the home of The Warlocks, though we did not know it at the time. We landed just as the sun was going down, and crawled ashore. We walked along the grassy paths until it was night. We didn't encounter anyone, and soon we were wondering where to spend the night. We decided to rest under a tree. The breeze was cool and there did not seem to be any signs of rain. Except for the odd hunger pang, there didn't seem to be anything to worry about."

"Well, there was one person who seemed very hungry..." laughed Jenna.

"Oh yes!" butted in Trix, chortling with glee. She looked sidelong at Percival. "His stomach began to rumble. At first I thought a volcano was starting to erupt, so I poked Basil in the ribs, and woke him up. Basil does often feel very hungry, you know. But no, this time it was Percival. He was groaning softly in his sleep, and I knew he was dreaming of food!"

She poked him in the ribs and laughed merrily. The sun shone through her silvery hair. She looked delightfully cheerful and wickedly pretty. There was a sparkle in her eyes. Percival glared and growled, "Witch!"

"That was when I heard the drums. At first I thought Percival's stomach had taken on a rhythmic beat. But it was the drums. There was no mistaking them. They were hypnotic. I woke Jenna up and we decided to go see what was happening."

"We walked for a long, long time," said Jenna. "Our feet were beginning to hurt when suddenly we came to a clearing where we saw a group of Warlocks around a fire. They were dancing in a circle to the drumbeat. The drumbeat was hypnotic, mesmerizing. It drew us in, and we felt ourselves beginning to dance to the beat. Then the circle opened up and Abramelin and Tamsin looked straight at us. They seemed to be saying something, but we had no idea what it was. We felt ourselves drawn by a strong force into the centre of the circle. The force was a malevolent one, full of anger and hate. We had no power to resist it and were soon down on our knees. Our last moments had arrived, or so we thought. But then, slowly, the malevolence and threat disappeared and we found ourselves looking into the eyes of the pair. Their mouths did not move, but we could feel their thoughts. They spoke of Threye, betrayal, vengeance, and foul magic. We found ourselves looking inside ourselves. We felt ourselves being lifted; our bodies seemed to float in the air. Then we lost all consciousness."

"When we awoke, we were in a room in beds. Percival and Basil were there too."

"Of course I was with Percival and she was with Basil," corrected Jenna hastily. "We awoke, changed into the new clothes that had been laid out for us, and went downstairs."

"'I smell heaven!' cried Percival," Trix continued. "Boy, oh boy, was he indeed in heaven, when he saw the spread that had been laid out for them. The next thing we knew Percival had buried his snout in bread, butter, jam, fruits, and sausages. Indeed, he seemed to disappear into the pile of food. He was young and happy again as he set about enjoying the meal. When The Warlocks walked in, however, he froze."

Trix closed her eyes and seemed to be meditating as her mind went back to the memory of Percival standing with a string of sausages dangling from his mouth, bread and fruit in either hand.

"Ooooh yes!" she giggled. "And then he fell back on his plump backside and all we could see were his legs thrashing about in the air.'Our conquering hero' I said, pointing to him as I introduced him to Abramelin."

"It was all we could do to keep a straight face," smiled Tamsin. "This was not a sight we had expected to see."

Percival glared but did not dare say anything to antagonize Tamsin. "Damn her and her powers!", he thought to himself.

Jenna stroked his head and laughed. "It took a while for poor old Percy to recover his sang-froid," she said.

"The greedy fella never did get over having his breakfast interrupted," chortled Basil. "You should have seen him standing there, eyes wide, mouth wider, sausages dangling...".

"Get on with it!" growled Percival. "What am I supposed to do if I am the only one who truly appreciates good food?!"

"Oh yeah, sure!" chortled Basil again.

"Anyway," Jenna continued, "We then told The Warlocks our story."

"It was then that Abramelin remarked that it was time we stopped being the hunted and became the hunters. That stunned us for a moment.

"We told them," said Tamsin, "What Threye was used to being the aggressor, that he could never imagine anyone attacking him or his allies. We would need to let him know that we were not afraid of him. And so we formulated a plan to attack his home and to reclaim it."

"We left soon after, continued Percival. They were all now taking turns telling the tale. "And Percival spent most of the time eating, not particularly listening to what we were saying, ot particularly lis"We left at night, two days after that fateful breakfast. Percy seemed to have swelled up in two short days. But that is besides the point..."

"Yes, we left at night and when we arrived home a day later it was dark. There wasn't a sound in the town," continued Percival. "It seemed so very peaceful. You would never believe that the town had been taken over by dark forces.

I looked at my home as we passed, and the smell of freshly baked cake and freshly brewed coffee seemed to waft it's way into my nostrils. I almost cried."

"You did cry," pointed out Trix.

Percival glared at her, "W....W....W..."

"Go on, say it, say it, say....", said Trix laughing..

"We were covered in a shroud of darkness," interrupted Abramelin, "which is why we were able to attack stealthily."

Jenna chipped in: "It was amazing, come to think of it. In the earlier days, when we were with Threye, we would march into a town, weapons blazing, scattering the townsfolk about us, laughing in almost murderous joy. Now we were cautious, quiet, waiting for the right moment to strike. Earlier, we invaded to conquer, to destroy, to see blood on the streets, and to revel in it. Now we went in to liberate. Blood would flow, we knew that, but it would be blood that needed to be shed in order to liberate. This was new for Trix and me. We spoke about it and how our lives had changed since we had escaped from the dungeon with all of you. We called you The Little Birds then, and since that night we have become part of The Little Birds..."

"The Little Birds?! " burst out Sally.

"Yes, that is what Threye calls us. He wants to catch us in his snare and destroy us. I know that he seethes with rage, a rage that consumes him. No one has ever escaped Mrod alive. No one has escaped from the dungeons. No one has defeated Azazel!"

"And," continued Trix, "no one had ever defeated our father, Esh. This is all too much for Threye to take in. At first he thought it was chance. Then he thought maybe he had underestimated you. Now he believes that we -- you -- have hidden powers. I am sure that behind the rage there lurks a degree of fear. It will drive him to eradicate any opposition to his power. This is why we must turn aggressor."

"So," she continued, "we walked into the town quietly. A sense of death, decay and evil hung in the air. No one seemed to suspect our presence, and finally we came to the house, the house where Bessie used to live. When we saw the lights on we knew that Blanche was awake. I crept up and looked in one of the windows. She was sitting with Christina and Julia. Her face seemed more mottled than I remembered it being. I must have made a noise because suddenly she looked up and I found myself looking into her eyes. There was death in those eyes, and an emptiness I had never seen before. Blanche opened her mouth and pointed. Then there was a flurry of activity. She moved with a speed I would never have believed possible. Christina was up, so was Julia. Alarm bells rang out and soon the streets were crawling with every sort of maggoty fighter and the rest of the Sangre clan."

"The battle was truly upon us, and we fought," said Jenna. "We went in, fire blazing in our eyes, swords in hand. The joy of battle consumed us. We lay waste the maggoty fighters who charged us. Every house we passed was set alight."

"And then I saw Percival climb to the rooftop of the restaurant he said he would visit before he was married.

Micla was behind him. I saw Micla grab Percival's ankle. His foot waved frantically in the air like a fluttering flag as he tried to escape Micla a flutter He seemed to lose his grip and fall. With him went Micla. I heard a squeal and then another one as Percival came crashing down upon him. Percival just flopped there, oblivious of the battle raging around him. He wheezed: 'Hee! Hee!' Even in that crazy hour, I stood and laughed."

"And you would have got your head chopped off," said Basil, "had I not been there!"

"Yes you saved me sweetie..." purred Trix, caressing his cheek and kissing him.

"What happened to Percival?" asked Thar.

"I will tell this part," said Percival gruffly. "I did indeed fall but it was a graceful fall and I think I broke some bones in Micla's body. He was under me, moaning in pain. As I lay there, catching my breath, the night sky was suddenly blotted from view by the ghastly mottled face of Blanche above me. I raised my right hand and focused on her destruction. I imagined a light emanating from my hand."

He paused for dramatic effect, and continued. "And then it happened. A blinding light emerged from the ring I was wearing. It seemed to burn Blanche. She screamed and turned away. I stood up, ring still pointed at her. She continued screaming as her skin burned. Soon all that was left of Blanche was a powdery skeleton."

There was an awed silence as all those wearing the ring looked down at it in wonder. They had not expected the power of the rings to be revealed to them in such spectacular fashion.

"The rings," said Abramelin, "cannot be used for evil. If you use them for evil, their power shall turn back on you. They must be employed only in times of stress, of danger, and of doubt. Use their power well."

Chapter 22

The Madness Of Azazel

The morning sun rose in all its glory, its fiery rays greeting the ships as they approached the Valley of Kings. Percival stood on deck watching land approach. He wore a pensive look as he marveled at the change that the past events had wrought in him. He was no longer the same pig that had set out on his honeymoon. He would never be the same. Yet he could not escape the occasional twinge of nostalgia as he recalled the old days, himself sipping coffee on the lawn, birds chirping all around him. What had become of Bessie? Had she changed or had Dragor simply given expression to her true nature? Why did she hate him so much? Why did she want to kill him? As he thought of her, he also realized that he could never deliberately kill her. If she were to die at his hand, it would be an act of self defense. He sighed, and wondered where she was, if she was alive or dead. Somewhere in his mind, he knew that their story was still not over.

What he did not know was that Bessie and Dragor were back in Mrod with the trolls and the few giants that had escaped destruction. In their anger and haste to destroy the Black Forest, the giants did not realize as they slashed and burned the trees that seeds from these trees had fallen onto their bodies. And so life for the forest began anew in the Land of Ice and Snow, and in the bodies of the giants on whom the seeds fell. What did they need to grow? Water, organic matter and air. Everything was available on the bodies of the Giants. There was a deep anger in the forest, a deep anger of nature slighted. As the Giants made their way around, the seeds began their growth. Slowly, the roots emerged from the seed cover, latched themselves onto the bodies of the Giants, with a fierce anger, and started to grow. They found sustenance in the bodies of the Giants whom they devoured, and grew again in a malevolent fury.

The Black Forest was reborn.

A cool breeze passed over Percival, and he shivered. He looked around and saw Jenna standing near him. His face brightened immediately. The past may have gone forever, but it had in a most unexpected manner brought him and his true love together. He reached out and touched her hand, and she smiled. The Fates are strange, he thought, as welcome electricity passed between the two as their hands touched and stroked each other. They were meant to be enemies, one hunting the other, but Fate had something else in mind. Two of the most unlikely creatures had found love in each other, and their lives would never be the same again.

It was a glorious morning, the kind of morning you would always wish for when setting out to liberate a land and its people. A morning meant for freedom, a celebration of the sheer joy of living, the kind of morning whose dawn heralded the start of a new age. The sun burst forth in radiant joy, and the rays shone through the billowing clouds in vibrant energy. Everything about the morning seemed to speak in words of optimism, hope, and a new dawn. The Brethren and the Warlocks looked at each other and smiled. They each took a deep breath, raised their faces to the Heavens and allowed the pure energy of the morning to wash over them.

As they emerged from their ships and walked into town, they were struck by the destruction that had been wrought in so short a time. Townspeople peeped through their curtains, windows began to open, and a slow cheer started up. People emerged from their homes to greet their Queen as she passed down the street. The sight of their Queen gave them strength and reason to cheer. They had experienced days of terror and pain under a changed Erissa. Gone was the gracious lady who smiled and healed. She had quickly become the cruel mistress who kept the king in a state of thrall, a state of near madness. She controlled both the army and the king's mind. By her side was her husband Azazel, and Esmerelda. The former did not speak much, but an air of wild malevolence hung about him. He would walk the streets, red hair flowing about his shoulders, green eyes full of madness and chaos. He was always accompanied by Esmerelda, she of the green hair and green eyes, eyes that were at once young and playful, old and empty. No one could ever look directly into those eyes. To do so was to look into the a bottomless pit, empty, cold, old and evil.

As they marched along, the warriors saw the gates of the palace open slowly. They were black, spiked and dangerous. Foul smoke rose from the palace chimney.

"Cover your noses!" ordered Abramelin. "This is no ordinary smoke. It is smoke that has been brewed by the Old One, designed to smother and send your mind into madness."

He yelled, "Prepare for battle! The moment has come!" and waded into the oncoming army, sword glittering in the morning sun. Heads flew and bodies fell all around him. The Brethren followed close.

Their recent battles had given them a previously untested strength, and it seemed as though the king's armies were no match for them as they cut huge swathes through the oncoming hordes. Googol's arm rose and fell as he fought those who had been his comrades in days gone by. Tears streamed from his eyes as he cut and thrust his sword into the bodies of his earlier friends. The joy of victory could not compensate for the sadness at killing so many of his former friends and comrades, and as they fell, the weight of memories past fell heavily on his heart, almost weighing him down.

The battle seemed to be almost at an end, the armies decimated. It was all too easy. The few remaining soldiers started the retreat. The trumpeter sounded his horn. It was not the sound of victory, it was the sound of despair. Then, as the Warlocks and Brethren approached the palace walls, they were stopped in their tracks by the sudden sound of laughter. Thin, evil and vicious, there was no humour in the laugh. Their blood almost froze at the sound.

Regina looked up and shrieked. Erissa was standing on the wall looking down mockingly. Next to her was Regus. Not the Regus of old, but a pale shadow of himself. He hung limply by her side like a rag doll. His face was grey, his mouth open. There was a half-crazed look in his eyes. As he took in the sight of the army below, he giggled with the madness of one whose mind is no longer his own.

Spittle dribbled from the corners of his mouth. Seeing him like this, Regina screamed in anger: "I will kill you, you witch!"

"Oh I am no witch," smirked Erissa. "Esmerelda is the witch. I am just your humble servant. I have served your husband well and now I think it is time for me to return him to you."

She paused, adding: "But do you want him back? Do you want the pretty boy back?"

She looked at Regus and slowly released her grip on his collar. She watched as he lurched forward like a drunken man. Just as he swayed on the very edge of the wall and was about to fall, she pulled him back.

"Do you want him back?" she asked again with a sneer in her voice. "He has served his purpose. Maybe it is time to return him to you." Erissa stood on top of the wall and laughed, and as her body shook with laughter, the almost limp and feeble body of Regus shook with her. He seemed to have no life of his own. The kingship had left him, leaving him to be a hollow shell.

"Wait!" said a sudden voice behind her. Erissa turned as Esmerelda joined her on the wall.

The two women looked down together. One, with black hair and black eyes; the other green-eyed. Black eyes that revealed cruelty; green, emptiness of soul. Finally Esmerelda spoke: "What price would you pay for your beloved husband? What price would you give to have him returned to you whole in full strength of body and mind?"

"Will you give us these raggedy warriors? We want The Little Birds and we want you to pledge allegiance to Threye for all eternity. Is this something you would do? Wait," she paused. "I am a reasonable person. We would be happy with just The Little Birds. In particular I want Jenna, I want Trix, I want Basil, and I want Percival. Give them to me and your husband shall be returned to you whole. You shall live out your life in comfort, and you shall both die in your beds, in old age. Is this too big a price to pay?"

The Old One laughed and looked down at the group. "What say ye?" she asked. Her voice was honeyed and sweet and she looked sympathetic. Regina felt weak inside. Her knees seemed to be giving way. Small price indeed! She looked up at Esmerelda and felt the power of the witch's eyes drawing her in. Despite the distance she was drawn to The Old One. Tears clung to the corners of her eyes as she watched her husband tottering on the edge of the wall, knees buckling under him. He would have fallen had he not been held tight by Erissa. As she looked away from Esmerelda and at him, she thought she saw a gleam in The Old One's eyes. Her heart overflowed with love for her husband. She could not forsake him. Regina lurched forward, a beseeching look in her eyes.

"Beware..." whispered Tamsin, standing close behind Regina. "Beware The Old Crone. Do not look into those empty pools. They have a power you cannot overcome. They will take over your mind and you shall become her prisoner for the rest of your life. Look past, look past!" Thus saying, she gave Regina a hard push. The Queen gasped and stumbled. It seemed to break the spell. She lay on the ground for a moment, her face stained with mud and the blood of fallen soldiers. As she rose, anger choked her throat.

"Be gone, you old witch!" she croaked. "I may be condemned to a life alone but I shall live a free woman! I shall not parlay with you!" She looked up, her face contorted with rage, and spat at the two women on the wall.

Erissa laughed. A murderous glee filled her face as she slowly released her grip on Regus's collar. The king toppled and fell slowly down the ramparts. His body twisted and turned as he made his way through space towards the ground below. Then it gained speed, hurtling faster and faster. At the point of impact, however, Thar and Basil rushed forward and caught him.

Erissa, still laughing uproariously, didn't notice the spear flying through the air towards her. It was Percival's. It struck her on the shoulder, passing through flesh and bone and emerging from the other side. Erissa screamed in pain and fell back. The pain was sharp and unexpected. Blood dripped from her body onto the ground. Esmerelda laughed. Pain was not new to her, she had experienced it before. Stepping up to Erissa, she pulled the spear from her body and put her lips to the bleeding wound. As she licked the blood, the wound seemed to close and heal.

Esmerelda stood up just as Azazel emerged from the shadows. He looked down at the army assembled below, and then jumped. A wild energy flowed from his body, fierce and uncontrollable, causing the Brethren and Warlocks to move back in surprise. Azazel's face was unrecognizable. The features were the same, but the red hair and green eyes were new. He raised his arms to the sky as though invoking the energy of a strange and malevolent god. He brought his arms down and the earth shook, knocking everyone down. He made his way towards them, enveloped in flames fanned by the wind. He seemed to control both the fire and the wind.

His body seemed to swell, and he felt a mad, almost uncontrollable power inside him. Chaos was he, and he was Chaos, as he inflicted his terrors on the warriors in front of him. The armies of The King were almost flattened in his wake, and he felt a joy that he had not felt in a long, long while. Gone was Azazel the Game Player. This was Azazel, The Lord of Chaos, and he reveled in it.

Wordless thoughts tumbled through his brain, and all that he was conscious of, was his awful power. Victory was at hand, but even better, total annihilation was in his grasp. It was at that time that he felt a tiny voice making it's way into his brain It grew, and he finally recognized the voice of Threye.

"Come", said the hoarse voice of Threye, and there was a note of urgency in the voice. "I need you here. We can deal with these miserable creatures later. But, you are needed here in Mrod, now...."

The Warlocks were dismayed at the chaos that Azazel was unleashing. They watched Esmerelda beside him. Her eyes were empty pools, as were Azazel's. Yet, the madness and chaos that gripped Azazel were offset by Esmerelda's emptiness. They made a horrific pair. The winds howled around them, the ground seemed to be on fire. Nature itself appeared to be in their grip. The worst fears of the Brethren had been realized.

Hope was beginning to fade. Was this the end? The end to all their dreams? The Warlocks stepped in front of the fallen Brethren. Abramelin and Tamsin raised their shields, blocking the wind and the flames. They strained heavily against the chaos unleashed by Azazel. Azazel opened his mouth wide as though to swallow everything around him. The fires were in his mouth. His eyes blazed and his body crackled. The wind blew even more fiercely. Then Azazel laughed and the madness of his laughter pierced the fallen Brethren causing unbelievable pain. They screamed in agony. Esmerelda laughed with Azazel, twirling a whip. Green fires ran up and down the whip as she advanced towards the group.

One thought, and only one thought went through Percival's head. He had to survive. He stood up and pulled Jenna to her feet. His body ached all over, yet he staggered around helping the rest of the Brethren to their feet.

"Put the rings together!" he gasped finally. "Put the rings together and think of freedom. Feel freedom. Feel strength and power. Feel through your pain. Cry freedom!"

They put the rings together and a blinding flash of light coursed through their bodies ridding them of the pain. They felt their strength return, allowing them to stand with the Warlocks and fight on.

Azazel continued to laugh with the wildness of one who controls chaos with the strength of his madness. Then suddenly it was gone. The madness was over, and the wild forces that he had unleashed were drawn back inside him. Azazel seemed to shrink. Something caught his attention and he looked at Esmerelda.

"He is calling us," he said. "We must go."

As quickly as the madness came, it disappeared. And the two of them were gone.

The Warlocks and the Brethren fell to the ground exhausted.

"We have never experienced anything like this before," said Abramelin, gasping. His voice was tired, weak. He could not sit up, and he lay there on the ground, speaking up at the sky. "It would appear that Azazel possesses the power to create and control chaos. He will be a formidable foe. I think he has been called away by Threye who will be preparing his army. We don't have much time. We must prepare to attack Mrod. The hour is upon us."

"Let us return to your house," said Tamsin. "We will gather our forces and plan the final assault."

The day was a beautiful one, and as the cool breeze blew about them the weary warriors closed their eyes and drifted off into a deep sleep.

Chapter 23

Interlude. Preparing For The End

Percival and Jenna lay in each other's arms in the shade of a tree. Once again, Percival's thoughts returned to the past, to days when he had been spoilt and innocent, and to the many adventures he had been through. Bessie, he had then thought, was the love of his life. But he had found love also in the most unlikely of places and people. He and Jenna had braved dangers together; she had lost her home and her people. They were now the strength in each other's lives. Percival sighed and stirred. Life was strange indeed. Basil had found Trix, and the two sworn enemies were about to become brothers-in-law. There was, of course, that they had to find a way to end the menace of Threye and Azazel. Love was in the air, it was in their hearts, yet there were obstacles that needed to be overcome before they could lay full claim to a life of ease and happiness.

Percival looked around and marveled at the calm that pervaded the valley. The madness of Azazel had been brief. He was now accompanied by a strange woman with green hair and green eyes. Who was she? She seemed powerful and cruel beyond measure. He remembered the look in her eyes, and shivered. While the expression was playful in her eyes, there were wells of deep knowledge hidden in those eyes. A deep evil resided in those seemingly empty pools. Along with Erissa, the three were a formidable force indeed. And then there was Threye. But what had been the reason for Azazel's sudden disappearance? The question buzzed around in his brain until he felt as though he was going crazy. He walked around and stamped his feet uneasily. Too many questions needed answering, questions that would not be answered.

What Percival didn't know was that far way in The Land of Ice and Snow, the giants had destroyed The Black Forest, or so they thought. They had hacked and burned the forest, destroying every plant, every shrub and every tree. Yet, as they hacked they loosened seeds that fell to the ground and onto the matted bodies of the giants.

The roots of The Black Forest ran deep into the ground, so deep that no fire reached them in their frozen depths. But the smell of the fires travelled down to the roots whose anger blazed forth in the shoots they sent soaring into the cold winter sky. Vines grew along the ground wrapping themselves around the ankles of the giants. As they did so, they held them in a vice-like grip, slowly sucking the life blood from their veins. Seeds that had fallen onto the giants found sustenance in their flesh and blood. This way the giants were slowly decimated, as the trolls looked on in horror. They were of the same earthy substance as the forest; they recognized the anger and malice that grew and grew.

"We must withdraw from this land," the Troll King told Dragor. "This land is now damned for us. If we stay, the roots shall spread and we shall all become part of the land.

"No," snarled Dragor. "We did not come here to withdraw. Let's dig deep and burn the roots."

"Fool!" hissed the Troll Queen. "This is no time for bravado. This is the time for prudence. We are of the same nature as The Forest. Withdraw, or perish!"

"Go if you must," snarled Bessie. "We are not cowards. We shall stay, and we shall destroy this forest."

The trolls prepared to leave. On their departure, the Troll King said: "We shall honour our last pledge and leave for Mrod. There, we will confer with Threye on what is to be done. If you survive, we shall meet you there."

Dragor watched the ships depart in the midday sun. He spat on the ground, saying: "We shall get to work tomorrow."

The day waned, and as the sun went down he and Bessie sat down to eat. What they did not know was that Sindar the Elder and his group had emerged from their hiding places and were paying homage to The Forest. The Lexters had lived in peace with The Forest for generations and had honoured them through the ages of their history.

Sindar approached the hut. He stood there silently until they became aware of his presence. Dragor snarled and charged. As he charged, Sindar withdrew into the cold night with Dragor giving chase. He paused and blinked to adjust his eyes to the sudden dark. He became aware of a luminous presence in the distance. Rollo was standing next to a woman bathed in a silvery light. His heart swam with a helpless rage, and the blood rushed to his head. He charged at Rollo, sword raised, ready for the kill. He did not see the woman move in front of Rollo, a beam of silvery light extending from her arm. The beam passed through his body and he slumped to the ground, blood staining the icy earth.

Bessie ran out screaming. Kneeling by Dragor as he died, she shouted:

"I will have my revenge!". Tears streamed from her eyes, as she wept for her fallen lover. Happiness had eluded her, and rage and sorrow filled her heart.

"Withdraw," said Sindar the Elder quietly. "This is no longer the place for you to stay. Go back to Mrod and give Threye the message that the tide is turning. Go now."

Screaming incoherently, Bessie ran to her ship and started the journey back to Mrod. There, a week later, as she stood in front of Threye, the Troll King and Queen by her side, she told the story of her withdrawal from The Land of Ice and Snow.

Threye's face was inscrutable as he listened, but it was just possible that a seed of doubt was planted in his heart. Hitherto he had had no opposition. No one had dared oppose him. Suddenly he was faced with the prospect of a sustained fight-back. As he withdrew into his quarters, his mind raced to Azazel, calling him back to Mrod.

Never before had he felt the cold fingers of fear and doubt clench around his heart. An icy wave swept through his body. Yes, this was the beginning of doubt. Was this the first sign of weakness in Threye? He would have to gather his forces. He waited with unease and impatience for Azazel to return.

Percival's idyll under the tree was disturbed by a prod in the ribs. He had dozed off. He opened an eye to find himself looking straight up into the grinning faces of Basil and Trix. Suddenly there was a rush of water as it made its way from a bucket to his face. Percival sat up with a jerk, sputtering and coughing.

"Witch!" he screamed in rage. He shook his fist at the laughing girl, growling: "Just wait till I get my hands on your neck!"

"Poor little Percy, he sleeps by night.

Poor little Percy, he sleeps by day

Holding forces with his might

Where are they, he could not say.

Poor little Percy, he dreams of food..."

Trix scampered off singing, a bellowing Percival in hot pursuit. Jenna and Basil howled with laughter, rolling on the grass until they could barely breathe.

"Come on Percival," said Basil finally. "We need to convene to plan. Don't be angry now."

Scowling, Percival followed them to the palace where Regina was waiting for them accompanied by Abramelin, Tamsin and the other Lexters.

"It is time for us to make the first strike," said Lucifer. "I fear that Azazel has returned to Mrod and that Threye has a plan. I have been discussing this with Tamsin and we feel we should try and reclaim your home. We shall then go to yours, Sally, where we shall meet Sindar the Elder and the rest of his group. Then we shall launch an attack on Mrod. We have to act now. There is no time to lose."

"What?" stuttered Percival. "No time?"

"Yes, dummy!" Trix said, poking him in the ribs. "While you and your lovely have been sleeping under the old willow tree, the rest of us have been plotting our next move. Ow!" Jenna stamped on her foot and smiled sweetly at Trix. "I never sleep lazily," she said with a smile.

"When do we leave?" asked Percival.

"Now," returned Tamsin. "We attack at the first light of dawn. We shall leave a small force of Warlocks here in the valley in case Mrod sends a punitive expedition. Gather your things. It is time to leave."

There was no time for farewells. They left quietly. What they did not see was May taking a boat and slipping away quietly to Mrod. The seeds that Erissa had sown had taken root. There was dissent in the land that would, in time, erupt in a manner no one could predict. The old days of peace and order had left the Valley of the Kings, never to return. A new world order was about to begin. No one knew how the pages would turn.

They arrived the next morning. It was still dark. The sun's rays had not yet lit the skies. The Little Birds, the Brethren, made their way up the harbour into town, killing any guard that stood in their way. No mercy was expected; none was given. When they reached the town square, the fires were blazing as Blanche, Christina, Mr. Benttwist, Kale and Micla stood in wait for them. How had Blanche come back to life? It was an evil miracle.

Battle horns were rung and the two sides rushed at each other, cutting, slashing and shouting their battle cries. Blood flowed and heads rolled. Limbs were cut, torsos slashed as the Brethren made their way through the defenses of the forces that had taken over Percival's Land. They were soon beaten back and Blanche found herself face-to-face with Percival. She turned her pale, blotched face towards him and stared at him through lidless eyes. Her tongue flicked in and out of her mouth. She smiled. Hers was the face of death and decay; her smile spoke of the horrors of hell.

"Come to die have you little Percy?" she crooned. "Do you remember the times we kissed and our tongues touched? Do you remember the times our tongues would touch and curl in passion?" she continued. "Let's do it again and maybe this time you will feel death."

"You think so?" asked Percival, circling her warily. Blanche's tongue flicked in and out as she watched him circle her with amusement.

Then she pounced. Percival thrust his knife into her stomach. She pulled it in, the knife melting in a smoky hiss.

"Poor little Percy, lost his knife...

He shall die remembering his wife," she sang and pounced again.

Percival's back was to the wall. Blanche approached him slowly, savouring the moment when her touch would melt his flesh. He raised his hand, and as he did so he remembered the ring on his finger. Concentrating all his will, he imagined her burning up in front of him. He opened his eyes to see her screaming in agony. She turned and ran, flames bursting from her body. Percival stood still with the shock of what he had done, and the spell was undone.

Elsewhere, Trix and Christina were engaged in a fierce battle, neither giving a quarter. Christina's sword knocked the weapon from Trix's hand and, with a blow, Trix was sent spinning. As she fell, she felt Christina's weight on her body and smelled the hot breath of the woman as she revealed her fangs, ready to bite. Trix opened her third eye and a flame burst from it, burning Christina's face. Christina screamed and fell back; before she could recover Trix had picked up her sword and severed her head from her shoulders.

Zalyts meanwhile had come face-to-face with his brother, Micla. The two looked at each other. Zalyts marvelled at the change that had come over Micla. Gone was the innocence that had been the hallmark of his brother's face and personality. Instead, he found himself looking at a creature that seemed to have been born from the depths of hell. He saw a ghoulish mask he did not recognise. The ghost of his brother. The two fought like ancient adversaries, no hint of brotherly love between them. Finally, Zalyts ducked a heave from Micla and, bending low, cut off Micla's legs at the knees.

As he watched his brother lying on the ground, tears dropped from his eyes. Pity and love welled up in his heart as he drove his sword through the heart of the creature that had once been his brother.

The battle was soon over. Mr. Benttwist, Kale and Blanche had escaped with some of the Sangre. They retreated into the shadows, boarding ships that would take them back to Mrod. They would never return to Percival's Land.

The victors stood around watching the embers die. They walked amongst the fallen bodies, driving their swords through the hearts of those that still survived and carrying off their own wounded warriors. There was no time for celebrations. Their tired bodies ached for rest, as they prepared two funerals. The bodies of their enemies were piled into a heap and burned. The fires shot up into the skies and sparks burst from the flames. No doubt, in far away Mrod, Threye would be watching the signs. News of the defeat would have reached him. He would prepare his forces. They needed to attack before this happened.

Their own fighters were given a more fitting farewell. Their bodies were cast into the sea to become one with the waves.

They left a small force behind to guard against any future threat and left for The Exotic Island where they would meet Sindar the Elder.

Meanwhile, in Mrod, Threye saw the flames shoot up into the sky and his heart burned with rage. It was a rage tinged with something new and alien. Was it fear that he was feeling? He paced the floor of his quarters, and waited. Azazel entered, with Erissa and Esmerelda besides him.

"The world is turning," said Threye when he saw them. "There will be a new world order. We need to crush The Little Birds once and for all. What say ye?"

He looked at Azazel, and felt the waves that seemed to pulse from his body. He looked at The Old One, and at Erissa. Erissa looked weak. Some of the strength seemed to have been sucked out of her. Her wound had healed, but when Esmerelda had sucked the wound, she had also taken something of Erissa's spirit into her. Not for a minute did Esmerelda dream of letting Erissa have Azazel. She was The Old One. No one could plumb the depths of her nature, her evil, her sense of perfidy. At once whimsical, playful and without any feeling, her's was a nature of primeval times. She existed destroy, to take what she wanted and served only one master, and only one.

Threye looked at her, and sensed this He looked at Azazel, and doubt entered his mind. At the crucial time, would he be true?

Over the next days, as he gathered his armies about him, he was thoughtful and pensive. He had suffered defeats one after another. This was new to him.

He had suffered defeats, not because he had been weak, or The Little Birds had been strong. But, there was a new fragrance in the air, one that was unfamiliar to Threye.

His armies were strong, but would Azazel and Esmerelda be true? Would the Trolls be true? He could rely on Kale, and Mr Benttwist. He could rely on Bessie, but without Dragor, she was weakened. Would they be enough?

Yet, the die had been cast. All that needed to be seen, was which way it would fall.

Chapter 24

The Final Battle

The day dawned bright, and at Mrod Threye sat with Azazel. They looked at each other in silence, thoughts moving between the two seamlessly. They were of one mind: to crush the Little Birds. They knew that ships were fast approaching Mrod. This had never happened in living memory. The Mrodics had always been the aggressors. They were feared. Now they were under imminent attack. This was new, and their minds adjusted rapidly to the situations. They knew they had to defend themselves, and that they had to convert their defense into attack.

Threye's face held a grimace; the skin stretched back tight glowing white like bleached parchment. Azazel could see through the yellow of his eyes to the skull sockets behind them, and he knew that Threye was enraged. He also knew that despite the rage, the kernel of fear was beginning to grow. He smelt it, and despite himself, he fed upon this fear. Azazel battled with his old feelings of loyalty towards Threye, but his own nature had changed too much. Instinctively, his mind, his soul started to feed upon the fear, and something dark began to take shape.

As the day wore on, other members of Threye's trusted group entered the room. Erissa, Esmerelda, Kale. They sat in a circle with Azazel and Threye. Slowly the room dimmed and the music began. The bodies in the circle started to move in unison, swaying gently to the music of death, of destruction. Then, suddenly, Threye opened his eyes and went outside.

The sun was dipping below the horizon, its rays giving off a reddish hue. "A blood sky," he mused. "The sky of death, of blood spilled, of madness."

The tide was turning; the sun seemed to signal the beginning of the end of days past. A new history was about to be written.

As the sun's rays lit the skies, The Raven, The Icy Petrel, The Firebird and The Black Shadow bore down on Mrod. Percival stood on deck, hand-in-hand with Jenna. Basil and Trix stood with them.

"There shall be blood tonight, and the world shall never be the same again," said Basil. Trix nodded slightly, adding: "I shall meet Azazel. If I live through the night I shall be both surprised and grateful. Never once did I imagine, when we were married, that I would have to battle him one day."

"You shall have to battle with him as well as Erissa," replied Jenna. "I wonder how it will turn out. Is Erissa the dangerous one? Is Esmerelda? Will she have a role to play before the end?" Jenna shivered, almost with anticipation. Her face was turned towards the setting sun, its rays warmed her face. The breeze blew her hair back. She raised her arms, fists clenched. Her eyes were cold and hard. She was prepared for battle.

Sunset gave way to night. The dying embers of light glowed and then suddenly went out. The winds were icy, and as the ships approached land they could hear the sound of drumbeats. The Trolls were preparing for battle; the drums were being sounded. It was a dark night. The winds blew with anger and spite, and the darkness was pierced by the red tongues of fire, by smoke and the sound of the drums. It was a night that spoke of death, a night that spoke of endings.

Veering away from the shores of Mrod, the ships bore down on a deserted bay. There was silence as they stepped onto Mrodic soil. The only sound that broke the night was the relentless, hypnotic drumming.

As they made their way through the bushes, a voice seemed to whisper: "Welcome to Mrod. I know where you are. I can feel you sneaking into my realm. This is mine and shall remain mine for eternity." There was a hissing as the voice seemed to slither along the ground, creating a fog that engulfed them and threatened to take possession of their minds.

"Oh yes," continued the voice. "Your mind shall soon be my mind. But I am kind. I am willing to let all of you live as long as you give me three of your company. Just three. Is that too much to ask for? Give me Percival so that he may pay for his sins. Give me Jenna and Trix. They too must pay for their transgressions. Three is all I ask for, and you shall go free."

Abramelin walked to the head of the group and fell to his knees, Tamsin close behind him. Their hands were clasped as they knelt.

"We shall not give up even one of our company," they seemed to say to the whisper. "We have not forgotten your treachery of the past."

"Ah, we meet again Abramelin! Three is all I ask for. You have my word." The whisper turned into a hiss. "Three is all I ask, just three!! Heed my words or you shall all die."

"We shall see who dies and who lives," was the reply that went from the kneeling Tamsin. "We shall see. The fate of those who follow us shall no longer be decided only by you."

"You refuse my offer?!" the voice hissed in rage. "You shall all die a horrible death! Don't say you were not warned."

"I sense fear," said Abramelin. "I smell fear. I smell death. We are ready for you."

The trees seemed to thin and fall away. Suddenly, a bright flash lit up the sky and they found themselves in a clearing. There before them were the Trolls, Bessie and the Mrodics.

The drumbeats became frenetic, and the Trolls laughed. A madness seemed to engulf them as the drumming continued. Then, suddenly, it stopped. The two sides faced each other. Looking across the gap that divided them, Percival saw Bessie after what seemed like an eternity. Gone was the winsome lass that he had married. Gone was the innocence, the almost childlike sensuality she once possessed. Before him now was a stony face, one that showed no remorse for people done to death, or crimes committed. He saw a woman who would kill him if she could, a woman who would exult over his dead body. Any shred of sympathy he may have felt for the woman he had once loved, vanished. All that was left was an emptiness. Blood would be spilled, and only one of them would live to see the morrow.

Meanwhile, the tension mounted. Neither side was willing to make the first move. And then there was a shriek that sounded like it came from the very depths of hell. Bessie charged at Percival, her sword held high. Her teeth were barred; she resembled a wolf on the hunt. Saliva flecked the corners of her mouth.

Percival stood rooted, petrified, as she charged at him with blood lust in her eyes. Something snapped, and the resentment that had been bottled up inside him for so long boiled up into a maelstrom of emotions. He felt anger, a deep anger, as he lifted his arm and charged at her.

Did she hesitate just for a moment? Did a brief second of doubt stir her mind? Was this the timid Percival bearing down on her with madness in his eyes? She charged nevertheless and the two bodies crashed into each other. Bessie was sent screaming to the ground.

The moment of hesitation was broken and bedlam ruled as the two foes set about attacking each other. The Trolls were driven by a strange force as they hacked at everything they came into contact with. Slowly, the Little Birds were driven back as the war chants of the Trolls grew ever louder.

In the midst of the battle, Sindar The Elder looked into the skies and sang softly, calling to the winds:

"Hear my call
Hear my call, heed my call
The time is now, for you to blow
Let the airs swirl and flow
It is time for the Trolls to fall."

A breeze began to blow softly. It grew in intensity. It swirled. It seemed to possess a life of its own. Alternately hot and cold, it blew around and around. There was madness in the wind, an anger that could not be denied. The Trolls paused as the wind seemed to singe them, then freeze them. Their stony bodies struggled to cope; small cracks began to appear.

Elsewhere, Bessie seemed to be getting the better of Percival as he slackened his attack. She was intent on murder and she laughed wildly, hacking at him. Suddenly, he feinted, ducked and kicked her feet out from under her. The point of his sword was at her throat.

"I cannot do it!" he said suddenly and walked away. Crawling to her feet, Bessie charged at his receding back. Just as she was about to bring her sword down, a sudden blast brought her to her knees. Turning round she saw Jenna walking towards her, cold determination in her eyes.

The battle raged on. Kale, Erissa and Mr. Benttwist had all joined in the fray. Erissa and Trix came face-to-face, their eyes filled with hate.

"The time has come," said Erissa.

"Yes indeed!" hissed Trix as she prepared to face-off Erissa.

"This is when lies and schemes come to an end," said Trix with a sneer as she circled Erissa. The two were soon locked in a battle unto the death. Neither gave an inch, not one trace of softness was seen on their faces as they fought each other. Years of hatred, long suppressed, suddenly found expression. Gone was the silvery laugh of Trix, gone were the schemes of Erissa. All that remained, was desire to kill and be triumphant. Blast met with blast, swords clanged, and the two punched each other without mercy.

Basil, the Lexters and the Warlocks battled the Mrodics and slowly the balance shifted as they started to push the Mrodics back. Bodies fell to the ground, blood flowed. The power of the Shadow Rings was unleashed as the Little Birds beat back the flames from the eyes of the Mrodics.

Percival pushed through the fighting hordes, hacking at anyone who came in his way. His mind was blank; instinct seemed to drive him. Jenna walked beside him, leaving Bessie's lifeless body on the field. Her head had been separated from the rest of her. Her brief life had come to an end as her soul rushed onwards to a private heaven with Dragor.

Erissa and Trix fought on grimly, their faces almost touching. Then Erissa drew back laughing like a mad woman. She raised her hand and screamed: "Die, Die"! Then she fell to the ground, dead. She had been hit in front by a blast from Trix's ring, and at the back by one from Esmerelda. She had been prepared for anything that Trix had in store, but she was not prepared for the attack from behind.

Seeing her fall dead, hope arose in Trix's heart. Was this, the lack of unity under the command of Threye, the small glimmer of hope that they needed? She had no time to pause and reflect as the battle raged on around her, and the Old One stood there, triumphant in her power, in front of her.

A cackle rose in the air as Esmerelda stood over Erissa's fallen body. Gathering it in her arms, she melted into the night sky leaving behind only the sound of insane laughter. Trix dropped to her knees in shock, oblivious of the battle raging around her, mindless of Kale and Mr. Benttwist bearing down on her. She would have died there had Abramelin and Tamsin not jumped in between and driven the two off. Hissing with anger, with fear Kale and Mr. Benttwist withdrew. They sensed that the battle was turning against them, and chose to withdraw and melt into the darkness of the night.

Percival walking with Jenna by his side saw a shape grow from the battleground and a rotten stench fill the air. Blanche started to move. Smiling the smile of death and decay, she walked through the Lexters felling whoever she touched.

Just when it seemed as though she would destroy them all, a fire seemed to build around her, trapping her. She looked through it into the eyes of Tamsin. The Warlock Queen merely said: "The time for decay is done. Burn! Burn! Let your soul be liberated from this cycle of decay." As Blanche burned and screamed for mercy in the last throes of her life, the stench from the fires that filled the air was borne away by the winds. The Trolls ran madly trying to escape the winds. Sindar the Elder and Indu blocked the path of the Troll King and Troll Queen as they tried to make their way back to the ships.

"What say ye?" asked Sindar, as the winds swirled around him gently. "Will ye return home in peace? Or will ye fight for the wrong cause? You lived in peace for many years. You were betrayed by Threye. Yet you fought for him."

"A madness overtook us," said the Troll Queen. "A madness that shall not afflict us again."

Indu walked up to her, her body shimmering silver. The gentle moonlight seemed to flow right through her, and as she looked into the Troll Queen's eyes, she seemed to drink in her soul. The two were locked in a gaze that held them. Then Indu stepped aside, smiling gently, and said: "Pass, oh queen. Live in peace."

And so the Trolls were gone.

Meanwhile, the battle raged on.

Suddenly Thar said: "Where is Percival?"

"Gone to look for Threye, I think," said Trix. "And I am going to join them. They shall find Threye and Azazel together."

She found them. The three of them walked in silence. Nothing stirred.

"Something is not quite right," whispered Trix.

"Be watchful," Jenna whispered back.

As they spoke the ground seemed to give way beneath them. Black shapes blotted out the night sky, and they found themselves face-to-face with Azazel and Threye.

Azazel looked down at them and laughed. As he laughed, the air swirled around him. His eyes had a deranged look; they gleamed red in his gaunt, skeletal face. Threye was beside him, palely white. They were a study in contrast: one with any icy cold power, the other the power of madness.

Basil and Trix stood behind Percival and Jenna, with Sindar and Indu. They looked quietly at the two men in front of them. In time they became aware of a third as Esmerelda manifested herself on the other side of Threye.

"Trix!" Azazel screamed. "We meet again, my dear. And who do we have besides you? A pig! A PIG!" His tongue flicked in and out of his mouth, small drops of phlegm falling to the ground. Basil and Trix started, but were held back by the restraining hands of Abramelin and Tamsin who had also caught up with them.

"You dare come to my land?!" a voice sounded in Percival and Jenna's heads. "You dare come and threaten me?! Me, Threye! Do you think that I can ever be overcome by the likes of you? Weak, so weak... So pitiful and small. Yet you come here with your friends?!"

A searing pain shot through Percival and Jenna's heads as they fell to the ground writhing in agony. The voice pierced their skulls and burned their souls. It was like a vice -- sharp, merciless, implacable. Threye spoke on, Azazel and Esmerelda dancing around him conjuring up whirls of chaos. The rest of the group felt themselves being dragged in and around in a whirlpool of madness, hate and spite. Their feet slowly lifted off the ground; they were losing control. They felt as though their souls were being ripped from their bodies, and that they were dissolving into nothingness.

The end was near. Basil reached for Trix's hand; she reached for Indu. They formed a circle, hands touching hands, spirits connected. The Rings flashed, a white light beamed and pierced the whirlpool. It danced and played; it grew and acquired a life of its own. It tugged at the chaos that was raging around them, and tamed it. The whirlpool died and they fell to the ground, stunned.

The spell was broken. Percival and Jenna rose unsteadily. They looked into the eye of Threye and saw doubt. There was just a moment's indecision, and then Threye's face contorted with rage. He raised his arms to the sky, his hair blowing wildly in the wind. And then his hands came down, his finger pointing at them. Guided by instinct, they held their ring hands together. A blast of red flame flew from Percival's ring; a blue flame from Jenna's. The blue met the flame coming from Threye's finger; the red pierced Threye's third eye.

Screaming in pain Threye fell back, a yellow liquid streaming from his eye. He stumbled about, wounded. His face was a snarl, and he raised both hands in rage. Stepping forward, he found himself trapped in the whirlpool of Esmerelda and Azazel's madness. Laughing wildly, they swung him about as his body twirled in the air.

Was Azazel the Lord of Chaos, or had chaos overcome him? As he danced about madly a door seemed to open behind him. Esmerelda danced into it, Azazel followed laughing wildly. The door shut behind them.

There was silence as the eight survivors fell to the ground in a faint. Then the air cleared. The clouds lifted. A gentle rain fell from the sky onto the bodies lying on the grass.

Epilogue

Some years had passed since the Final Battle. Percival was back in his home on the hill, and was content. Life was as it should be again, yet different. The events of the past had changed everyone. Percival no longer believed that he lived in an isolated land, a land where nothing else existed.

Mortimer's cooking made him feel that life was worth living again. And Jenna helped him realize the value of love. In the mornings he would sit drinking coffee under the trees, sunlight filtering in through the leaves. Life was good, even if Trix did occasionally poke him in the ribs or pour water into his snoring mouth. Basil and he had become friends, something no one would have dreamed of before.

Bessie's old home had been burned down, and the road on which she lived converted into a public garden. Corky's Top Hat Shop was back in business and now counted Thyme as one of its most loyal customers. He strutted about in his new possessions, Sally at his side. The proud husband of a beautiful woman, he loved his top hats and was often heard spouting its history.

Occasional trips were made to the Land of Ice & Snow. The old group would gather to reminisce about the past and to celebrate times of peace. The Warlocks were not to be seen; they had played their part in the battles and had disappeared. The Trolls too had retired to their island, behind strong fortifications. The Matted Giants had been decimated and the Black Forest stood tall on their remains.

Back at the Valley of Kings, Regina ruled in place of her husband, with as steady a hand.

Indeed there was peace, and the world rejoiced.

One day, a thin wisp of smoke was seen coming from the Grey Heavens. Sitting by a fire that gave off grey smoke, surrounded by shadowy creatures from days gone by, Mama Kuko opened her eyes: grey they were, colourless and empty.

"I am the Medicine Woman," she proclaimed. "My time has come."

About the Author

Rajiv has always been interested in the world of fantasy and magic. This is something that has always inspired and motivated him. These are worlds into which you can escape and live out great adventures. His writing reflects this love of adventure, philosophy, and romance, with a hint of mystery.

Printed in the United States
By Bookmasters